Jane Lane was born Elaine K Dakers and her first novel was published when she was just seventeen. She adopted the pen-name of Jane Lane to reflect the historical nature of her books, Lane being the maiden name of her grandmother, a descendant of the Herefordshire branch of Lanes who sheltered King Charles II after his defeat at Worcester. A versatile and dynamic author, Jane Lane has written over forty works of fiction, biography, history and children's books.

BRIDGE OF SIGHS
A CALL OF TRUMPETS
CAT AMONG THE PIGEONS
COMMAND PERFORMANCE
CONIES IN THE HAY
COUNTESS AT WAR
THE CROWN FOR A LIE
DARK CONSPIRACY
EMBER IN THE ASHES
FAREWELL TO THE WHITE COCKADE
FORTRESS IN THE FORTH
HEIRS OF SQUIRE HARRY
HIS FIGHT IS OURS
THE PHOENIX AND THE LAUREL
PRELUDE TO KINGSHIP
QUEEN OF THE CASTLE
THE SEALED KNOT
A SECRET CHRONICLE
THE SEVERED CROWN
SIR DEVIL MAY CARE
A STATE OF MIND
A SUMMER STORM
THUNDER ON ST PAUL'S DAY
A WIND THROUGH THE HEATHER
THE YOUNG AND LONELY KING

JANE LANE

Sow the Tempest

This edition published in 2001 by House of Stratus, an imprint of Stratus Holdings plc, 24c Old Burlington Street, London, W1X 1RL, UK. Also at: Suite 210, 1270 Avenue of the Americas, New York, NY 10020, USA.

www.houseofstratus.com

Typeset, printed and bound by House of Stratus.

A catalogue record for this book is available from the British Library and The Library of Congress.

ISBN 0-7551-0848-5

Contents

PROLOGUE

Early Brilliance

On midsummer eve in the year 1509, King Henry VIII rode to his crowning.

All up and down his little green kingdom, the bells proclaimed the event to his four million subjects. Bells solemnly christened, forming almost the only source of news, their clappers muffled for passings and funerals, ringing backward to warn of fire or invasion, marking off the day with hours of the Divine Office, bidding men pause in their toil to salute the Mother of God with the Angelus. From some eight hundred monasteries and abbeys and convents strewn over the face of this small land, from great towers soaring up into the sky, and from humble little belfreys, the familiar voices of the bells rang peals of joy; for this was a day of days.

For the first time for nearly sixty years a son was following a father to the throne of England. The violent vendetta of the Wars of the Roses, thirty years of treason, bloody battle, and murder, which had shaken the monarchy with the continual making and unmaking of kings, all was over and could never be repeated. Over too was the reign of the first Tudor, with his uncertain title, his long nose sniffing out rivals, his predatory hands groping for money.

The White Rose and the Red were truly united at last; and in a youth whose beauty, learning and manliness promised England a glorious reign.

From the window of an inn at Rochester a young man named Thomas Cromwell watched the solemn procession of the Guilds, with their religious banners and treasured images, marching to the Cathedral to give thanks.

It had been mere chance which had brought Mr Cromwell to England at so historic a moment; since quarrelling with his ruffianly father, a brewer of Putney, he had lived abroad, chiefly in Italy, the Italy of Machiavelli, where he had learnt the art of getting the better of everyone, of turning everything to his own advantage. It was upon a matter connected with his trade of money-lending that he was in England now; and it occurred to him that his native land might be a good place to return to permanently. A golden age had dawned, folk were saying; to Mr Cromwell, the word 'golden' was synonymous with money.

In his tiny room in Jesus College, Cambridge, Mr Thomas Cranmer, aged twenty, short-sighted, timid, plodding, the younger son of a petty squire, worked at his theology, irritated as usual by a scholasticism grown rigid and lifeless, and distracted this morning by the clamour of the bells. His purse lay on the table, and in it the few shillings his widowed mother sent him weekly for his commons; would it be extravagant to spend a penny or two on some ale? This was a great occasion; the College was filled with the traditions of the Tudor claim; and only three years previously he had been among the cheering crowds who had watched a golden, sturdy boy, now the new King, ride with his parents through Cambridge to the great Shrine of Walsingham. Yes, it would be only loyal and fitting to drink to King Henry's health; and, where else but at the Dolphin, the best inn in the University?

But as Mr Cranmer peered myopically into his slender purse, he was not really thinking of King Henry, nor even of ale. He was thinking of the Dolphin's barmaid, commonly known as Black Joan.

In London there had been one long round of merrymaking ever since the funeral of the old King on May 9th, what with his heir's romantic marriage, the procession through the City of the immensely popular bride, and now the climax on St John's Eve with the gorgeous spectacle of this fairytale couple riding from the Tower to their crowning in the Abbey.

Conduits spouted wine; the intruding booths and the heaps of refuse had been cleared from the streets which were decently sanded. The pasteboard pageants, stored in Leaden Hall, has been refurbished and set up at traditional spots; the City Companies in their parti-coloured gowns and with their banners embroidered with the figures of their patron saints, stood in strict order of precedence along Cheapside. Every alley and casement was a cobble of heads; the ancient wall enclosing the City was black with sightseers; at the door of each of the one hundred and twenty-six churches within this square mile stood priests and singing clerks and censers; and overtopping the frenzied cheers there thundered the bells.

Three men in that multitude had a personal reason for rejoicing today. By a curious coincidence all three, like the pasty-faced money-lender in Rochester and the short-sighted theological student in Cambridge, had been given the baptismal name of Thomas.

Mr Thomas Bullen (or Boleyn, as he preferred to spell it), wealthy merchant, sat enthroned among his family at a window of the town house belonging to his father-in-law, the Earl of Surrey. Mr Boleyn had always been of the opinion that he had conferred a favour on the semi-royal Howards by marrying one of their daughters; not only was it clear that the day of the great feudal families had passed with the Wars of the Roses, but the first Duke of Norfolk had fought on the wrong side at Bosworth, and his son, Mr Boleyn's father-in-law, had been attainted and kept in prison for three years. Even when released he had not been allowed to assume his father's title, and most of his lands still remained with the Crown. Now, however, almost certainly he would be restored to favour, and would advance the interests of his son-in-law.

Not that Mr Boleyn was incapable of advancing his own interests under a young and open-handed King. Henry VII had made it dangerous for any subject to grow too rich, unearthing ancient laws and creating new ones whereby he could mulct the wealthy; so that the vast fortune inherited by Mr Boleyn from his father had been a source of worry rather than of comfort. Now all that would be changed, and there would be offices and honours for rich men with smooth tongues and a spoonful of noble blood in their veins. (Mr Boleyn's plebeian father had married a daughter of Sir Thomas Ormonde).

So here he sat complacent, come up from his manor of Hever in Kent for the occasion, with his well-brushed beard and moustache partly concealing his weak mouth, with his French bonnet worn so much on one side that in profile it looked like a halo, with his flirtatious wife beside him, and his surviving children gathered about. There was George, the baby, on his mother's knee; Mary supported on the window-seat by her nurse; and the eldest, Anne, a lanky girl of seven, her brilliant dark eyes, slightly protuberant, watching the procession, whilst she sucked the rudimentary sixth finger on her left hand.

On a stand set up in front of Lincoln's Inn was another family group, the family of Mr Thomas More, barrister and butler of that learned institution. For Mr More it was a double celebration, for his delicate little wife Jane had just presented him with a son after a succession of daughters. At what an auspicious moment to be born! All of Mr More's own youth had been passed under the shadow of the mean, ill-educated first Tudor king; and as he cheered himself hoarse this morning he had the sensation of one awakening from an evil dream.

There had been no flattery in the beautifully illuminated Latin verse he had composed for the occasion. His new Sovereign really did remind him of the legend of Achilles in woman's disguise, so perfectly did young Henry combine manly strength with feminine beauty; Mr More genuinely believed that the blond giant riding to his Coronation possessed the prudence of his father, the piety of his grandmother, the sweet kindliness of his mother, and the noble heart of his grandfather, Edward IV. And he would prove the patron of the New Learning; no longer would England be left without some of those treasures of Greek art and scholarship which, scattered by the sack of Constantinople by the Turks half a century before, had been transforming Italy and France.

'I shall write to Erasmus to hasten to England,' exulted Mr More. 'He will not lack now for a patron.'

'You attend to your law business, son,' advised old John More, shrewd, humorous, and rubicund, in his bar-gown and sergeant's coif, 'and leave this heathen Greek alone.'

The third Thomas of the trio, he whose surname was Wolsey was actually riding in the procession, though in a humble place, and, as became a cleric, upon a mule. He was thirty-six years old, already stout, with an unconscious grandeur of carriage which, together with his high intelligence, his vitality, and his full, rolling voice, impressed all who came in contact with him. The son of a prosperous Ipswich butcher, he had been destined from childhood to live on the endowments of religion, the ordinary lot of a younger son who showed talent at his books. He was to be part of that vast clerical body who undertook three-quarters of the administrative and official work of Christendom. He had done well at Oxford, and it was during his time there that he had begun to attract the notice of the great.

In the school attached to Magdalen, of which school he was Master, there had been the two young sons of the Marquis of Dorset. The boys had liked their hearty, jovial Master, and had invited him to spend Christmas at their home. The father had liked him so much that he had presented him with the living of Lymington; it was the first rung on the ladder of fortune. Two years later Wolsey had become one of Cardinal Morton's chaplains; with a now established reputation for cheerfulness and an enormous capacity for work, he had been passed on in due time to the service of Sir Richard Nanfant, Deputy-Governor of Calais. Nanfant had died in 1507, but not before he had recommended the useful Wolsey to the King himself.

In his determination to destroy for ever the almost sovereign power of the great nobles, Henry VII has established in their place a bureaucracy, entirely dependent on his favour; and into this band of officials had Thomas Wolsey entered. Scarcely had he so entered than he made his mark. He was sent by his royal master on an embassy to the Emperor Maximilian. Two mornings later, King Henry caught sight of the stout cleric as his Grace went to Mass, and chided him for not having started on his journey. Under his Highness' favour, replied the decided voice, he had already been with the Emperor and had fulfilled his mission, he trusted with his Highness' liking. His Highness' liking had been so great that there and then he had rewarded Thomas Wolsey with the Deanery of Lincoln.

And now here he was, left as an inheritance to the new young King, who was already drawn to him because of his joviality, his vigour, his love of display. Intoxicated by the roars of acclamation about him, he felt the stirrings of an ambition he had scarcely realized he possessed. He looked at the arms of the French provinces carried in the procession, provinces held by the legitimate Plantagenets and lost only within living memory, and he thought: If I can win his Grace's confidence, I could make real those empty claims. He looked at the Bishops in their scarlet mantles and white fur hoods, and he thought: If I can win his Grace's confidence, I could have not only a mitre but a Cardinal's hat…

The cheers of the crowds redoubled and black woollen flat-caps were flung into the air, as there came riding in her jewelled saddle-chair upon her Spanish mule with its housings of white satin, Catherine the Queen.

If Thomas More had the sensation of one awakening from a nightmare, so also, and with better reason, had this daughter of Spain, now in her twenty-fourth year. She was no great beauty, though there was a long-drawn 'Ooh!' of admiration from the crowds at the sight of her unbound russet hair which fell almost to her feet, but today she was so radiant with happiness that her somewhat statuesque features were transfigured.

From the age of sixteen, when she had been sent to England to marry sickly, puny, precious Arthur, Prince of Wales, she had known nothing but misery and humiliation. A few months of nominal marriage and the adolescently nasty Arthur was dead; and she had learnt exactly what kind of a man was her father-in-law. When her parents had rejected with horror his suggestion that he marry her himself, Henry VII had refused either to let her go home or to give her an allowance. There had been a moment when he had demanded that her dowry be settled on himself, and Catherine's mother had written frantically to the girl, bidding her touch no food save that prepared by her Spanish attendants; Henry VII had sent to the grave, openly or secretly, so many who had thwarted his greed.

And now she was Queen of England. She who, only two months ago, had been selling her remaining plate and even her gowns to buy food for her household, was married to the generous young Prince to whom she had lost her heart when they were children, acclaimed by London who had always pitied her sorrows and resented her wrongs, resolved in her good and simple soul that she would fulfil the destiny settled for her in her cradle, that she should be the ambassadress of great Spain to this small, rich northern land.

Again the voices completed with the thunder of the bells, as under a canopy of cloth of gold borne by the Barons of the Cinque Ports, there came riding his great charger, Henry the King.

For three weeks past while, according to custom, he had lived in seclusion in the Tower, he had sensed the eagerness of his people for him under their conventional grief for his father. He himself had felt no grief; always his father had seemed to him old, a ghastly pale man, strangely faceless. Childhood humiliations had engraved themselves upon his mind; his father beating him for some fault, and exclaiming to the embarrassed courtiers, 'This child will be the ruin of England!'; his father inviting himself to feast with the Earl of Oxford, and immediately afterwards fining the Earl fifteen hundred marks for his extravagance. No wonder London had cheered with one voice when the Heralds had cried, '*Vive le Roy Henri le Huitième!*' No wonder a Court poet had exulted, 'The heavens laugh, the earth rejoices, all things are full of milk, of honey, and of nectar; avarice is expelled from the land.'

It was the dawn of a golden age indeed, and he was a golden king. He was the royal young bridegroom of the 44th Psalm, beautiful above the sons of men, grace poured abroad from his lips, proceeding to reign prosperously. He looked the part; he was not quite eighteen, a giant in stature, fair-skinned and auburn-haired; he was, so men assured him, the handsomest prince in Europe. And he was the richest man in England. In the Mint within the Tower he had opened his father's treasure-chests, boyishly plunging his arms up to the elbow in the gold hoarded by that royal miser. And when those chests should be emptied there would replenish them the rents and dues from manors and forests, from mills and fisheries, from ports and markets, an income greater than any in England save for that of the Church.

He would spend it freely, joyously. He would show all Europe how a great king should live. He would give his people the show and the pageantry in which they delighted; and he would revive the age of chivalry, now in its decline. He had read his Malory, and truly it seemed to him that he was another Sir Tristram, 'in all manner of hunting, hawking, jousting, tourneying, dancing, singing, and wrestling, excelling all others.' His zest for life was unquenchable, as was his thirst for renown.

So he rode to his crowning, gorgeous in crimson mantle furred with ermine and coat of raised gold, surrounded by the great Officers of the Household, the Kings-at-Arms and Heralds, the Yeomen of the Guard in the Tutor colours of white and green, with the bride whom he had squired when she was a lonely child widow, with the arms of his royal dominions carried before him, England, Cornwall, Wales, Ireland, Gascony, Guienne, Normandy, Anjou, and France, with the City maidens disguised as Graces and Muses addressing him in Latin orations, with his three Standards unfurled, the Red Cross of St George, the Black Bull of the Nevilles, and the fiery Dragon of the prehistoric Welsh kings from whom his father had claimed descent.

The walled City was behind him now, and crossing the Fleet Bridge he heard the bells of the Blackfriars, the Greyfriars, and the Whitefriars taking up the tale of welcome. Past St Mary-le-Strand on its village green; past the great Episcopal Inns and the Hospital of the Savoy, with open country on his right; past the little hermitage at Charing Cross, where, on a sudden impulse, he dismounted and begged for the prayers of the holy anchorite there; and so down to the old Palace of Westminster, nestling under the shadow of the great Abbey, where tomorrow the Archbishop would place upon his head the Crown of St Edward, and in his hand the Confessor's staff, with its relic of the True Cross, to guide the feet of a Christian king ruling one small province of a united Christendom.

PART ONE

Noon Overcast

Chapter One

King Henry had suffered a restless night. Several times he had been awakened by the Wait piping the watch through the courtyards of the Palace, and each time he had roused the Gentleman of the Bedchamber, who slept on a mattress before the door, demanding wine and biscuit from the Night Cupboard. But such refreshment had failed to give him his usual sound sleep; his huge body tossed and turned between the scented sheets and his soul, strangely defenceless when he was alone, longed for morning and action.

Why could not his small army of physicians cure this irritating, recurring rash? It was such a trivial thing; of course it was a trivial thing, he told himself emphatically. It had made its first appearance when he was sixteen; the doctors had diagnosed measles, and had turned out to be wrong. The rash had continued to recur at intervals, yielding temporarily to ointments; it was fantastically absurd for him to entertain for a moment the suspicion that the thing dated from his first amorous episode, a brief affair which had been a kind of celebration of his manhood and of his release from the destiny marked out for him before his elder brother's death, that he should be Archibishop of Canterbury and thus save his father from having to provide for him.

15

The morning light began to filter through his bed-curtains, and he sighed hugely in relief. He would forget the rash in his busy day; it was Michaelmas, and in honour of St Michael he had arranged an especially grand tournament, that mimic war in which his soul delighted. He flung back the curtains on one side and sprang naked from his bed; it was an hour before his usual time of rising, but as though his attendants who slept in the anteroom, the Privy Chamber, and the Presence Chamber, had sensed the royal restlessness, there was already a discreet bustle in these apartments which all opened out of one another. The Yeomen of the Wardrobe brought the King's clothes to the door of the Presence Chamber; they were received by the Pages, who handed them to the Grooms in Privy Chamber, who in turn handed them to the Esquires of the Body in the ante-room, who, entering the Bedchamber with profound obeisances, advanced to dress the King.

He hummed to himself as he was arrayed in a shirt made for him by his wife, of white lawn ornamented by her skilled fingers with black floss in the Spanish fashion, his short slops, his sleeveless, open-fronted vest to which were attached the short skirts known as bases, divided in front to expose a large codpiece, and his slashed tunic with its rubies in gold mounts. He was himself again; the abominable word 'pox' was banished to the region of nightmare. It was outrageous to imagine that he, Henry, by the Grace of God King of England, Cornwall, Wales, Ireland, Gascony, etc., etc., could be the victim of so disgusting a disease. He began to sing loudly a song with which some Court poet had greeted his accession:

> *'Adonis of fresh colour,*
> *Of youth the goodly flower,*
> *Our prince of high honour,*
> *Our wealth, our earthly joy… '*

He moved into the Privy Chamber where the Gentlemen of that holy place waited to claim their privilege of putting the finishing touches to his toilet. The Groom of the Stole presented the surcote with its huge puffed sleeves; reverent fingers knotted about his waist his silken girdle from which depended his dagger and pouch; his plumed bonnet was placed upon his auburn head; a chain of white sapphires and emeralds was hooked upon his shoulders to give the fashionable wide effect; from a scroll of parchment on which they were kept he chose the finger-and thumb-rings he would wear that day; and his buskins were exchanged for a pair of white satin shoes shaped like a bear's paw. He surveyed himself in the steel-glass; was well pleased with the reflection of the best-dressed Sovereign in Europe; and passed beaming into the Presence Chamber where the Lord Great Chamberlain and a crowd of officers, clerical and lay, waited to conduct him to Mass.

It was his custom to hear three Masses daily, and he heard them with genuine devotion. But this morning, perhaps because of his restless night, he was somewhat distracted, rustling the leaves of his exquisitely illuminated Primer, glancing now and again at the Queen who knelt on a crimson velvet *prie-dieu* near him, thinking to himself how good she was, how much he admired and loved her, pitying her because so far she had presented him only with a stillborn daughter and a son who had lived seven weeks, revering her rather rigid piety; and all the while his body was aching for hard exercise. The tourneying would not commence till ten; he had a couple of hours in which to fly his hawks. Leaving his wife to her long thanksgiving, he made a profound genuflection to the Blessed Sacrament, strode out of the chapel, gulped down a draught of ale, changed his clothes again, and was away in the September sunshine.

(ii)

In the first few months of his reign, King Henry had added a tilt-yard to Placentia, the palace at Greenwich he so much preferred to that at Westminster; and this morning the lists within their seven-foot high palisades were filled with colourful and noisy preparations. The three Kings-at-Arms solemnly conferred beside the breast-high barrier; the Heralds were busy affixing blazons of arms to each pavilion; the Pursuivants were inspecting the armour of each combatant to make sure that the order which required lances to be blunted had been observed, and that the swords to be used were 'bastards', having no edge. Trumpeters practised their martial music; pages hung the palisades and the spectators' galleries with arras; esquires laid out the tilting harness to be worn by their respective knights.

In his pavilion, Lord Thomas Howard, the Earl of Surrey's son, groaned in spirit.

He was a short, spare, black-haired man in his early thirties, the pouches under his eyes giving him something of a resemblance to a blood hound. With his high feeling for rank, and the impoverishment of his youth, he had become permanently exasperated; and especially did he hate the plebeian tribe of officials whom Henry VII had created and Henry VIII encouraged. And Henry VIII was making it ruinously extravagant to live at Court, while on the other hand the royal favour was extended only to those who did so live.

'To achievement, knights and esquires! To achievement!' the voices of the Heralds rang out.

Lord Thomas glowered at the innocent squire who, at this signal, began encasing him in his armour. He heard in memory the voice of one of these *'Novi homines',* as he contemptuously called them, enquiring in feigned surprise:

'Your lordship wears ordinary harness for tilting?'

Yes, he did wear ordinary harness, because, as the new man knew very well, he could not afford tilting armour. The game was expensive enough as it was, he thought, as his esquire screwed on the extra pieces on his left side which received most of the blows, the small wooden shield, the heavy elbow-guard, the large knee-plate, and the queue which supported the buttend of the lance. The Heralds were waiting outside to collect the nail-money for affixing his blazon of arms; as an earl's son he would have to pay fifteen marks for the privilege of entering the lists; and if he were vanquished (which undoubtedly he would be, since he was jousting with the King) his arms and armour fell to his conqueror and he would have to ransom them.

'Come forth, knights and esquires, come forth!' shouted the Heralds.

Shut up in his steel case, Howard stumped out of his pavilion, followed by his esquire carrying his great jousting-helm with its beak-shaped front, by his minstrels, and his varlets whose duty it would be to keep his horse on its feet – a formidable task, since the horse was weighted down by steel bards, its ears stuffed with cotton wool, and its head protected by a chanfrein without ocularia.

As usual King Henry had made the tilting into an elaborate masque. Two damsels representing the Lady Pallas and the Lady Diana came forward in pasteboard castles drawn by wildmen, to present the champions; the 'novi homines', Seymours and Wyatts and Howard's in-laws, the Boleyns, small lords of the manor or rich merchants, pandered to Henry's love of display by entering the lists on cars drawn by dragons, or perched upon artificial mounts. Just before he was almost completely blinded by his helm with its few narrow sight-slits, Howard had a glimpse of the man whom he and his class had come to see as the embodiment of all they hated most, the upstart son of a butcher, Thomas Wolsey, sitting up there in the gallery in his silk gown, and round his shoulders the heavy gold chain he had put on when made a Privy Councillor last month.

Wolsey, watching the sparks struck from armour, the splintering of lances, the tossing of plumes and bobbing of ladies' favours worn by their knights, said the right thing, cheered at the right moment, and thought about preferment. Already he had done extremely well for himself. Within a few months of the Coronation he had become a Prebend of Lincoln and Dean of Hereford, with a fine house next door to the Ecclesiastical Inn of Lincoln in the Strand, an Inn, a great palace, upon which he often looked with an envious eye. There had followed the post of Royal Almoner, with which went many perquisites, including the confiscated goods of suicides, and the 'deodands', objects which had caused accidental death. And then last month he had got upon the Council, where he was busy showing the King his extraordinary grasp of details and his great intelligence in dealing with the problem immediately under discussion.

'Fold up the banner, knights and esquires!' commanded the Heralds.

Amid laughter and cheering and brazen of trumpet, the tournament, so tedious to some spectators, came to an end. The Marshall of the Lists presented to Queen Catherine the names of the combatants, begging her Highness to award the prizes as she thought best. With an affectionate smile she bestowed the palm on a certain vast figure that bore engraved upon its guard the motto *Sir Loyal Heart,* and tried to look properly astonished when, the helm being lifted off, the unknown champion turned out to be the King.

Throughout the long performance she had kept seeing in memory a very different kind of combat. Her early childhood had been passed in the camps and sieges of her parents' holy war against the Infidel; when she was six, her heroic mother's tent, always in the front line of battle, had been burnt, and Catherine and her sisters had been rescued with difficulty. A year later she had watched the surrender of Granada, the last Moorish stronghold, she had seen the Silver Cross of the Crusade hoisted on the watch-tower of the Alhambra and the heathen Crescents thrown down, had heard Christian bells drown Moorish horns, and the *Te Deum* proclaim that her mother's oath to 'take the Cross through the south' had been fulfilled.

She listened now, not only from her strong sense of duty, but because of her deep affection for him, as her husband, over an elaborate collation, described to her the intricacies of the tourney and the jousting. She was unaware of her own lack of tact, and could not understand his reaction when she remarked kindly:

'Your Grace and your courser must be quite exhausted after so much frolicking.'

He had just been describing to her exactly how he had unhorsed Lord Thomas Howard by striking him upon a particular point in his helm, and how expertly he had dropped his own lance directly contact had been made, to avoid splintering the weapon. He felt a sudden sharp irritation with her; she must think the whole thing childish or she would not have used that expression, 'frolicking'. He turned from her in a huff, and heard the full, rolling voice of his new Councillor, Wolsey, discussing in the proper jargon and with almost boyish zest the feats of the day.

Wolsey had not missed the King's frown, nor the reason for it. Often of late he watched the Queen with the eyes of a rival; one of his chief defects, which was also a source of his strength, was his furious and sustained desire to govern others, to be pre-eminent above all others, and supremely to have the guiding and directing of the inexperienced and vain young King. That his Privy Councillorship was but a prelude to much higher office he did not doubt; but whereas he could dominate at the Council-board by his rapid thought and high intelligence, he sensed in Catherine a more serious rival than the aristocratic clique who hated him. She was like some squat rock in his path, he thought spitefully, a rock he could neither uproot nor get round; he hated her high Spanish manners, her rigid piety, her royal dignity which nothing could ruffle, and above all her influence over the King.

Though she did not give her husband the flattery he demanded from others, she gave him a love which combined that of wife and mother, she who was nearly six years his senior, gently advising him, bearing with his restlessness, his vanity, and his casual infidelities, and she had bound him to her by a multitude of little personal things. She made his shirts, even as her dead mother had made King Ferdinand's in her tent during the Moorish wars; she saw personally to the washing and mending of his linen; she shared Henry's love of music and his sincere religious devotion; she had interested him in horticulture, importing vines and fruit trees from Spain. And he consulted her on all his foreign policy; it was she who had persuaded him to ally himself with her father, King Ferdinand, in the Holy League formed to defend the Papacy against the French in north Italy.

If I could get him away from her for a while, mused Wolsey, then, while giving him the toys he loves, I could persuade him to leave public matters to me. And then when I have power, real power, he thought, I would set about reforming the abuses in religion. He said this to himself automatically; it was a sop to his conscience which occasionally informed him that while talking about reform, he himself gave a glaring example of the need for it.

That very evening, fate presented him with the chance he had been looking for.

(iii)

The long ceremonial of the King's retiring had begun.

The Page of the Bedchamber, with a cresset in one hand and a baton of the Tudor colours in the other, had come to fetch the Gentleman of the Bedchamber and the four Yeomen on duty, lighting them to the Wardrobe of Beds and back again with their load of bedding. The Gentleman laid out the night-gown furred with polecat and set the King's sword at the bed-head, while, lighted by the Page, the Yeomen got to work. First they must prod the palliasse with a dagger; then they must tumble upon it to make sure there were no hidden weapons; and then, two on either side, they made up the bed with feather mattress, pillows stitched with golden fleurs-de-lis, fustians, and counterpane. Lastly they kissed the sacred thing their hands had touched.

The Gentleman, with due reverence, was just placing the golden chamberpot beneath the bed, when through the series of rooms which opened out of the Bedchamber there advanced the rapid thump of feet and a voice resembling the warning growl of a lion. One of the Yeomen who was warming the royal nightcap at the fire, dropped it from his trembling fingers as the great blond giant, the master of England, strode into the room, followed by a gentleman in riding clothes which were plentifully bespattered with mud.

'Be off! Be off!' thundered Henry to his Bedchamber entourage.

While they backed hastily to the door, he flung himself down upon his chair of estate beneath its canopy, and gnawed his thumb. When the door was shut:

'God's body, it cannot be as you say!' he snarled. 'If it is, we shall write our brother Ferdinand to cut their throats, every whore-son mutineer among them. Nay, you must be mistaken, man; tell us again.'

Thomas Boleyn, Sir Thomas now, cleared his throat a little nervously. To be the bearer of ill news, and to such a master, was not consonant with his usual good fortune.

'Your Grace will see in these dispatches that my Lord Dorset did all that any commander could do. But from my personal observation I assure your Grace that the plight of our army was pitiful. It is true they saw no fighting, but that was not their fault; and they were so stricken with disease in a southern summer that if my lord had not brought them home as they demanded, scarce one of the fifteen thousand of them would have been left alive.'

'We will have their blood!' raged Henry, crashing his heavily ringed hand upon the chair arm. 'We engaged in a holy war; our quarrel with France is God's quarrel. The king of France has favoured detestable schisms; he has caused the Holy Father to flee to St Angelo, while his Frankish hordes encamp about Rome, and we have sworn that we will free the Church of God from the menace of this Louis who is the common foe of all Christians.'

His solemn words had both sobered and relieved him. The intolerable suspicion that he had been made to look ridiculous had disappeared. He was again that which he would always be in his own estimation, the romantic cavalier, the chivalrous champion.

'We must teach this King of the French to know himself by force of arms,' he said pompously. And then, on a sudden impulse: 'Send to us our Master Almoner.'

24

More and more frequently of late he found himself sending for Thomas Wolsey. Wolsey never hampered or delayed or fumbled like the older men on the Council; Wolsey understood better than anybody how avid his master was to make England great again abroad. And he had a genius for co-ordinating a mass of information whereof the rest of the Council only possessed fragments. Yes, Wolsey was the man.

He came. His very presence was heartening, so stout and vigorous, so sure of himself and yet so absolutely devoted to his master. He listened in respectful and intelligent silence while the doleful tale was told, and then said briskly:

'Have I your Grace's permission to speak my mind?'

'It is what we do require of you.'

'Then, Sire, first I would advise your Highness to announce publicly that your troops have returned by your Highness' orders. That will suffice to silence spiteful tongues abroad. And then, Sire, to organize a new and greater expedition, which, in my poor opinion, should be delivered at close range, with Calais as our base, and with your Grace in personal command. I feared from the beginning, though it was not my place to say so, that the former expedition could serve no end but Spain's.'

He talked on, his eyes blazing with enthusiasm. As usual, the thing of the moment absorbed him, as it did the man who listened and who fell more and more under his spell. His religion, like Henry's own, was not mere convention, and there was genuine sincerity in the rolling voice as Wolsey spoke of the intolerable insults given to the Pope by Louis of France. But mixed up with such talk were grandiose schemes of winning back the lost Plantagenet possessions in that kingdom, even of gaining the French crown; and above all there was the broad hint that the failure of the late expedition had been due to a lack of cooperation by England's ally, King Ferdinand, father of the Queen.

'Let other men have their councillors, here is the councillor for me!' cried Henry, clapping a hand upon the stout shoulder.

'If,' said Wolsey, dropping his voice and looking up earnestly at his master, 'if your Highness would be pleased to honour me with your full confidence, I should not doubt but so to establish your Highness' authority both at home and abroad as to make you the greatest and happiest prince living. Neither should I fear to fall, if any benefit might grow to your Grace thereby.'

Impulsively Henry pulled from his thumb a turquoise engraved with the Tudor Rose.

'Whensoever there shall be need,' said he, 'for privy and urgent communication betwixt us, send this ring to me by a gentleman and you shall have instant audience.'

It was the hour of which Wolsey had dreamed.

While the King, forsaking his tilting and his hunting, went daily to the docks to inspect his fleet, having his portrait painted on board a man-of-war, in a vest of gold brocade and holding an enormous gold whistle encrusted with gems, Wolsey set about organizing an expedition on a scale greater than any within living memory.

Though still subordinate on the Council, he gave his orders, and suddenly showed himself implacable to all who opposed the least of his designs. But though he enormously increased the hatred felt for him by the aristocratic party, they were forced to admit his superior powers. In person he bargained with graziers and horse-breeders; he had worked out the number of carcases to be salted, the number of draught-mares to draw the twelve great siege guns named after the Apostles. He ordered water-mills to be built for the making of biscuit; he went down to Paynter Stayner's Hall in the City to inspect the banners and standards being painted there. Since there was no time to import gunpowder from Spain, he bought saltpetre and sulphur and had it made in the Tower; he even designed for the King a new suit of armour, calling in modellers, steel-, silver-, and gold-smiths, inlayers, engravers, and polishers to make a harness so richly decorated with hammer-work that the like had never been seen.

Throughout England reluctant vassals and artisans said farewell to their families at the bidding of this hitherto unknown cleric; at every forge bills and halberds were sharpened; trees were felled for battering-rams; in workshops a strange nauseous mixture of sulphur, bitumen, and naptha was prepared, the ancient 'Greek-fire' for the war machines; peasants collected stones for their slings; on every waste ground the bowmen of England practised at the butts.

To Henry it was the most glorious of games. In his new armour, upon a horse barded as decoratively as himself, with drum and trumpet sounding before him, he made his gorgeous progress to the coast where his ship with cloth of gold sails awaited him. The ship and the great siege guns and the whole fleet having been solemnly blessed, he set sail, heartily concurring with his admiring courtiers who assured him that he was another St George.

(iv)

Catherine the Queen was inspecting the new garden laid out for her at Greenwich by a Spanish gardener who had imitated here the clipped myrtle hedges and the box borders of the Alhambra in which she had passed her girlhood. It was well enough, but she still missed the scarlet flare of the cactus flower, the roses drooping in long trails from the cypresses, the heat of the southern sun, the view from the dramatically high red walls of the Alhambra, of the rich plain of the Vega and on the horizon the Sierras and their eternal snows.

She had never liked England, with its rain and fogs and lack of colour, though she had tried hard to do so, for from her cradle she had been called 'the Princess of England'. But with her steel-strong sense of duty she had disguised her feeling, and as a reward had found that the English had taken her to their hearts as devotedly as they had taken another daughter of Castile, the well-loved Queen Eleanor of the Crosses.

And today she was very happy. She was with child again, and surely this time she would be able to fulfil her principal duty in life, to bear an heir to England; moreover there had just arrived the news of a great English victory. Her husband's letter was jubilant; it appeared that the Emperor Maximilian had been so impressed by King Henry's martial aspect that his Imperial Majesty, the veteran of many wars, had insisted on serving as a private soldier under this great new Hector. And in the rout of the French troops, known as the Battle of the Spurs, France had been taught what she must expect at the hands of his Grace of England if she dared to cross swords with him; a week or two later the great commercial city of Thérouanne, so vital to French power on the borders of the Low Countries, had surrendered to English arms. He was now marching to encamp before Tournai, concluded Henry, and made no doubt of taking that likewise.

Yes, it was very good news, she thought, as she sat down with her ladies in an arbour, her small Spanish verdingale and black velvet mantilla incongruous in this English landscape. Her beautiful hands set to work upon her embroidery, filling in the design of a pomegranate, her chief emblem, with her motto, *Not for my crown* – for the crown of the pomegranate is worthless and is thrown away.

Beyond the gardens flowed the great river, with its ships and barges passing up to London on the flood; in the smokeless air the white turrets of the Tower rose clearly, and beyond could be glimpsed the towers and spires of London's many churches, with the Gothic pinnacles of St Paul's overtopping them all, seeming to float, strangely ethereal, above the gilded weathercock on the cross glittering in the sunlight. From the great Abbey of Bermondsey near at hand, a solemn bell rang for Vespers.

Upon this peaceful scene intruded urgent footsteps, agitated voices. An Esquire of the Body ushered into the Queen's presence a haggard messenger who stammered out his news; King Henry's brother-in-law, James IV of Scotland, had invaded England as the ally of France.

Those who knew Catherine only as a domesticated, pious lady were astonished by her reaction to these dreadful tidings. The mantle of her mother, Isabella of Castile, seemed to fall upon her, Isabella who had driven from Spain the Infidel, entrenched there for seven hundred years. Catherine laid aside her embroidery; she was quite certain what must be done and how to do it, even as her mother had been. She sent for all those Privy Councillors who were in London, and because she had never learnt to speak English easily, she addressed them in the French with which all the nobly born were familiar.

They regarded her in wonder, this motherly little woman already growing stout. As though it was a thing she had been doing all her life, she took charge in this crisis, reminding them that as Regent and Captain General of the Forces in his Grace's absence, she had power to raise men and impose taxes for the defence of the realm. She appointed the old Earl of Surrey Commander-in-Chief, and she announced that she would follow him to the North with reinforcements. Even her pregnancy did not seem to concern her now; it was an essential part of her character that she knew what was right and would do it, no matter what the cost.

Before she dismissed Surrey and his fellow commanders, she made them an impromptu oration, passionately eloquent, reminding them that English courage excelled that of all other nations. Then, while beacons flamed on headlands and bells rang backward in alarm, she sat up with her ladies far into the night, making banners displaying the Tudor Rose, the Beaufort Portcullis, and the Castle of Castile, while the yeoman of England, their ranks gravely diminished since Henry had taken the flower of them for his aggressive war, rushed with enthusiasm to the standards which called them to defend their native soil.

Wearing a steel cap in place of her mantilla and a corselet over her gown, Catherine rode north through a countryside where she was cheered to the echo. She had reached the Midlands when news arrived that Surrey had routed the Scots on Flodden-field, King James himself being among the dead. She turned aside to give thanks at one of the most hallowed spots in England, whither pilgrims from all over Europe had flocked for five hundred years, the Shrine of Our Lady of Walsingham.

And here she wrote a letter to her husband, an innocent letter written from her heart.

'To my thinking,' she wrote, 'this battle hath been to your Grace and all your realm the greatest honour that could be, and more than should you win all the crown of France. In return for the captured banners your Grace was pleased to send me, I send you a piece of a dead king's coat.'

It was tactless; but then lack of tact, and an inability to deal with complex characters or situations, were Catherine's chief defects. And this letter, though she could not know it, was one of those tiny clouds which were veiling the brilliance of her morning, and England's.

(v)

A month later, King Henry returned.

The road from Dover was gay with triumphal arches; the Mayor and Aldermen met him on Blackheath with the Trained Bands; the ancient stone Bridge with its crowding houses had rich cloths and greenery hung from every window; in the City there were pageants and ringing of bells and caps flung skywards, while the cannon boomed salutes from the Tower.

But at the back of Henry's mind, a mind now completely under the influence of Wolsey, was an intolerable suspicion that the most popular figure in the procession was not himself but his wife, and that the City was celebrating not his showy successes abroad but the deliverance from the threat of invasion at Flodden.

Other suspicions nagged at him. He had covered himself with glory, while, indulging Wolsey's urgent pleadings, he had not once risked his skin. He had a gift for self-deception amounting to genius, but no man can completely deceive himself at twenty-two; therefore he had work to smother the voice deep inside him which said that he had been very glad indeed to yield to Wolsey's persuasions, that while he revelled in rough sports and bloodless jousting, he had no taste for cold steel upon a field of battle. And if he had the glory of the late campaign, his allies, King Ferdinand and the Emperor, had the results. Ferdinand, his left being covered by the English forces, had annexed Navarre, the disputed Basque province for the sake of which he had entered the holy war. Cunning old Maximilian had demanded the destruction of Thérouanne, the symbol of French power in the Low Countries; and King Henry had paid for the destruction, having already advanced one hundred thousand pounds to a Maximilian pleading poverty, and playing him ten thousand crowns a day for playing at being a private soldier under his Grace's command.

To the cheering crowds of London he appeared the familiar Henry; the wide, square face was jovial, the oddly flat eyes under white lashes looked with apparent approval upon two citizens disguised as Job and the Archangel Raphael who for some strange reason greeted him out of the moon; his small pursed mouth smiled at the maiden garbed as St Catherine who welcomed her namesake, his wife, from the top of the Lud Gate.

But under his bluff exterior a dangerous anger glowed; and he had not been home long before a piece of the news fanned it into flame. It was Wolsey who broke the news to him; those four months abroad had made Thomas Wolsey, who had given his master the toy of military renown, and who had just been consecrated Bishop of Lincoln. From one of the messengers who had come to arrange the ransom of certain noble French prisoners, Wolsey had learnt that the King of France had absolute proof that King Henry's allies were proposing to arrange a secret peace treaty with him without reference to his Grace of England.

Henry had been playing tennis when this appalling thing was disclosed to him by his faithful adviser. He flung aside his guitar-shaped racket and the balls of white kid stuffed with hemp; and just as he was, all sweaty from the game, in his square-necked shirt and his slops with their slashes outlined in gold cord, he strode straight to his wife's apartments, his flat eyes red with rage.

She looked her worst this morning. She was near her time, and her skin had a grey tinge to it, her thickening figure strained against her shapeless gown. He felt at that moment that he hated her, and everything connected with her, from her shifty realist of a father to the Spanish translation of the *Epistles of St Jerome* she held on her lap.

'I embarked upon a holy war,' bellowed Henry, 'risking my life and reducing France to extremities, emptying my treasure-chests, sacrificing my comfort, and all for the sake of Christ and His Church. And now I am stabbed in the back by my allies, one of whom is your father.'

She could only stare at him with her china-blue eyes. She had grown accustomed to his outbursts of childish temper, but she was utterly unprepared for this uncontrolled fury which made her amiable, genial husband seem a stranger.

'Your father! – do you hear me, Madam? I refused to hearken to what men whispered of his lies and treacheries, but now I see for myself what manner of rogue he is. I should have known. He cheated my father of your dowry, and endeavoured to persuade him to take your mad sister to wife after my mother's death.'

'Oh no! It was the other way about – '

'God's body! do you dare to contradict me, Madam? It was an ill day for England when you were named Princess of Wales. What have you brought us, eh? An unpaid dowry and stillborn children. And now your father using me as his voider. But he shall not! I will oust him from Navarre, ay, from Spain also. I will not sheathe my sword until I have taught these foreign princes that I can make and unmake them at my will.'

She tried to reason with him, and as usual was tactless. The new Pope, Leo X, begged his Grace to desist from avenging him, she reminded Henry; to talk of making and unmaking kings, whose dominions were at least three times the size of England was childish. No one except Wolsey was taking seriously his resolve to conquer the whole of France. If her father and the Emperor were making peace with King Louis, it was only what His Holiness begged for; and if Henry really wanted to engage in a holy war, there was the menace of the Turk sweeping through Europe.

Her attempts to soothe and argue only served to madden him still further. He now saw the whole Spanish-Imperial connection, including his wife, in the light of his wounded vanity. There was no question, he snarled, of conquering France; on the contrary he would give his sister Mary, betrothed to Maximilian's grandson, to the aged Louis instead. Again she tried to make him see reason; France was England's hereditary foe, while peace with the Empire and Spain, which meant trading with Flanders, was the desire of nobles and merchants alike. He swept this aside; *he* had been crossed; *he* had been betrayed; he would avenge the insults put upon him.

In the midst of such horrible scenes as these, Catherine's son was born prematurely and lived but a few hours. The catastrophe sobered Henry for the moment, and he became again the kind and attentive husband. But the influence Catherine had wielded over him was gone for ever; it had been transferred to the man who never thwarted him, who shared his love of show and renown, who pandered to his appetites and his vanity, and fed him on grandiose dreams.

Henry needed comfort. Having sacrificed his unfortunate young sister Mary to the elderly Louis of France, a few months later Louis was dead, on purpose, Henry felt, to spite him. And instead of Mary being Queen of France, she had made a clandestine marriage with the Duke of Suffolk without Henry's permission; while on the French thrones sat a monarch younger than Henry, handsome, dashing, of brazen energy in arms. And what must this young Francis do but win a really brilliant victory against the Emperor, Europe ringing with the tales of his mad valour, and the Pope, on meeting him at Bologna to sign a Concordat, actually embracing him and refusing to permit him to kiss his toe.

But there was always Wolsey to comfort and encourage. Arm-in-arm the stout cleric and the huge King paced the galleries of Greenwich or held private conference in the Privy Chamber, the holy of holies, planning how, on the Emperor's death (which surely could not be long delayed), they would persuade the seven Electors to bestow on Henry the Iron Crown of the Empire; and how they would prevail on the Pope to send Wolsey, only just consecrated a bishop, a Cardinal's hat, even to bestow on him a Legacy *a Latere* for life, which would mean in effect handing over the Papal powers in England to the King whom Wolsey served, and who was now wholly under his influence.

Chapter Two

Since the beginning of the reign, Mr Thomas More had become one of the best known and best loved figures in the City.

He was a freeman of the Mercers', his father's Company; in the Parliament of 1510, which lasted only a month, he represented the City; in the same year he was elected Under-Sheriff, trying cases which came before the Court of the Poultry Compter, and here he had become famous not only for his legal brilliance but for a strict integrity combined with a real kindness of heart. He was the City's natural choice when an Orator was needed for the reception of the Venetian ambassador, or a Latin interpreter when the Pensionary of Antwerp came to discuss some problem with the Merchant Adventurers, or as London's representative to go to Flanders to conduct negotiations with the Hanseatic merchants who had their English headquarters at the Steelyard on the Thames at the mouth of the Wall Brook.

It was beside the Wall Brook, covered over in the previous century, that Thomas More had his house, a good, solid City dwelling called the Barge on the south side of Bucklersbury. It was roomy, and needed to be so, for besides his four children there were several City orphans entrusted by the Mayor to his guardianship, his foster-daughter, Margaret Gigs, his step-daughter, Alice Middleton, a crowd of young scholars eager to study the new Greek under his guidance, and always a coming and going of humanist friends.

The domestic side of this large household was ruled, not by the dear little wife, Jane, who had died at the birth of her only son in the year of King Henry's Coronation, but by a sharp-eyed, rough-tongued widow of a London mercer, now the second Mrs More. She was seven years older that her new husband, who had married her, to the astonishment of his friends and the strong disapproval of his father, within a month of Jane's death.

'Matrimony,' Mr More senior had warned his son, 'is as if you should put your hand into a bagful of snakes and eels, seven snakes for one eel. I have put my own hand into that bag four times, and it is my advice to you that you stay a widower.'

On a fine summer evening, Mrs More was standing on her doorstep, inhaling the pleasant aroma from the herb-market near by, and gossiping with her neighbours, when she perceived her husband wending his way between the crowding booths of the street, with his young son John riding on his shoulders. She began at once to chide.

'Tilly vally, Mr More, here are you, come straight from discharging your honourable office at the Compter, and behaving like some foolish boy for all your neighbours to see, neighing like a horse and playing the fool.'

He doffed his cap to her, and said with his native cheerfulness:

'You remember, Mistress Alice, how I have told you that my name in Greek means 'fool', and therefore must I live up to the part.'

'You have been running at the Saracen again, boy,' declared Mrs More, turning her displeasure upon her stepson, 'or else how came you by that tear in your pourpoint? It is sport for men and not for children; and you must be beaten for engaging in it.'

'I have told him so,' said her husband, very solemn. 'We are agreed upon it.'

The child buried his face in his father's shoulder to hide his chuckles. It was Mr More's habit to inflict chastisement upon his children with a bunch of peacock's feathers.

'Now upon the matter of my feigning to be a horse,' continued More, taking his wife's arm as they went into the house, 'you must know, Mistress Alice, that this was a sport well known to antiquity. The Persian ambassadors found Agesilaus, the Lacedemonian monarch, engaged in it; and Socrates also did the same, for which his pupil Alcibiades laughed at him.'

'And I suppose these heathens played at leap-frog, at cat-after-mouse, and marbles, as I have seen you do in one minute, and the next stuffing your girls' heads (and mine likewise if you could, but you can not) with Latin and Greek and such-like which is only fit for boys who are to be clerics,' remarked his wife tartly.

'Indeed,' said More with interest, 'Augustus often amused himself at marbles with little Moorish boys, only then they used nuts. Which reminds me, though I know not why it should, that I promised to send Erasmus the second book of my *Utopia* which I have at last completed.'

'*Utopia*!' grumbled Mrs More. 'It sounds like a disease of the bladder. What a good year, man, will you waste your time writing books about a place called "Nowhere", when if you would but put yourself forward you might be Mayor of London – '

Her voice was drowned in shouts of welcome, as the young people of the household came running at the sound of More's footstep. His wife smiled despite herself; she could never be cross for long with this gentle, cheerful man who had so merry a humour, such friendly blue-grey eyes, and such a charming way with him.

Supper was eaten as usual in monastic fashion, all keeping silence while Meg, the eldest daughter, intoned a portion of Scripture, and her formidably learned sister Cecily followed with the *Commentaries* of Nicholas de Lyra. But then, again as usual, Mr More clapped his hands and cried that it was time for play.

'And let us act my droll of the Sergeant and the Friar,' said he, 'and it is my turn to be the wife with her distaff.'

It was wild knockabout stuff, such as he loved to write for the entertainment of the young people; they had reached the point when the Friar turned out to be a Sergeant in disguise, come to arrest a bankrupt, and Mr More, dressed in one of his wife's snoods and kirtles, was in the thick of the mimic battle, when Mrs More gave an exclamation of dismay. Standing on the threshold, vainly trying to make his voice heard in the din, was a gentleman wearing the King's livery.

'I knocked,' said this personage, 'but could get no reply. Master More, the King's Grace desires you to wait upon him at Greenwich.'

(ii)

More came home a couple of hours later in an unusually pensive mood, and taking his wife's arm drew her out into the garden, where, to her often expressed disgust, he kept a collection of strange pets, a fox, a badger, a beaver, and several conies, studying their habits and discussing these with his learned friends.

'For some while now,' he began, 'his Grace has been pressing me to enter his service, hearing, as he is pleased to say, that everyone is praising my diplomacy on my embassies for the City. Then, says he, when the 'prentices rose against the foreigners on Evil May Day, it was I who persuaded them to go home (though indeed, poor silly souls, it was rather the armed retainers of the nobles). And of late, says his Grace, I displayed such learning in arguing the case of the Pope's great ship which was driven on our shores and claimed by his Highness, that, though the verdict was given for the Pope, the King will not rest until he has persuaded me to come upon his Council.'

'And why should you need pressing, Master More?' his wife demanded sharply.

'It would mean my breaking old associations with the City, and I foresee I should have but little time to spend with my family,' More replied; but his tone was evasive.

He walked among his flowers, one shoulder raised higher than the other, a sure sign that he was disturbed. One of his deepest beliefs was in that of a strong central government; no man more reverenced authority than he. But on the other hand the past few years had shown that King Henry plunged into aggressive wars for personal aggrandisement, and that he was ruled by a cleric whose ambition was always put before his duty, and who urged the King to greater and still greater extravagance. The thought of living in such an atmosphere as he would find at Court was altogether hateful to Thomas More.

'I really believe, Mr More,' his wife said with marked patience, 'that if you would take meat to your dinner like an honest Englishman, you would not get queer maggots in your head as you are wont to do. It is no wonder that you run upon fancies and imaginings when you live on milk slops and green-stuff. Was it not only the other day that you interrupted me in the midst of my candle-making to tell me that the earth is the lowest spot in creation whence everything ascends in all directions? Good God, man! If you continue in this way they will put you into the Hospital of Our Lady of Bethlehem.'

She paused to take breathe.

'And then there are these friends of yours who encourage you in folly. I would not speak evil of a priest, but when Master Linacre pretends to a knowledge of medicine, and calls me superstitious because I send your hosen to a wise woman to have an ague charmed away, and when this Erasmus, of whom you think so much, though he is a bastard and for ever carping about what he terms the abuses of religion, and turning up his nose at good English beer, and demanding a skin of Greek wine, and terming honest folk ignorant because they cannot speak the Greek tongue, which is a heathen tongue, and – now I have forgot what I was going to say.'

'I believe you were about to advise me on the King's most gracious invitation to come upon his Council, Mistress Alice,' her husband said meekly.

'Why, to be sure I was. And what would you do, pray, that you will not put yourself forward with the rest of folks? Will you sit still by the fire and make goslings in the ashes as children do? Nay, go forward, man, go forward, for as my late husband, Master Middleton, used to say (God assoil his soul), it is ever better to rule than to be ruled. And therefore I would not, by God, I warrant you, be so foolish as to be ruled where I might rule.'

'In this I daresay you speak the truth, wife,' observed More, bending down to fondle a little dog which, to his wife's disgust, he had christened Cerberus. 'For I never found you willing to be ruled yet.'

This Mrs More took as a compliment, and being mollified eagerly enquired what a Councillorship was worth. Informed that the salary was one hundred pounds a year, and would almost certainly carry a knighthood, she clapped her hands and exclaimed joyfully:

'Why then we can afford a fool! Bless me, how I have longed for a Fool in Parti-coloured tunic sewn with bells, to cheer me with his merry quips when I am out of humour.'

'I had supposed that poor *Morus*, your fool of a husband, was enough,' he murmured, giving her a kiss.

And then he went on seriously, speaking half to himself:

'I remember what I wrote in *Utopia:* "Suppose wrong opinions cannot be plucked up by the root, and you cannot cure, as you would wish, vices of long standing, yet you must not on that account abandon the ship of state, but by indirect approach and covert suggestion you must strive to the best of your power to handle all well, and what you cannot turn to good, you must make as little bad as you can." '

'I cannot understand one word you are saying,' sighed Mrs More.

He smiled abstractedly.

'I took the liberty of discussing with his Grace my hesitation in accepting his honourable offer, for there be some about him (to speak frankly, wife) with whom I fear I might fall out if I were on his Council, some who infect him with their own overweening ambition and love of empty show. His Grace told me very solemnly that if I entered his service he would expect me to be God's servant first, and then my King's; the which has made me more easy in my mind,' he added, becoming his cheerful self again.

At the time when Thomas More entered the King's service, it seemed that the little clouds which had threatened to dim the golden morning of the reign had dispersed.

The Queen had borne a living child, the Princess Mary, and though disappointed that is was not a boy, Henry had exclaimed optimistically:

'We are both still young. The sons will follow.'

He was quite delighted with his new Councillor, whose *Utopia* had made him famous throughout Europe, and often would send for More of an evening to accompany himself and the Queen to a watch-tower on a hillside behind Placentia, where they would consider the diversity of the stars and admire the magnificent view of the estuary with its shipping and of the Epping woods to the north. Here More would entertain the royal pair by recounting how the Egyptians had determined the beginning of the year by the morning appearance of Sirius, the brightest star in the Northern Hemisphere; how the Phoenicians had directed themselves on their voyages by the Little Bear, called by them 'the tail of the dog'; and how until recently Venus had been considered as two different stars, Hesper in the evening and Lucifer in the morning.

'We shall know more of this wondrous science of astronomy,' said he, 'when we are better acquainted with Greek literature.'

He lost no opportunity of trying to persuade the King to become a patron of letters and to make England what she had been in the eighth century, the centre of European scholarship whence learning had spread over a war-ridden world. They had lost Erasmus for want of a rich patron; but there were other scholars to be encouraged. Henry listened solemnly; he sent for More's learned daughters to hear them dispute in philosophy before him; he praised them extravagantly, and was large in his promises to encourage the New Learning. The reluctance with which More had entered the King's service was swept away; though he secretly deplored Wolsey's amassing of pluralities and his vainglory, he was ready to admit that the Cardinal's vanity was to some extent offset by his kindness to the poor, whose suits he heard instantly, expecting lawyers to plead for them without fees; and best of all, even Wolsey seemed converted to the cause of international peace.

What More did not know was that the King's graciousness was the result of a secret and abominable suspicion being dispelled from his mind.

He had tried to persuade himself that it was his wife's poor health which prevented her from bearing living children; but still the abominable word 'pox' had continued to haunt him. A year or two previously a small lesion had appeared in his leg; he had fallen into uncontrollable panic, though his doctors had assured him it was perfectly harmless and innocent, and indeed it had yielded to treatment. But then there was his rash, which still recurred; and when it was on him he suffered from sudden violent rages which alarmed even himself. He had heard or read somewhere that syphilis affects the brain.

He had tried to stifle the preposterous fear by flinging himself more and more into strenuous sports, by arranging ever more elaborate masques and tournaments, by composing Masses, by reckless gambling, by inventing a new harness such as no armourer had ever seen. But still he had been restless, walking out in the middle of a morality play, moving constantly from one royal manor to another, simmering with impatience during Council meetings, humming his own songs under his breath, dreading to be alone.

Well, thank God all that was over now. His wife had produced a daughter who throve, and a mistress, Elizabeth Blount, had given him a healthy son. He was not particularly amorous by nature; sexual affairs were to him like any other sport; but to be defective as a lover not only wounded his vanity; it increased his dread that he was the victim of a foul disease. He had proved his virility now, and believed himself satisfied; as for Elizabeth, there was the faithful Wolsey to marry her off respectably to some docile knight, while her child was brought up in semi-royal privacy. Meanwhile he was in the brief exciting stage of

44

another amour, this time with the younger daughter of Sir Thomas Boleyn. No doubt he would soon tire of this rather cloyingly sweet Mary; but again there would be Wolsey to find her a husband.

His public affairs, too, seemed to him to be going excellently. True, he suffered a sharp disappointment when, the Emperor Maximilian dying at last, Henry did not receive a single vote in the election of the new one; all those bribes for nothing! But, as Wolsey impressed on him, the lay headship of Europe remained now only in theory; and since the new Emperor, young Charles V, Catherine's nephew, had become lord of all Spain, Austro-Germany, and Italy south of the Papal States, King Francis of France was courting King Henry's alliance, as was Charles himself. To be courted was what Henry liked best in life (and was expecting ever more and more as his right); and Wolsey was planning a stupendous love-feast with Francis, while making a secret treaty with Charles behind his back. To Wolsey it was to be the golden frame of high politics; to Henry an opportunity to show all Europe how much richer and handsomer and more athletic he was than these younger kings.

Never had he been in higher spirits than on this fantastic occasion which came to be known as the Field of the Cloth of Gold; it did not occur to him, and even if it had he would not have cared, that so costly a love-feast would require a war with its loot to replenish his coffers and put his nobles in pocket again.

It seemed to him that his dear Wolsey, to whom he had given carte blanche to arrange the treaty with Francis, had even been able to arrange the weather; the June sun shone dazzlingly upon the silken city of three thousand white tents pitched on the French plain, the gentlest of breezes fluttered the coloured pennons which decorated each tent, a bright moon glittered on the glass palace designed by

Wolsey and shipped over from England piecemeal. In the courtyard of this mushroom thing, the King's beasts, as large as life, guarded a fountain spouting wine, while Alexander, Hercules, and Julius Caesar adorned the walls. A splendid chapel was served by thirty-five priests, and a kitchen by two hundred servitors. Everything that could be gold, was gold, hurting the eye but rejoicing Henry's heart.

He was almost beside himself with pride as he rode out for his ceremonial meeting with Francis who was at his much smaller town of canvas at Ardes, and who was content with a marquee while Henry had a glazed palace. The cannon boomed from the ridge in salute, and the knights and archers of either side, with standards displayed and bows bent, gave an ironically martial air to this love-feast. Trumpets and sackbuts blared; the two hosts halted; and across the clear space Henry spurred his great charger, even his reins and saddle flashing with jewels, to meet the tall young man whose workmanlike armour bore the dint of many a battle. The Kings reined-in simultaneously, dismounted, embraced, and walked arm-in-arm to the inevitable cloth of gold pavilion and the two chairs of estate and the elaborate refreshments, while both hosts roared out their acclamations.

'He is well enough, well enough,' Henry commented to his wife afterwards. 'But I would not call him handsome, and though he fancies himself a poet, he was fain to admit that I was his master there. I sang him my *Pastime with good company*, and he begged for a copy. And he is very spare in the legs,' Henry added, glancing complacently at his own calves.

Never had Henry so excelled as he did at the jousting and the pageantry of that week. Within the English pale he had caused a tiltyard to be set up, with artificial trees around it, bearing among their leaves of green damask and their fruits of silver the Arms of England and of France; and day after day, in tourney and joust, Henry carried off the palm. He beat the younger King at tennis, outdistanced him in hunting; but he was not content until he had shown Francis his skill at archery, an art the French had never mastered.

Forsaking gold for once, he arrayed himself from head to foot in green which well became his auburn hair and set off his tall figure with its flat stomach and enormous width of shoulder. He would have the butts set at the extraordinary distance of twelvescore yards apart, carefully explaining to Francis that this was almost unheard of. The whole plain watched in reverent silence as he strung his bow, well aware of the graceful figure he made, with left foot turned slightly inwards and one hand reaching for a clothyard shaft from his belt, grasping it a few inches above the grey-goose feathers. He was in his element, the cynosure of all eyes. The thumb of his drawing hand came into light contact with his right ear; he loosed without a second's pause; and ere his arrow had made half its flight he knew that it would split the peg which affixed the white mark to the centre of the butt, a superlative feat of archery.

Again and again he repeated this feat, while the whole plain shook with applause. He was in an ecstasy when at last he walked with Francis to the cloth of gold pavilion where his wife and Queen Claude of France awaited them with their ladies to partake of a banquet. Francis might be a charging sort of man who risked his life recklessly in battle, but he, Henry, had shown him during the past week, and especially today, that in all true manly sports he was the Frenchman's superior. His little mouth grinned suddenly with sly pleasure; with a lightning movement he seized Francis by the collar, crying joyously:

'Brother, I will have a wrestle with you!'

The tall young Frenchman was taken off his guard. He nearly fell; recovered himself; and by some quick skilful movement flung Henry flat upon his back. In that fraction of a second, Henry had a glimpse of Wolsey, the fleshy face surprised into a smile.

As the whole gaudy multitude stood petrified, Queen Catherine's voice came clearly:

'*Madre de Dios!* I have never seen your Grace take such a tumble!'

He rose slowly. His face was purple with rage, and in his heart was something almost maniac. Courtiers and ladies stepped hastily into the breach, and Francis himself, exercising all his native charm, speaking of the slipperiness of the turf, explaining that he had used a cunning trick taught him by a professional wrestler, brushing Henry down with his own hands, helped in the soothing.

But Henry, though he laughed it off, would remember that trifling little incident. Especially would he remember his wife's tactless remark, and the smile, gone again in an instant, he had surprised on the face of his faithful Wolsey.

(iii)

The first thing he did on his return to England was to marry off Mary Boleyn to William Carey, a Gentleman of his Chamber, relishing her tears; and then, feeling a crying need to teach everyone he was master, he summarily cut off the head of the Duke of Buckingham who, so Wolsey had informed him, had dared to say in private that he had better title to the throne than King Henry. If that sort of treason went unpunished, England might be plunged into a civil war again.

So he told himself; it was for his kingdom's sake that he had sacrificed this man who had been to him a kind of elder brother. But he sensed that his new Councillor, Thomas More, from his silence on the subject, disapproved, possibly believing that Wolsey had struck at

Buckingham as being the very embodiment of the old nobility who hated him, even that the execution of the Duke had been judicial murder. To question the purity of Wolsey's motives was in effect to question those of Wolsey's master; and Henry watched for an opportunity of showing More, whom he really respected, that he was a man of the very highest principle. Such an opportunity occurred in the matter of Martin Luther.

Some three years previously, this obscure Augustinian monk had nailed his ninety-five Theses to the door of the church of Wittenburg, and in the spring of 1521 he was summoned to the Diet of Worms to answer a charge of heresy. He had become a power; his heretical writings were gravely disturbing a Christendom already menaced by Selim the Grim who was building up a huge Turkish empire; and Henry had ordered the public burning in St Paul's Churchyard of Luther's book, *The Babylonish Captivity of the Church.*

But this was not enough. It needed a reply, and who so fit to write one as his Grace of England who, at least in his own estimation, was a brilliant theologian, and at the moment was aching for that sense of moral integrity which would convince himself and all the world that he was the very pattern of a Christian king.

Jousts and hunting were neglected while the thick fingers, ablaze with some of his two hundred and thirty-four rings, covered sheet after sheet of parchment in a work which must turn out to be a masterpiece. He would smite Luther hip and thigh; and in return he naturally expected from Pope Leo some special title such as had been bestowed in former ages upon other royal champions of the Papacy. Drawing largely upon the learning of Bishop Fisher, his old tutor and a very great scholar, Henry finished at length his *Assertion of the Seven Sacraments*, and sent the untidy mass of manuscript to Thomas More, just appointed his Under Treasurer, to sort out.

He expected as a matter of course the highest praise from a subject he had so honoured, and who himself was a scholar famous throughout Europe. Henry was hunting at Richmond when More brought back the manuscript; and after the long ceremony of supper he took More out for a walk in the courtyard to regale his Grace with compliments. It was a windy May evening, and the gilded vanes on the many towers made quite an orchestra, as the two figures, the one so huge and gaudy, the other with his clothes put on anyhow as usual, and with his right shoulder raised slightly higher than his left, walked slowly towards the fountain from which water sprang from artificial roses.

It appeared to Henry that his companion must be quite overwhelmed by what he had read, for he said practically nothing. To give him time to recover himself, Henry burst out:

'This Luther is a serpent, a plague, a mad, raging dog, a trumpeter of schism and calumnies! What a great member of the devil he is who endeavours to tear the Christian members of Christ from their Head upon earth!'

His face was flushed with genuine passion.

'But I have drawn his teeth! Come, Master More, tell me if I have not muzzled this mad dog. And especially in the matter of the Sacrament of Matrimony upon which he voided his venom.' He quoted in solemn accents what he himself had written in reply: ' "Who does not tremble when he considers how he should deal with his wife, for not only is he bound to love her, but so to live with her that he may return her to God pure and without stain, when God who gave shall demand His own again." '

More bowed his head gravely, but it seemed that his thoughts were elsewhere.

'We bid you to speak your mind on what we have written,' Henry said sharply.

'It has come into my mind while reading your Grace's book,' said More in a hesitating manner, 'that perhaps it is beneath your Grace's royal dignity to write a reply to this lowborn heretic.'

'Eh?' barked Henry, bitterly mortified by the lack of the praise he had expected.

Again More was silent for a space. He could scarcely say what was in his mind, that the King had written the book simply in order to get a new title for himself, and that he, whom everyone knew to be a faithless husband, was not the one to write a sermon on the Sacrament of Matrimony.

'It is of course, for your Grace to decide,' More said at length. 'But with all submission I would suggest to your Grace that you may think it in your royal wisdom a little to soften certain phrases in the chapter upon the Pope's authority.'

'And why, pray?' demanded his Grace, even more sharply than before.

'I must put your Highness in remembrance that the Pope is a temporal prince as you are, at present most happily united with other Christian princes in the affairs of Europe. But it may hereafter so fall out that your Grace and His Holiness may vary, as two temporal princes, where-upon may grow a breach of amity between you. With great respect, therefore, I think it best that that place be amended, and his authority be more – more slenderly touched.'

'God's body!' Henry cried with vehemence, 'that shall not be. We are so much bounden to the See of Rome that we cannot do it too much honour.'

For yet a third time More was silent, for again his reverence for his royal master prevented him from saying what he thought. And what he thought was that the extravagant and fulsome way in which Henry had written of the Medicean Pope Leo, who had been loaded with abbeys from his youth and made a Cardinal at thirteen, was exactly the sort of ammunition of which Luther would make good use in his reply.

'I am, of course, at one with your Grace,' he said gravely, 'in reverencing the spiritual authority of the Pope as the key-stone of the arch which supports our Christian society. I am moved to obedience to that See not only by what learned and holymen have written, but because we find that on the one hand every enemy of the Christian faith makes war on that See, and on the other, no one who has ever declared himself its enemy has not also shortly afterwards shown most evidently that he was the enemy of the Christian religion. Nevertheless, in time past His Holiness' predecessors and your Grace's have fallen out over temporal matters, and therefore – '

Henry interrupted with an impatient gesture.

'Whatsoever impediment there be to the contrary,' he said, very stiff, 'we will set forth that authority to the uttermost, for we received from it our Crown Imperial.'

A copy of the masterpiece, bound in sheepskin covered with cloth of gold, was sent to the Pope, who replied by bestowing upon Henry the title of Defender of the Faith. But Henry, while flattered, was in a restless, touchy mood. He had been thwarted in his ambition to win the crown of France, even to recover the lost Plantagenet possessions in that kingdom; he was thwarted again when, Leo X dying suddenly, Wolsey did not receive a fifth of the votes cast in the Papal election. Henry had talked optimistically of having sons by his wife; but Catherine had borne another daughter who lived only a few days, and it was plain she could have no more children. So he brooded; and all the while inside himself he was collecting little grievances.

Catherine had referred to jousting as 'a frolic'; Catherine had written to him that the victory of Flodden was more important than if he had won all the realm of France; Catherine had laughed at his mishap on the Field of the Cloth of Gold, and Wolsey had smiled at it. Unrealized by himself, a change of attitude was growing up in Henry towards his wife and his favourite. He still regarded Catherine as his dearest companion, and admired her simple goodness; on Wolsey who, as Papal Legate and Lord Chancellor, had in his hands both the ecclesiastical and civil machinery of the realm, Henry still relied in all public matters. But within him what was to become a familiar process was at work; his abandonment of the initiative to a stronger will was being followed by an irksomeness growing into resentment against those who had mastered him.

It was in such a mood of childish sullenness and secret rebellion that he met the young woman named Anne Boleyn.

Chapter Three

Despite his wealth, his smooth tongue, and his noble connections by marriage, Thomas Boleyn had not done so very well for himself in the new reign. All he had secured so far was a knighthood, the Governorship of Norwich Castle, and the honour of being sent with his father-in-law, Surrey, who after his victory of Flodden had been allowed to assume the title of Duke of Norfolk, in the train of the King's sister when she was being sacrificed on the altar of international politics to marry the elderly invalid, Louis of France.

That was in 1514; and since the French Court was considered the most refined in Europe, Sir Thomas had secured for his elder daughter, Anne, a place in the young Princess' household; when the widowed Princess had married her early love, the Duke of Suffolk, Anne had remained in France at the Court of the new French Queen, who took great pleasure in the company of young girls. Anne's letters home testified to the benefits she was receiving from this refined education; but towards the end of the year 1521, relations between England and France becoming strained once more, Sir Thomas sent Anne a letter bidding her to come home.

She took her time about it; and meanwhile her father was busy arranging a good marriage for her; he was determined that Anne should help raise the family prestige and not make such shipwreck of her life as her younger sister had done. He blamed Mary for not being able to retain the King's heart; true, it was a fickle heart, and all his Grace's amatory affairs had been extremely brief; but Mary was a Boleyn and ought to have made a good thing out of the liaison. And here she was, married off to this William Carey, who was not even a knight; that, raged Sir Thomas to himself, was Wolsey's doing, or rather it was the doing of Wolsey's new Steward, a bullet-headed, pasty-faced man named Thomas Cromwell, who nowadays managed the more seamy side of the Cardinal's affairs.

It was not until well on in the new year, 1522, that Anne Boleyn returned to the moated, fortified manor-house in Kent, known as Hever Castle, where her father was wont to spend several months in retrenchment after his fantastically expensive spells of living at Court.

To her family it was as though some exotic bird had come home to the nest. All through supper on the evening of her arrival they kept glancing in wonder at her French gown, with the bodice cut close to fit the figure, her enormous cuffs turned back on the forearm to show the lining of lynx fur, her hood with its horseshoe-shaped frontlet set well back on her head to expose her luxuriant but coarse black hair, her sleeve clasps of yellow topaz and jacinth which flashed and winked with every vivacious gesture. She talked incessantly, pouring out a stream of airy anecdotes, punctuating them with her high laugh which had an edge of hysteria. Her French ways, her arts and graces, made them feel gauche and ill-bred. She jingled whenever she moved, for she wore bracelets, most unusual in England, and on the bracelets were trinkets engraved with mottoes.

'Queen Claude was generous with gifts, it seems,' remarked her father, when the family had retired into the dais-chamber for the confections and muscadine.

Anne laughed again, giving him a sly glance, fluttering her fan of peacock's feathers on its ornamental handle, peeping at herself in the little mirror set in the centre of the toy.

He began presently to speak of the marriage he had been arranging for her.

'You know that through my late mother (God assoil her soul), I have a claim to the Ormonde estates in Ireland. Now this claim is contested by Sir James Butler; therefore have I persuaded his Grace that you shall marry this Sir James and unite our two families; and in due time you will become Countess of Ormonde, my girl, and – '

'And live in a tumbledown castle, watching the Nore flow by for my amusement, and as a special treat going to thatched Dublin for a Parliament,' Anne interrupted in her deep, husky voice. 'I thank you, *mon pere,* but after Paris – '

'But it is all arranged,' Sir Thomas exclaimed in weak indignation. 'Your grandfather, my Lord Norfolk, has given the match his blessing, the King's Grace approves, and Sir James and I are agreed upon your dowry.'

'So that only the consent of the bride is wanting.' Anne said pertly. 'And that, I am afraid, sir, will not be given. I am twenty years of age, you may remember; obtain for me a place at Court, and trust to me to find a husband who will please both of us better than can this Irish chieftain.'

'You have learnt strange ways in France, it seems,' grumbled her father; but he admired her poise, and he felt he could trust her not to make a fool of herself as her sister had done. She took after him, he thought complacently; she knew what she wanted and would be ruthless in pursuit of it.

56

In the bedroom they shared, Mary watched the unpacking of her sister's trunks, staring wide-eyed at the rich gowns, the furred mantles. In her tight-laced *basquine* worn over her chemise to give her a small waist, and her backless pantoufles which made an elegant little clatter as she walked, Anne wandered over to the window and surveyed the gardens.

'I must have a merry-trotter hung from that oak,' she remarked. 'In France it is all the rage to swing.'

Her sister said nothing. She was red-eyed, and had been silent all through supper.

'Are you with child, or what ails you?' Anne demanded, sitting down on the window-seat and nursing one knee.

Mary's pretty face crinkled up with misery.

'I hate to come home now,' she whimpered. 'It was here his Grace wooed me; he was for ever riding to Hever. He kissed me for the first time in the pleached alley. We were so h-happy – oh, where is my napkin?' she sobbed, groping for her handkerchief.

'Napkin,' scoffed Anne. 'Well-bred folk call it a *mouchoir*. Here, you may have mine.'

Mary took the tasselled square of cambric edged with Flanders lace, and momentarily forgot her broken heart in her curiosity.

'Did the Queen of France give you all these fine things?'

Anne closed one brilliant black eye in a wink.

'My child, are you really so innocent? She did not.' She took out a little filigree comfit-box and popped a sweetmeat between her sensual, obstinate lips.

'You mean that you had lovers?' persisted Mary.

'I mean that I had admirers. And if you think it the same thing, you are a fool. I held my admirers at arm's length,' she said, suiting the gesture to the word, 'and lo! they put rings on my fingers and bracelets on my wrists. I learned in

France the art of coquetry, the most necessary art for any woman.'

Her sister fell to studying her afresh. Anne was not beautiful; she was tall, thin, flat-chested, with a sallow complexion. Her brow rose bald above her sparkling eyes, and round her neck she wore a jewelled collar to hide a distressingly large mole. At supper their mother had remarked on so odd a fashion, and Anne had replied that she had made it *a la mode* in France. And perhaps to conceal the rudimentary finger on her left hand, she affected long ruffles to her sleeves. When they were children, Mary had been half fascinated, half repelled, by that deformity; she remembered their nurse shaking her head over it, and muttering:

'Bewitched at birth, was Mistress Anne. She will always have a finger in the pie, mark my words.'

'But did you never fall in love?' Mary inquired at length.

'Oh la la la!' cried Anne airily. 'Love is for green girls and poets. A brilliant marriage and a great estate, these are for me. I will have nothing under an earl's son, and I shall find one, never fear, when I am at Court and have looked around.'

'How hard you are! Yet you do not look hard; you look passionate. But you are like Father; he thinks of all things in terms of money and advancement. Whereas I – '

'Fell a victim to the wooing of his Grace,' interrupted Anne mockingly. 'And how has that advanced you? I tell you, you are a fool, Mall, and more of a fool because you made nothing out of your armour with a King. I'll warrant you have not so much as a pension.'

'I did not want to *make* anything!' Mary cried tearfully. 'I loved him. And I cannot understand why he should be so unkind. I did nothing to displease him, except that I did not bear him a child like that Bessie Blount, but that was not my fault. He is defective as a lover, for all he looks so strong and manly.'

'He has the pox,' Anne remarked, yawning. 'It is the talk of the French court.'

Her sister stared at her aghast.

'Anne! How can you say such a thing about his Grace of England!'

'Oh *mon Dieu!*' whispered Anne, mock-terrified. 'Will fire descend from Heaven and consume me? Or are there spies behind the arras?'

Mary lay a long while sleepless, inhaling her sister's heavy French perfume, looking at the face beside her on the pillow, the night-light glinting on the jewelled collar Anne wore even in bed. She is vain, thought Mary, and cold-blooded, and she is not nearly as pretty as I. How did she get all these admirers? And then poor Mary thought of her own faithless royal admirer, and wept afresh.

(ii)

The sedate round at Hever was turned into a whirl of gaiety. The country sports, the hawking and the hunting and the archery which formed the recreation of all such families as the Boleyns when they were staying at their country seats, were given a touch of the exotic by the mere presence of Anne. She wore a man's bonnet, rakishly on one side; she sang French songs, slightly *risqué,* as she rode homeward; she was bored with shovel-board, the usual evening game, and taught her family Mount Saint, at which, it seemed, the French Court lost fortunes every night.

The house was filled with her perfume, the rustle of her taffeta skirts, the jingle of her bracelets, the echo of her high laugh. The sober-coloured kersey and broadcloth of her family looked drab against the bright colours she affected, violet and fig-purple, crimson cloth of gold for feast days, tinsel which glittered with its coating of silver. Mary regarded with an envious eye the variety of head-dresses her sister wore; she could make an ordinary gable look daringly *outré* merely by a dextrous twist of the lappets into the shape of a whelk shell; sometimes she wore the *béguin,* like a nun's hood, its white silk lining showing off to advantage her thick black hair; next day she would appear in the long-tailed caul, bound and cross-plaited and stuffed with tow, reaching to her heels.

There was no doubt that she had profited by her French education. She spoke that language, and Italian, fluently; she played not only the lute and virginal, but the harp, rebec, and flute. She was adept at inventing new steps to a dance, new games, new everything.

But what most puzzled the simple Mary was Anne's relationship with men. There were always Boleyn relations or connections visiting the house, and there was not a male among them, from staid grandfathers to young boys, but Anne set herself out to flirt with them, to practise on them her arts of coquetry. The majority of them, while infected by her high spirits, obviously remained indifferent to her in their hearts; but there were a few among them who seemed to find in her something violently attractive. Of these the chief was her cousin, Thomas Wyatt.

He was a gentle, sensitive creature, a poet, and a happily married man. One cold winter's morning, when the frost sugared the grass, he came through the woods of Hever with a present of hares for his relations, and entering the gardens, paused in astonishment. Seated on a swing which was attached to a large bare oak, was Anne, her underdress drawn up to expose a generous length of black silk stocking, her thick black hair, unbound, without so much as a coif upon it, floating and tossing about her shoulders as she swung herself to and fro, her sallow face flushed like a child's with excitement. Like a child too, utterly unselfconscious, she called out to Wyatt in her husky voice:

'Oh come swing me, cousin, come swing me higher! I feel like a hawk released from the fist when I am on my merry-trotter!'

He pushed her to and fro, inhaling her perfume as she came swooping down to him, watching her whirling skirts and floating hair as she went soaring up again. Her bracelets rang like silver bells; her hair brushed his face. At last she sprang suddenly full into his arms, panting, laughing, murmuring that she was dizzy and that he must hold her tight. It was crude, perhaps, but he was a simple man; and as he held her he felt the beginning of a sort of madness tingle in his veins. She released herself and danced away from him towards the house, looking back over her shoulder with enticement and mockery in her full black eyes, running her fingers through her wildly disordered hair, begging him like a child not to tell her father, who disapproved of her swinging, glancing at him with the eyes of a woman.

He was captured by her, body and soul. He, hitherto so faithful to his young wife, now shamelessly wooed his cousin, pouring out his passion, begging for her favours, blissfully happy when she gave him a kind word, a surreptitious kiss, plunged into misery when she refused him more, lurking under her window just for a glimpse of her shadow on the panes.

On the last night of her stay at Hever, while she and her sister were undressing, there was a strange little sound against the window, and Mary cried out in alarm as she saw a blunt-headed bolt used for killing small birds sticking through one of the panes of thin horn. But Anne gave her high laugh, opened the casement, drew out the arrow, and unrolled the paper bound with thread about the shaft.

'It is a dart from Cupid's bow,' she said complacently. 'It is my love-lorn cousin's farewell.'

She sat down by the fire and read aloud:

> ' "*Whoso list to hunt? I know where is a hind,*
> *But as for me, alas, I may no more.*
> *The vain travail hath wearied me so sore,*
> *I am of them that farthest come behind.*
> *Yet may by no means my wearied mind*
> *Draw from the deer, but as she fleeth afore*
> *Fainting I follow. I leave off therefore,*
> *Since in a net I seek to hold the wind.*" '

The enchantress poor Wyatt thus described went off next day to become one of the Queen's Maids of Honour, taking with her her deceptive air of passion, her French gowns and graces, the trinkets she had collected from a score of admirers, and her cold-blooded purpose to make a brilliant marriage.

It was a dull household into which she entered. The Queen, though still under forty, was in temperament and body middle-aged; and repeated miscarriages and stillborn children had undermined a constitution which had never been strong. She was occupying herself with the education of her one surviving child, the little Princess Mary, passed more and more time at her religious devotions, wearing the habit of the Third Order of St Francis under her robes, spent two hours each day in spiritual reading, suffered in dignified silence her husband's capricious amours, and taught her ladies the art of lace-making, hitherto confined to nuns. But though she and Henry were no longer living together as man and wife, he treated her with affection and respect, still wore her favour in the lists, and relied on her to provide him with a multitude of little comforts.

With her black head bent over the cushion on which a parchment pattern, tricked out with small fishbones, was laid, Anne Boleyn plaited the thread for her lace from a number of minute bobbins; and looked about her.

Even in the Queen's seclusion, there was always a coming and going of gentlemen; there was her Highness' own entourage, her Great Chamberlain, her Master of the Horse, of the Purse, of the Wardrobe, esquires and pages, ushers and yeomen; and on public occasions, or at the joust, there were his Grace's gentlemen as well. Here as at Hever, while most of the courtier's found nothing particularly attractive in the new Maid of Honour, a few, like poor Wyatt, were drawn to her as steel is drawn to a magnet. Among the latter was young Lord Henry Percy, son and heir of the Earl of Northumberland, one of the oldest and greatest families in England, petty kings of the North. In the fashion of the day, Percy had been sent to learn the ways of the fashionable world in some nobleman's household, in this case Cardinal Wolsey's, who had no less than eight hundred high-born gentlemen to attend upon him.

It was soon plain to everyone that Percy had fallen head over heels in love with the Boleyn girl; and it was plain also that for once the flirtatious Anne was serious. Heads were shaken darkly, for Percy was already betrothed to Lady Mary Talbot, daughter of the Earl of Shrewsbury. But it appeared that Anne cared nothing for that; she had looked about her and she had made her choice of a future husband, not because Percy was particularly attractive (indeed he was a spindly, weak-chinned youth), but because of his wealth and social status, and she was going to waste no more time.

There came an occasion when Wolsey gave one of his lavish entertainments at York Place.

He had transformed the old building erected in the reign of Henry III, bequeathed to the Black Friars and sold by them to the Archbishop of York. It sprawled now almost from Scotland Yard to Westminster, new stone mingling with ancient lath and plaster, the numerous courts filled with his enormous retinue, his servants with TC for Thomas, Cardinal, embroidered on their breasts, his gentlemen in his livery of crimson and black with thick gold chains about their necks, the Hat borne before him on a crimson silk cushion when he went to dine, his wall tapestries changed daily, his cupboards displayed gold mazers, cups, and platters, which were duplicated on his table, his ante-rooms crowded with petitioners.

Among the guests invited on this occasion was Norfolk's son, Lord Thomas Howard, now the Earl of Surrey – invited so that the still impoverished Howard might feast his eyes upon the wealth of the butcher's son. With Surrey came his brother-in-law, Sir Thomas Boleyn, who was always ready to eat a free dinner; and with Sir Thomas came Anne.

From his crimson velvet chair of estate upon its dais, Wolsey presided over the feast, full of bonhomie, glorying in his magnificence. Above the canopy a great crucifix blazed with jewels, and about him stood his gentlemen holding golden maces with knobs as big as heads. In the midst of the pompous ceremonial, just as the Carver, his hand wrapped in a white towel, had uncovered a dish, had touched it in four parts with a roll of bread, and had given it to the Pantler to test for Assay of poison, an usher came running in great agitation to the foot of the dais, genuflected, and whispered to his master that some gentlemen arrayed in strange garments had arrived at my Lord Cardinal's water-gate; they were speaking French, which he did not understand, but from their gestures they seemed to be demanding admittance.

Wolsey beckoned forward his Great Chamberlain.

'I shall desire you,' said the Cardinal, 'because you can speak French, to go down and receive these strangers according to their estates, and to conduct them into this chamber, where they shall see us sitting merrily at our banquet, desiring them to sit down with us.'

The strangers were ushered in, a motley company, some in Turkish costume, others garbed like shepherds, all of them masked. They saluted the Cardinal, and being escorted to a table proceeded to play at mumchance with a cupful of gold pieces as the stake.

'I pray you,' said the Cardinal, again addressing his Great Chamberlain, 'show them that it seems to me there be among them some nobleman whom I suspect to be much more worthy to occupy this chair than I; to whom I would most gladly, if I knew him, surrender my place according to my duty.'

The Chamberlain, wearing a proper air of solemnity (though indeed he had had the arranging of this elaborate farce), picked out from the company of strangers one whose rich dress seemed to indicate that he was the nobleman in question. Suddenly from among his fellows there was a great roar of laughter, and up leapt a huge figure garbed like a shepherd, plucked off his vizor with its beard of silver wires, and disclosed the enormously wide face, the little pursed mouth, the flat eyes under upshot brows, of Henry the King.

Everyone present did their best to simulate astonishment; but Anne Boleyn's was genuine. She was too new to Court to have become bored by Henry's constant childish love of dressing up. She clapped her hands delightedly, and her prominent black eyes looked into the flat and narrow ones of Henry, instantly shifted in her direction.

He had seen her at Court, but he had not particularly noticed her. He noticed her now. He knew instantly that

65

she was really astonished and delighted by his little farce, where others, and especially his wife, only feigned to be. He noticed her again later, when the perfumed cloths had been withdrawn and the company danced. Henry danced as he did most other things, for the sheer joy of physical exercise; this Boleyn girl made it into an elaborate art, arching her leg, pointing her toe, swaying and mincing, but all the while vital and gay and full of high spirits. As he passed her in the Hey, the rhythmical interlacing of two groups of dancers moving in serpentine fashion in opposite directions, several times he caught a glance of fond understanding exchanged between Anne and young Lord Henry Percy.

The King experienced a sudden sharp annoyance; and before he left York Place that evening he had a private word with Wolsey, giving him certain orders.

(iii)

On the following morning Lord Henry Percy received a summons to his master's presence, though he was not on duty that week. He went unsuspecting of trouble, and found Wolsey in his Great Chamber and in his full pomp, with his gentlemen about him. His long red silk train made a shimmering pool upon the dais on which he sat; his tabard-shaped chimere strained across his stout but majestic person; through the slashes in his glove his rings glittered; and his expression was as lowering as a thundercloud.

Almost before the young man, greatly wondering, had made his genuflection, the full rolling voice, robbed now of its usual geniality, burst forth in icy scorn:

'I marvel not a little that you would entangle yourself, out of your peevish folly, with a foolish girl about the Court, I mean Mistress Anne Boleyn.'

Percy turned scarlet with humiliation. To have such a thing said in public!

'His Grace and I,' continued Wolsey, 'require to know how far you have proceeded in your intentions to marry this chit.'

The youth stammered with a touch of defiance:

'May it please you, we – we have plighted our troth.'

'Then,' thundered Wolsey, 'You have done like a lewd boy to attempt any such thing without the knowledge of the King's Grace, your father, or myself. After the death of your father, you are like to inherit one of the worthiest earldoms of this realm, and your father has already matched you according to your estate and honour. And therefore I command you that you go no more into the company of this girl, upon pain of the King's displeasure and mine. By the honour of my cardinalate, I will signify to your father your bold and rash attempt, whereby it is likely you will be disinherited for ever.'

Percy's lip was quivering, but he made an effort to be firm and dignified.

'I most humbly desire your Grace's favour herein, that you will stand so much my good lord as to entreat the King's Highness for me. For truly I have now gone so far in this matter, and that before many worthy witnesses' – (Anne had insisted on that) – 'that I know not how to discharge my conscience before God, nor yet excuse myself before men.'

'Do you still harp upon that string?' snarled Wolsey, his fleshy face almost as red as his cassock. 'I thought you would have shown yourself penitent for your foolish doings, and here have promised to relinquish from henceforth any further attempt therein.'

Percy, terrified, but deeply in love, persevered.

'Sir, though Mistress Anne is but a simple maid, yet is she descended of right royal stock. For by her mother she is of the Norfolk blood, and of her father's side lineally descended from the Earls of Ormonde. Why should I then, sir, be anything scrupulous to match with her, whose descent is equivalent with mine?'

Wolsey rose majestic in his crimson silk; he wagged a white-gloved finger at this impertinent youth who dared to argue with him.

'Think you,' he roared, 'that the King and I know not what we have to do in so weighty a matter as this? Now I will tell you that his Highness intends to bestow Mistress Anne on another person; and although she knows it not, yet has the King, like a most politic and prudent prince, contrived the matter so that she, I doubt not, will be right glad and grateful to do as he has arranged.'

He flapped his hand in dismissal. The affair was settled.

Now utterly miserable and cowed, and further bamboozled by his father who, summoned by the Cardinal, treated his son to another public rating, Percy contrived to see his beloved for a few moments before being hauled off to Northumberland. Anne's black eyes snapped with anger as he narrated what the Cardinal had said.

'So he called me a foolish girl about the Court, and a chit, did he? I shall remember that.'

Without mentioning it to her father, she begged leave of absence from the Queen and went down to Hever. Thither, a day or two later, came Sir Thomas in hot haste; how dared she leave Court without the King's permission! His Grace had enquired for her, and was much put out hearing that she had left London.

'I had permission from the Queen, in whose household I am,' Anne replied with the utmost calm.

'He stroked his silky beard and looked at her askance; for the first time he noticed how obstinate was her sensual mouth, her large chin. All trace of the vivacious butterfly had vanished; she was a hard young woman, and as such he appealed to her.

'I do not know whence you have got these silly notions that you can marry where you list, but you must void them, else will you bring ruin on your family. The nobles of England are now the King's servants, and as such he will arrange their marriages, as he has done that of Lord Henry Percy. I have worked hard to gain his Grace's favour, and look for greater honours yet, and I am not to be cheated of them by my daughter's folly.'

'Is it folly to look high when one would wed? It is what you did yourself, sir.'

'It is folly to cross his Grace in any matter. You do not know him yet; but in France you should have learned this new supremacy of princes.'

'I have not crossed him. I would not wed with Percy now were he a royal duke, the spineless fool!'

'You must return to London instanter; the King requires it.'

'By your leave, I am not well,' said Anne, suddenly demure.

'My name has been so cheapened and bandied about the Court that it has given me the migraine. You must be pleased to make my excuses.'

Failing to move her, Sir Thomas rode back to Court, and fearfully stammered his apologies for his daughter's conduct. He had expected a storm, for more and more of late the King was inflamed by the slightest opposition to his will. But Henry appeared distressed rather than wrathful. Mistress Anne must take care of her health; she must remain at Hever until she was quite recovered. He sent her a very gracious message to that effect, together with a copy of his portrait by Gerard Hoorenbault, set into the lid of a little enamelled box.

(iv)

It was some weeks later when Mary Boleyn came running to find her sister, her face radiant with joy.

'The King! He is hunting in the neighbourhood, and his horns sound so near that I am sure he will visit Hever. Oh he has not forgotten me after all! I knew he could not, I love him so.'

Henry was at his most amiable. He was like an overgrown child, showing off by making his horse curvet, boasting of the number of harts he had killed, ceremoniously presenting a fat carcase to Lady Boleyn, graciously agreeing to stay to dinner, slightly absurd in his over-elaborate hunting costume, with his yew-wood bow of his own gigantic height and his arrows adorned with peacock's feathers, pausing for appreciative laughter whenever he made a jest. But he did not receive it from the elder daughter of the house; she sat silent and sullen, and the King's flat eyes kept glancing at her in hurt bewilderment. After dinner he asked her to show him the gardens, just laid out in the new fashion; and he made it plain that he did not wish other company.

They climbed the artificial mount and strolled around the 'knots' where patterns were arranged in coloured cloth.

'They look like jam-tarts,' Anne observed flippantly, referring to the knots.

He laughed. He was excited, his little mouth pursed and moist, his narrow eyes glancing at her lustfully. That night at York Place when he had first noticed her had reminded him how much he liked the family type, how much he had enjoyed the considerable liberties allowed him by the mother when she was a buxom young matron in the first year of his reign, how exciting he had found the adoring younger daughter until her possessiveness had irked him.

'We had hoped to see you at Court again ere this, mistress,' said he, 'but seeing you did not come, we are here in person to sue for your return.'

'Your Grace honours me,' remarked Anne, bending to pick a pansy and smoothing the plush petals with one finger.

'We delight to honour those who please us. We are about to appoint your father the Treasurer of our Household.'

'My father is fortunate in pleasing your Grace,' said Anne, still formal and impassive, still intent upon smoothing the flower.

He stood in his favourite attitude, his great legs straddled, hands on hips, and surveyed her indulgently. Obviously the poor girl thought she had offended him.

'And so may you be also, sweetheart. It may be you have heard that we were at some travail to arrange an alliance for you before you left London so hastily.'

'I was told it at the second-hand, Sire,' replied Anne tartly. 'Indeed, all London seemed to know of it except me. Is it permitted that I inquire the name of my intended bridegroom?'

He rumbled with laughter, and closed his huge hand upon the slim white fingers which still played with the pansy.

'We said not that we would give you a bridegroom, mistress,' he whispered. 'We intend for you an alliance which will do you more honour than if you were to wed with the greatest of our subjects.'

The secret was out. He confidently expected her to be overwhelmed; never yet had he met a woman who could resist his wooing, or indeed who tried to. There was a moment's silence. She did not seek to withdraw her hand,

and in fact he was sure he felt a slight returning pressure; but she did not seem either bashful or ecstatic. She looked at him, and her prominent black eyes were enigmatic; so was the tone of her husky voice as she said at last:

'Under your Grace's favour, so hasty a wooing is strange to me. In France, where I was bred, they take pleasure in the chase. And I assure your Grace, I am not to be taken by a bird-bolt.'

He pressed her hand to his lips, that rudimentary sixth finger on it strangely titillating his desire. This was to be a new experience, and one he thought he would relish greatly. He would chase this fleet hind since she demanded it, and bring her down at length with a broad-arrow; it would serve to increase his appetite jaded by women who fell into his arms.

She sat a long while by the fire that evening, when Mary had sobbed herself to sleep; and her eyes were very thoughtful.

Anne was her father's daughter, but she had more than his smooth tongue, his selfishness, and his sycophancy. She possessed, as she had found in France, a complete command over her physical inclinations, and an astonishing tenacity until she had attained her objective. Also she had courage, high courage, and she would need every ounce of it if she were to play the difficult and dangerous game which had occurred to her, and which seemed to her now the only game left to play.

Her sister was a living warning to her, if she needed one, to avoid an amatory affair with the King. On the other hand it seemed that a brilliant marriage, such as she had determined on, must have the King's consent, a consent that would not be given.

There was another alternative; and sitting here with her feet crossed, her jewelled collar flashing in the firelight, her obstinate chin sunk upon her breast, she reviewed her assets. Besides brains and a will which could be as fixed as death, she had a violent attraction for certain men, and it seemed that King Henry was one of them. She had learnt to perfection in France the art of enticing and at the same time holding off. And the Queen was sickly, past child-bearing, and no longer co-habiting with her husband.

Anne smiled slowly and secretly, remembering how an astrologer had forecast for her a brilliant marriage. Her black eyes snapped with excitement as in the glowing logs she saw, or thought she saw, the shape of a crown.

Chapter Four

The gossip-mongers of the Court soon began to notice how very much more frequently his Grace visited the Queen's apartments, and it was not long before the reason became obvious.

'We have a mind to dance, ladies,' he would say jovially to the Maids of Honour; but though he spoke to them in general, his eyes spoke only to Mistress Anne Boleyn.

He was tired, it seemed, of the old English group dances which tended to communal enjoyment. Pair dances were all the mode in France, and Mistress Anne must teach them to the English Court. The elder ladies were shocked, for the Church frowned heavily upon this new mode; they too frowned when they watched the indecent or suggestive kind of dancing Mistress Anne taught Henry. She hummed the old airs of the troubadours as she mimed a teasing figure, a sulking figure, and a reconciliation; she took swirling leaps, her skirts billowing out like a balloon, exposing her legs to the knees. He followed her excitedly, snapping his heels high in the air, imitating her obscene pantomime.

'Your Grace has not mastered La Volto yet,' she would say. 'See, you must place your hands firmly on my waist – so – and in this third figure your Grace must take your

74

weight upon your left foot and make a half turn in order to support me while I, with my arm about your neck, make my spring – oh *mon Dieu!*' – (in mock dismay) – 'I forgot then that I must keep my skirts down with my other hand.'

Or she would sit herself down at the clavichord, softly playing while Henry sang a new song he had composed, bending over her, his hot breath on her neck. They were always love-songs nowadays.

> *'The daisy delectable,*
> *The violet wan and blue!*
> *Ye are not so variable,*
> *I love you and no more'.*

He wore a new favour in his helm when he jousted, and as he made his horse perform marvellous feats he glanced through his eye-slits at a certain figure in the gallery, a figure always dressed in the vivid colours he loved. His wife had always been slightly scornful of his showiness in dress and his attachment to heavy perfumes; Anne loudly admired each new costume, begged for the name of each new essence. She entered into the spirit of his masques, clapping her hands and exclaiming in delight when the stranger in Venetian costume or disguised as a Saracen, invariably turned out to be the King. The pair of them sat for hours over the chess-board, while she taught him fresh varieties of the game.

'This one is called "Take if you can",' said she; and her prominent dark eyes looked meaningly into his.

The Court took it for granted that Anne had replaced her sister in the royal bed, and wondered at the length of this new amour. Only Henry and Anne herself knew the secret; she was refusing to give him full satisfaction.

So far he still found it diverting to chase this fleet hind, never doubting that he would bring her down. But as the months went by he found that, like Wyatt, he was seeking to hold the wind in a net, and that it was he who was entangled. For the first time in his career the mighty master of England was being thwarted in his primitive will by a woman, and he could not understand it. He mistook, as so many other men had mistaken, the promise of passion in her sensual mouth and inviting eyes; he was unaware of a frigidity which used flirtation merely as a weapon to gain an end. To him she remained a teasing, passionate creature, more desirable even than the toy of military renown which Wolsey was offering him in a new war with France.

She had hooked him, and she was playing this great fish with the hand of an expert. She knew perfectly well that, while refusing to yield, she must make her company indispensable to her lover, yet at the same time she knew that he would tire if he saw too much of her. So off she would go to Hever, whither there would follow messengers bringing her the latest love lament from the royal pen:

> *'Whereto should I express*
> *My inward heaviness?*
> *No mirth can make me fain*
> *Until we meet again.'*

The poetry was poor, but the promises began to be more definite. He sent her a gold tablet inscribed with the motto:

> *'Whoso loveth should love but one;*
> *Change who will, I will be none.'*

There were love-letters too, breathing ardour.

'My mistress and friend,' he wrote, dropping the customary royal "we", 'I and my heart put ourselves into your hands, begging you to recommend us to your favour.

For it were a great pity to increase our pain which absence alone does sufficiently, and more than I could ever have thought; bringing to my mind a point of astronomy, which is that the longer the days are, the father from us is the sun, and yet his heat is more scorching; so it is with our love, we are at a distance from one another, and yet it keeps its fervency, at least on my side.'

She answered evasively, or sometimes not at all. At her own vile game she was displaying extraordinary patience and courage. By allowing him liberties without once losing her own self-control, by checking, enticing, by drawing him to her by a glance or touch, by going off to Hever when he became too demanding, she was so increasing her spell over him that what had begun as a simple infatuation was becoming to Henry an overmastering obsession.

Except to the gossip-mongers the affair was of little interest. The Queen, poor lady had seen so many light o' loves come and go, and she herself was so ill at this time that her life was despaired of. The fact that her young daughter Mary had been sent away to keep her Court as Princess of Wales at Ludlow, was far more distressing to Catherine than a marital infidelity to which she had become inured. The very thought of Ludlow made her shudder, for in that dank and isolated castle she had passed the miserable months of her nominal marriage with the sickly Arthur.

And the realm at large was far too preoccupied to be interested in his Grace's amatory affairs. Wolsey had launched the war which was to prove his last; he was in an irritable mood since once again he had been denied the Papacy on the death of Adrian VI, this time not receiving a single vote; and because of the enormous expense of this war with France he had been obliged to advise Henry to call a Parliament. And the Commons refused him the eight hundred thousand pounds he had proposed to raise by a tax of four shillings in the pound on lands and goods. There was not in the whole realm, they asserted, the sum demanded.

'Would to God, Master More,' he cried in half humorous exasperation, meeting More at Court, 'that you had been at Rome, on one of your beloved pilgrimages, when I made you Speaker.'

'Your Grace not offended, so would I too,' sighed More, to whom Wolsey's whole war policy was hateful.

While the war dragged uselessly on, and the people cursed Wolsey, and Wolsey confidently assured his master that in the end he would 'attain' all France, the Queen unexpectedly recovered her health. Seeing for herself now the flagrant way in which Henry and Anne were behaving, she spoke to him of it, with unaccustomed tact appealing to his love for their daughter Mary. Having being played with like a shuttlecock between prospective bridegrooms, at the moment Mary was betrothed to Henry's ally and Catherine's nephew, the Emperor Charles V; as such she was to be brought up to Court to be shown off to Charles, who was paying a flying visit to meet his bride-to-be; and a clever child such as she was, devoted to both her parents, might well be injured for life if she heard of this scandalous thing.

'Consider, sir,' begged Catherine, 'how when you used to carry her about in your arms and show her to your people from the window, you were wont to say, "By the Eternal, this little girl never cries!" Would she not cry now, ay, and bitterly, if she heard what all the Court is whispering?'

To stand well in the eyes of everyone, particularly in those of the daughter he genuinely loved, was essential to Henry, and for the moment Anne's spell broke. A message was brought her giving her an indefinite leave of absence from Court. Henry expected a flood of tears, bitter reproaches; but once again he had reckoned without Anne.

She went with the greatest calm; she even seemed glad to go. The last sight he had of her was of a gay figure in the vivid colours they both loved, riding her palfrey towards the gatehouse, with a long train of sumpter-horses, loaded with the presents he had showered upon her, following behind.

(ii)

He waited to hear from her.

He was convinced that she loved him as passionately as he loved her, and he was bewildered by the cat-and-mouse game she was playing. That she was ambitious was plain, and he admired her for it; but what could she want that he had not given or promised? For her sake he had raised her father to the peerage as Viscount Rochford; for her sake he had honoured her incapable brother George by sending him on a foreign embassy. If she would yield he would give her any title in her own right she might fancy, but when he suggested it she merely shrugged her shoulders. Then what did she want?

The days passed, and the weeks; and still she did not write. Her absence and her silence only increased his obsession; he could not think of anything except those enticing black eyes, that sensual, poppy-red mouth, that extra finger which so intrigued him.

The appalling news arrived that Rhodes had fallen to the Infidel and that all the eastern sea was in his hands. Hard upon this came the tidings that Francis of France had been beaten and captured at the Battle of Pavia by the Emperor, who was now in no mood to share the spoils with an ally who had contributed very little besides money. Henry listened; he nodded his head sagely when Wolsey whispered that they must make peace with France and so avenge themselves on the perfidious Emperor who had promised his Grace the old Plantagenet possessions; but all the while Henry's mind was elsewhere. It was at Hever; in fancy he walked in the garden among the 'jam-tarts', watching slim fingers caress a pansy, hearing a husky voice sing a French song.

He would not go down there; it was beneath his dignity; but he would write. He did so stiffly, venturing a threat. Her absence grieved him; he admitted it, 'but if I heard for certain that you yourself desired it, I could do not other than complain of my ill fortune, and by degrees abate my folly.'

Again he waited in a fever of anxiety; her reply, when at last it came, both maddened and further ensnared him. She was perfectly cool; she had left Court in obedience to his Grace's command; her absence grieved her as much as it did him, but his least wish was to her a sacred thing; and so on. She was his very humble subject and loving bedeswoman, Anne Boleyn.

'By turning over in my thoughts the contents of your last letter, I have put myself into a great agony, not knowing how to understand them, whether to my disadvantage or not. I beseech you now with the greatest earnestness to let me know your whole intentions as to the love between us two. For I must of necessity obtain this answer of you, having been so long a time struck with the dart of love, and being not yet sure whether I shall fail, or find a place in your heart.'

He paused in his writing, fraying out the feathers of his jewel-studded quill. 'Whether I shall fail.' Those words made him uneasy, called up to the surface of his mind a horrible suspicion he had tried to stifle, a suspicion that he had been relieved by Anne's refusal to give him full satisfaction, because he dreaded his virility being put to the test. But it was ridiculous; with her, the one real love of his life, he would prove himself a great lover.

'This uncertainty,' he continued, 'has hindered me of late of naming you my mistress, since you only love me with an ordinary affection; but if you please to do the duty of a true and loyal mistress, and to give yourself, body and heart, to me, I promise that I will cast off all others that are in competition with you out of my thoughts and affections, serving you only. I beg you to give me an entire answer to this my rude letter, that I may know on what and how far I may depend; but if it does not please you to answer me in writing, let me know some place where I may have it by word of mouth, and I will go thither with all my heart. Written by the hand of him that would willingly be entirely yours, Henry Rex.'

She received the letter at Hever; and having read it, told the messenger that he must wait for her answer until next day. She consulted no one, not even her grasping and ambitious father, but shut herself in her room and bolted the door.

The time had come to land her fish or lose it for ever; a crisis was at hand. She had pinned her hopes on Catherine's dying; but the Queen had recovered and was still comparatively young. And still Henry believed that he could have Anne without having to face where he stood with his wife; he must be made to face it, and face it now. She must jerk him into decision by her stronger will, her superior intelligence, her greater courage; she must strike hard; she must win or lose everything at a blow.

Next day she despatched the messenger back to Court with a brief message; she was going with her brother George, who had just returned from abroad, to hunt in the forest near Hever, and would be staying at a hunting-lodge her father had there. If his Grace's affairs permitted him to visit her, she would, according to his suggestion, let him have his answer by word of mouth.

She arranged the *mise en scène* with care. She was a born actress. George had his orders and kept out of the way; on the walls she hung a set of tapestries the King loved, depicting hunting scenes; his favourite collation was set ready, a barrel of oysters with a relish of onions, washed down with red wine. She put on the gown she had been wearing when the King had made his first approaches to her at Hever; she wore on her girdle his gold tablet with its motto which promised that whoever changed in love its giver would not.

He came in trembling expectancy; almost he was humble, like a boy in the throes of first love he saw that she had been weeping. He was so moved he could find nothing to say, and it was she who opened the conversation, sitting on her hair, and his recent letter held in her lap.

'Your Grace says here that you put yourself into a great agony. So has you Grace put me likewise.'

'Sweetheart – '

'No, pray let me speak. I desire to know what mean these words: 'I promise that I will cast off all others that are in competition with you out of my thoughts and affections, serving you only.' And again your Grace ends by describing yourself as 'him who would willingly be entirely yours.' I cannot tell what such words mean.'

'They mean what they say, my entirely beloved,' Henry cried earnestly, hands on knees, body bent forward, huge face solemn. 'My heard is dedicated to you alone, and I wish my body were also. But you will not have it so; you do not love me.'

'You would have me as your mistress?'

'What else?' he cried in genuine astonishment.

She gathered all her resolution.

'I will be no man's mistress, not even your Grace's. You deem me light, but I am not. I came a maid from France, avoiding all the pitfalls of a licentious Court; and so I have remained since it seems it is not your Grace's pleasure that I should marry, though I am long past the age when it is the custom to wed. Therefore must I beg your Grace's leave to retire into some convent, where, though I shall never forget the one man I have loved, I am very sure he will soon forget me.'

A tear glinted in the firelight, caught like a pearl upon the bosom of her gown. He was intensely moved; the vivacious, coquettish Anne he knew had altogether vanished. And his vanity was flattered, whilst at the same time it was pricked by her implication that he was a lecher.

'If I have offended you, my darling,' he murmured, 'I beg of you to give me absolution. But if could cut out my heart and show it you, then would you perceive that it is indeed yours entirely.'

She was silent. He rose and began to pace the room, his immature will fighting against having to make a decision, longing for it to be made for him; his mind shying away from the knowledge that she was offering him an ultimatum. He took refuge as usual in asserting his own moral integrity.

'I cannot tell,' he burst out, 'Why God should punish me thus, seeing that I have always served Him faithfully, entering into a holy war, defending His Church against the foul tongues of heretics scrupulous in observing all His precepts. I am conscious of no sin whereby I have offended Him, save for those for which I have been shriven; and yet His hand is heavy upon me, denying me the son so necessary for the security of the Succession – '

He stopped abruptly. She had not spoken, but he had seen her black eyes glance swiftly up at him in the firelight, and down again. He stood over her, waiting for her to speak; and at last she said, very low and hesitant:

'It may be that your Grace is punished for the sins of others who offended against God's divine law in your Grace's regard when you were but a child.'

'Eh?' he said, startled.

She paused for the last time. She knew him well by now, and especially did she know that an idea once put into his head could never be put out again. On this she had staked all.

'In the matter of your Grace's marriage,' she said, very deliberate and solemn, 'to your brother's wife.'

PART TWO

The Gathering Storm

Chapter One

St George's Day was always kept at Court with great pomp and magnificence in honour of the patron saint of England. Even greater splendour than usual was displayed when the Bishop of Tarbes, Ambassador of the King of France, timed his visit to coincide with the national feast; since the defeat of Francis by the Emperor at Pavia, Wolsey had veered round to a French alliance, and the Bishop of Tarbes had come to negotiate a marriage which would cement that alliance, the betrothal of the little Princess Mary with the widower Francis himself.

The day began with solemn High Mass, at which Wolsey, old Archbishop Wareham, and ten mitred prelates officiated. Then came a particularly elaborate tournament. Unfortunately it was pouring with rain, so that the silver tissue sewn with pieces of money and embroidered with the motto. *By pain nor treasure, truth shall not be violated,* and the cloth of gold embossed with mountains full of olive branches, worn by the combatants, were ruined. This particularly distressed the new Duke of Norfolk, Thomas Boleyn's brother-in-law, who had spent a fortune on his costume; but the important visitor was snug enough, seated between the Queen and the Cardinal under a roof of purple cloth lavishly adorned with pomegranates, roses, and fleurs-de-lis, on one side of the tiltyard. It was observed by all how gracious Wolsey was to the Ambassador of a country with whom England had so lately been at war.

When the drenched combatants had changed their clothes, all adjourned to a specially erected banquet house, where a seven-storied cupboard displayed the King of England's wealth in the shape of gold plate. Minstrels played in the gallery, and St George himself, made all of sugar, with his Dragon bleeding red wine, was drawn in on a car by men disguised as horses. The elaborate ceremony of supper ended, there came the masque. Over a great rich arch painted to look like marble, the King's astronomer had most cunningly devised the earth girded by the sea, the Signs of the Zodiac, and the seven planets, each in its proper house. Latin orations, full of compliments to the King of England for granting peace and to the King of France for sueing for it, were made by a person in a mantle of blue silk embroidered with gold eyes and wearing a laurel wreath; six knights contended over a gilt bar as to whether riches were better than love; the Children of the Chapel Royal sang; and to a roll of drums the masque proper began.

A curtain being withdrawn, there was disclosed a crystal mount with rocks of ruby, among which grew flowers representing England, France, and Castile. Upon this were perched six lords in white satin and black velvet mantles sewn with pearls, who presently danced with the Princess Mary and her ladies who emerged from a cloth of gold flap in the side of the mount. Another roll upon the drums, and conventional alarm was simulated as there entered maskers whose faces were concealed behind ferocious vizards. One seized the Queen and commanded her to dance with him; there were cries of wonder and admiration as he bounded and skipped; the Bishop of Tarbes applauded more vigorously than any when at last came the moment when the Queen plucked off her captor's vizor, and lo, it was the King.

The Bishop was rewarded by being presented with his Grace's masking costume, and by having the royal arm thrust into his own as the company returned to the banquet house where more than two hundred marvellous 'subtleties' awaited the revellers. The wine flowed free, and after the ladies had withdrawn the gentlemen drank and gambled until morning. Her head spinning with the music and the excitement, the Princess Mary lay in her state bed, living over again this wonderful day.

She was eleven now, a small, thin child, with the quick temper of her father and his passion for fine clothes, and the loyalty, unwavering affection, and piety of her mother. That the occasion was that of her betrothal did not concern her; ever since she was born she had been engaged and disengaged to a succession of prospective bridegrooms as the political wind and Wolsey's ambition veered. Meantime she had been fully occupied with the formidable scheme of education worked out for her at her mother's request by the great Spanish scholar, Vives, learning Latin, Greek, French, Italian, Logic, and Mathematics, reading Erasmus' secular works and Mathematics, reading Erasmus' secular works and More's *Utopia*, recreating herself with the music for which she had a natural bent.

Though she missed her parents sadly, she was happy in her little Court at Ludlow, making Progresses through the lovely Marches of Wales, with her servants in her livery of blue and green damask, embroidered with her emblem, a sheaf of arrows, and with her dear Governess, the Countess of Salisbury, to mother her. Her real mother wrote to her every week and always cheerfully (for it was Catherine's policy to keep all unpleasant matters form her little daughter's knowledge while she could).

89

But though Mary loved Ludlow, to come to London was a special treat, chiefly because she would be with her parents. Both Henry and Catherine had always been indulgent to this their only surviving child; to her her father was the most wonderful person, so big and jolly, hurling himself over ditches with a fen-man's pole after his hawks, always victorious in the lists, excelling all his courtiers at every manly sport. But deeper still was her love for her mother, her love and her pride. Though for some years she had lived so retired, Catherine was cheered to the echo whenever she appeared in public; the common people had always loved this high-mannered lady with her real kindness of heart; and her conduct at the time of Flodden, and again on Evil May Day when she had gone on her knees in Westminster Hall to the King to beg for mercy on the rioters, had made her a heroine in the eyes of simple folk.

Mary was so tired tonight she could not sleep. Her father, who seemed to be in a particularly good humour, had shown her off all day, making her discourse in Greek on Erasmus' *Paraphrases of the Gospel;* then she must play the virginal and afterwards the lute, singing her father's own songs of which he was so fond, and which were full of promises of faithful love. It gave her a wonderful subconscious sense of security to know that all these promises were addressed to her mother.

> *'As the holly groweth green*
> *And never changeth hue,*
> *So I am, ever have been,*
> *Unto my lady true.'*

She had smiled up at her mother as she had sung verses like that, and seen tears in the big blue eyes. But they must have been tears of happiness.

90

She wished she could sleep, but the Palace was so noisy. Then as she tossed and turned, she remembered suddenly that at some time during that hectic evening she had hidden behind the arras a gift the Bishop of Tarbes had brought her from King Francis, an ornament for her head-dress, of lapis lazuli and rubies formed into a little sheaf of arrows. It was when she was called upon to play on the virginal; there had been no time to pin on the ornament, and she had meant to fetch it from its hiding-place afterwards, but had forgotten. Suppose some palace servant had come upon it and stolen it? The mere thought made her spring out of bed, wrap herself in her bedgown, and without waking her ladies, tiptoe from the room.

She went down the private stair, waving aside the yawning pages and the yeomen of the Guard with their partisans; and reached the room where she had hidden her treasure. In the customs of the times, the arras stood out a foot or two from the stone of the wall, and she slipped behind it, feeling among the floor rushes for her jewel. As she did so she heard to her dismay the door open and men's voices; for the Princess of Wales to be discovered in her bedgown was not to be thought of, and crouching her thin little body behind the arras, she waited anxiously for the gentlemen to depart again.

But instead came the closing of the door and a rustle of gowns slowly sweeping up and down the chamber. Two voices informed her who the intruders were; they spoke in French, which Mary understood perfectly and they seemed to be carrying on a conversation begun before they entered the room.

'You are a man of the world, my Lord bishop,' said the resonant voice of Wolsey, 'and therefore will not misunderstand me when I say that these scruples of conscience which have beset his Grace could not have come more timely. True, if the Princess Mary be declared illegitimate it is not to be thought of that she should marry your royal master; but in that case his Grace himself would be free to wed with King Francis' sister. What greater tie could bind England and France against the all-conquering Emperor?'

'That is to say,' the voice of the Bishop of Tarbes replied drily, 'if the Pope can be persuaded that the dispensation given by Julius II for his Grace's marriage with the Queen was invalid.'

'Speak soft, I beg you, my lord. Walls have ears when so privy a matter is mentioned. His Grace has enjoined the utmost secrecy concerning this great business, lest it comes to the ears of the Queen. Out of his great tenderness of her Highness, he has expressed the view that it is far kinder to spare her all pain and anxiety until the matter is settled.'

'But settled by whom, my Lord Cardinal?'

'Am I not Papal Legate? Have I not, though permanently resident in England, the plenary powers usually bestowed by the Pope only for a special occasion, but on me for life? I am, and I have. I purpose, therefore, to set up a private ecclesiastical court wherein myself and my Lord of Canterbury will sit as judges, and we will try this case put to us by his Highness as to whether he is living incestuously with his dead brother's wife, since, we shall maintain, her former marriage was consummated.'

'The dispensation allowed for that.'

'No power on earth can dispense from the divine law. We shall hear pleadings on the Queen's behalf by advocates appointed by the King, and these pleadings will be put on record. A summons to appear will be issued to Her Highness, and when she appears not (for I may tell you that she will not receive the summons), she will be declared contumacious and sentence pronounced against her.'

'My Lord of Canterbury concurs with you in this?'

'He does. He has always been doubtful of the validity of the King's marriage. Her Highness having been declared contumacious, she will be debarred from appeal; the sentence will be sent to Rome as a matter decided by myself as Legate, and His Holiness will be presented with a *fait accompli*. No more now, my Lord Bishop; I hear the trumpets announce that the King is retiring. Keep all close, and ere you return to France I trust to have some good news for you...'

The door opened and closed again, and there was silence.

The child crouched as still as death behind the arras, like some little animal that has heard the feet of the hunter. In intelligence she was a hot-house flower, forced into premature bloom by her lack of playmates and her formidable education' she knew the meaning of the words 'incestuous' and 'contumacious'; she saw, stark and hideous and shocking, the whole vile device. Her father was to put away her mother so that he could marry the French King's sister; she herself was to be declared a bastard; meanest of all, her mother was not to hear a word of it until the thing was done.

But her mother would hear.

Mary had gone behind the arras a happy child of eleven. She emerged a woman, a small fierce champion whose security had been broken in pieces, whose childhood was left behind for ever, who was ready to outface kings and cardinals in defence of her mother's rights.

(ii)

It was not long before Wolsey was made aware that his device of a private ecclesiastical court somehow or other had reached the ears of the Queen. He supposed that the Bishop of Tarbes had been indiscreet, or else that Mendoza, the Spanish Ambassador, who had a perfect genius for worming out secrets, had heard it from one of his spies. However it may have been, Wolsey was extremely vexed, for the plot was ruined; unless laid aside, undoubtedly the Queen would expose the unsavoury device.

While he was pondering what to do next, there arrived like a thunderbolt the news of the sack of Rome. A mixed body of imperial mercenaries, under the command of the French traitor, Bourbon, and mad for lack of pay, had stormed the Eternal City and were besieging the Pope in his castle of St Angelo wither he had fled. Wolsey, outwardly distressed, sought how he could use the disaster for his own and his master's advantage; if he went to France and got Francis on his side by promising that Henry should marry Francis' sister if Henry's present marriage were declared invalid, might he not persuade the French Cardinals to elect him as acting-Head of the Church during the Pope's imprisonment?

Always exaggerating his own power in Europe, he liked the scheme; but it would give him an excellent advantage if, when he went he could tell Francis that all the English Bishops concurred with him in deeming his Grace's marriage invalid. He was certain they would so concur; that Warham, a man of unblemished character, could have lent himself to the idea of a private ecclesiastical court, testified both to Wolsey's influence and to the prince-worship which Henry had instilled into his subjects. The majority of the Bishops were mere Court officials, and because they had been given so many secular offices they were hated both by the remnants of the old nobility and by the new men; they were wholly dependent on the King's good-will.

Of one thing Wolsey remained completely ignorant; the real reason why his Grace, after nearly twenty years of marriage, had suddenly been smitten with doubts as to whether that marriage was valid.

The Bishops, summoned to attend his Grace, were ushered into the Presence Chamber. As they doffed their blocked felt caps and kissed the heavily ringed hand, they noticed that the king had a world-weary air, and a Bible laid open on his knee.

'Graces and lords,' he began solemnly, 'it is a heavy matter on which we have to consult you. Chancing one day to open at random the Sacred Scriptures, our eye lighted upon this passage in Leviticus: "He that marrieth his brother's wife, doth an unlawful thing; he hath uncovered his brother's nakedness. They shall be without children." '

His narrow eyes roved round the assembled prelates.

'Our conscience hath been so tormented with the knowledge that we have, it seems, broken God's law by marrying our dead brother's wife, that we can neither eat nor sleep. Applying ourselves to the Lord Cardinal, we find him of our opinion, and futhermore so is his Grace of Canterbury and our own confessor. And the Lord Cardinal has drawn our attention to the fact that this is not the worst of it; if we were a private person the case would be ill enough, but seeing we are King of England, by this crime we have deprived our realm of a legitimate and undoubted male heir.'

He paused again before crying dramatically:

'Graces and lords, for near twenty years we have been living in mortal sin.'

While they looked at each other in astonishment and dismay, Wolsey spoke with his usual vigour. It was indeed a cruel thing that his Grace should be attacked thus in his sacred conscience, and it was the duty of his spiritual advisers either to remove these scruples or else to suggest a remedy.

'The King and I,' said he imperiously, 'desire your opinions whether a Papal dispensation can be valid when it sets aside the eternal, unchangeable law of God.'

Again they looked at each other, none wishing to be the first to speak. In the pause, Henry sighed deeply. He was not being hypocritical in the ordinary sense of the word; he could never believe himself unprincipled, since if his behaviour did not agree with his principles, he simply rearranged the latter. He would have rejected with honest indignation the suggestion that his desire to get free from Catherine had nothing to do with the Succession, and that he was simply being driven by, was bound hand and foot by, Anne Boleyn.

Gardiner, Wolsey's Secretary, taking his cue from his master, at last spoke up. He feared that no Pope could dispense from God's unchanging law. Old Warham said truthfully that from the first he had doubts about the validity of the marriage, and had mentioned them to the late King when his present Highness was betrothed. Edward Foxe, the King's Almoner, a violently ambitious man, expressed his horror at the thought that his Grace's sacred conscience should be left in this tormented state; and one after another the Bishops of England, who scarcely ever visited their Sees, whose main thought was the amassing of pluralities and offices, and who dreaded the wrath of the King of England far more than that of the King of Kings, vied with one another in offering sympathy and in promising to do whatever could be done to quieten his Grace's conscience.

But one among their number remained silent; and Henry, after waiting in vain for him to join the chorus, addressed him in flattering tones.

'My Lord of Rochester, we desire in particular to hear from you, not only because of the reverence in which our father held you and because you guided our youthful studies, but because you are beloved throughout our realm for your holy life and your great learning. Our conscience being in such torment, we desire you now to speak freely.'

It was a very tall, emaciated figure whom the King thus addressed.

In an age of clerics avid for preferment, John Fisher was almost unique in his absolute indifference to it. In youth he had been confessor to Henry's grandmother, and had persuaded her to found Christ's College and St John's College at Cambridge, where he was Vice-Chancellor and already famous for his learning. A little later he had received from Henry VII the vacant See of Rochester, rejoicing that its revenues were less than any other in England; except when summoned to London he had remained in residence, adored by the poor for his charity, renowned throughout England for his wisdom. Of late, while preaching and writing continually against the Lutheran heresy, he had not scrupled to attack the worldliness of the great prelates who gave Luther an excuse for his assaults upon the Church. Though so humble, and ever courting obscurity, the Bishop of Rochester was a man to be reckoned with; and even Wolsey now waited in some anxiety for his answer.

'I beseech your Grace in God's name,' Fisher said tenderly, 'to be of good cheer, and no further to dismay yourself in this matter.'

His big brown eyes in his thin face glanced for a moment reproachfully at Wolsey. He made no doubt that it was Wolsey who, for some end of his own, had insinuated these scruples into the mind of the King whom Fisher still thought of as the able and lovable boy he had tutored.

'For,' he continued, 'there is no heed to be taken of these men who account themselves more wise than were all the learned father and divines, both of Spain and also of this your realm in your late father's time, neither yet so much credit to be given unto them as to the Holy See, by whose authority this marriage was confirmed, dispensed, and approved as good and lawful.'

'You have heard what his Grace has said upon the passage in Leviticus,' said Wolsey, very sharp. 'And also what I have said upon the invalidity of a Papal dispensation when it sets aside God's unchangeable law.'

'I heard my lord Cardinal,' Fisher replied evenly. 'But I need not remind you, a learned divine, that in the 25th chapter of Deuteronomy, verse 5, it is written; "When brethren dwell together, and one of them dieth without children, the wife of the deceased shall not marry to another, but his brother shall take her, and raise up seed for his brother." '

He turned back to the King.

'Truly, truly, my Sovereign Lord, you may well, and justly ought, to make conscience of casting any scruple or doubt of this so clear and weighty a matter by bringing it by any means into question; and therefore by my counsel you shall with all speed put any such thought out of your mind.'

'And is his Grace to put Leviticus out of his mind likewise?' tartly enquired the Cardinal.

'As it is impossible that God should contradict Himself,' the tranquil voice replied, 'the Church and the Fathers have always applied the text in Leviticus to marriage with a brother's wife during his lifetime, thus emphasizing that prohibition against adultery in a case where it is particularly abominable. Thus it is evident, and has always been held to be evident, that the prohibition against marriage with a brother's widow is not part of God's immutable law, and that therefore the Pope has power to grant a dispensation for the same. And this, under favour, you know as well as I, my Lord Cardinal.'

'You take too much upon yourself, my Lord Rochester, ' cried the fiery Foxe. 'You stand alone in your opinion, for we are all agreed that it is our duty to devise some remedy for the easement of his Grace's conscience in this so weighty a matter, the which is not to be done lightly.'

'His Grace desired that I should speak my opinion freely,' said Fisher. 'and I have observed his command. The duty of his spiritual advisers is to remove this scruple from his mind; I will take upon my own soul any danger that may ensue. And I most earnestly beg your Grace to believe that it is a very perilous and unseemly thing that any question of the validity of your Grace's marriage be spoken of.'

Henry sat sucking his thumb-ring. His small eyes glanced resentfully at his old tutor, and he did not seem at all relieved to hear that his tender conscience had been troubling him unnecessarily.

(iii)

Sir Thomas More had been rising steadily in the King's favour.

While at times his quaint wit made Henry treat him as a sort of learned buffoon, his legal brilliance had moved the King to bestow on him the Chancellorship of the Duchy of Lancaster, which carried executive and judicial powers second only to those of the central administration. He was Under Treasurer, High Steward both of Oxford and of Cambridge; and his salaries, gifts, allowances, fees, and the customary pensions from foreign princes when treaties were concluded, had made him a rich man.

Though he loved the City in which he had been born and where he had lived for so many years, his business and his writings demanded a more retired home; some years previously, therefore, he had rented the Barge to John

Clement, his children's former tutor, who had married More's foster-daughter, Margaret Gigs, and buying a piece of land in the secluded village of Chelsea, had erected a spacious but unpretentious house, large enough to accommodate his married daughters and their families, for it was his delight to have them all live with him. It was a most pleasant retreat, its garden sloping to the river, where there was a water-gate with a flat roof from which could be had a fine view of the woods and pastures of Surrey.

But with all his new honours and wealth, More remained as he had been, careless in dress, intensely disliking formality and infinitely happier romping with his grandchildren than in partaking of the splendours of the Court. Mrs More could not understand it; she revelled in her new grandeur, and continually lectured to Thomas on behaving himself as befitted his dignity.

'His Grace's Under Treasurer to be seen going barefoot on pilgrimages!' chided Mrs More. 'And here you still go, man, with your hair upon your neck, when all the fashionable world is close polled, and I warrant were it not that I keep so sharp an eye upon you, you would forget to put on your gold chain when you go to Court. And then you must needs carry the cross in parish processions; his Grace would be much displeased, Mr More, at the idea of his Under Treasurer performing the office of a common clerk.'

'It cannot be displeasing to my lord the King,' said More mildly, 'that I pay homage to my King's Lord.'

To this she paid no attention, but continued with her scolding. On one occasion a messenger had arrived to summon Mr More to Court on urgent business, and had found him serving Mass in his parish church; he had refused to leave until Mass was ended, and had earned a sharp rebuke from his immediate superior, the Duke of Norfolk, Lord Treasurer. He was for ever following literally the Gospel precept of charity and inviting the poor to his table. Which made men laugh at him. And so on, and so on.

'Dame Alice,' said he, when at last he could get a word in, 'I will tell you a little tale, I heard t'other day. A friar was preaching in the country, and spied a poor wife of the parish whispering to her pew-fellow. Being angry he cried aloud upon her, "Hold thy babble, I bid thee, thou wife in the red hood!" Which when the housewife hears, she waxed angry again, and suddenly she start up and cried to the friar, so that all the church hang thereon, "Marry, sir, I beshrew his heart that babbleth most of us both. For I do but whisper a word with my neighbour here, and thou hast babbled there all this hour." '

Mrs More laughed ruefully.

'How you run on, man! But I will not scold you any more, for it was but yesterday that I was shriven and voided my shrewishness, and now I will begin afresh.'

'I verily believe you will, sweetheart,' drily replied her husband.

On a July evening he sat with family in his favourite place, the flat-roofed water-gate. He was about to leave England with Wolsey on an embassy to France, and had been telling his family how he expected them to write to him every day. The girls were not to say they had nothing to write about; they could always find something to *talk* about.

Presently a silence fell. It was the hour of the evening when the great brown-sailed barges, which had taken fruit and vegetables to the City markers, were sailing slowly home again. Fishermen set their eel-pots, and in the tall reeds by the river bank the swans dived their long necks for the pieces of bread More's grandchildren threw to them. The peace of it all was so great that even Master Patenson, the Fool, had ceased his antics and crude jests, and sat at his master's feet idly playing with the jester's head on the baton of his bauble.

'How happy we all are!' impulsively exclaimed More's favourite daughter Meg, now Mrs William Roper.

He laid a hand upon her head, softly stroking it.

'And therefore do we find it easy to be good,' said he, 'seeing virtue rewarded and vice punished. We are carried up to Heaven by the chins.'

His blue-grey eyes were meditative, and his mood a little sad. He detested these embassies which took him away from his family.

'But if you live the time that no man will give you good counsel, nor no man will give you good example, when you shall see virtue punished and vice rewarded, if you will then stand fast and firmly stick to God, upon pain of my life, though you be but half good, God will allow you for the whole good.'

As Meg looked at him wonderingly, there came from downstream a sudden fan-fare of trumpets and then the noise of many oars swiftly approaching. Roper, springing up and shading his eyes, exclaimed in excitement:

'It is the King! But not in his great state; perhaps he is coming here, sir, as he did once before.'

'My God!' wailed Dame Alice, rising in a flurry. 'And all of us in our week-day clothes!'

She bustled into the house, driving her family before her with confused directions as to what they must put on and what they must do in case his Grace was really intending to honour them with a visit.

It seemed that he was. He was in his most accessible and friendly mood; the evening was so fine that he had slipped away from the cares of Court, he said, to give himself the pleasure of calling on his friends. He desired no formality; he would eat what was to hand. At supper he was positively boisterous, joking like a boy; and afterwards he would have

Mr More stroll with him in the gardens and show him the New Building he had errected there, with a library, chapel, and gallery, a little retreat where More entertained his humanist friends, pursued his studies, and spent his entire Fridays in spiritual exercises.

As they emerged again and began to walk up and down the flagged paths in the garden, the King, actually laying his arm round his companion's neck, said pleasantly:

'In sending you with my Lord Cardinal to conclude our new treaty with France, we hope to show how much you have pleasured us. For we have not forgotten how, when you were Speaker in our last Parliament, you were so set against the French war that you prevailed upon your fellows to refuse my Lord Cardinal the sum he demanded.'

More glanced at the jovial face and away again.

'All war is hateful to me, Sire,' he said quietly. 'We English are a small nation, but we live upon an island, and our skill with the long-bow has made us the equal of any force that might invade us. But we are too few in number to make any impression abroad; in my poor opinion there is neither danger to be averted nor advantage to be gained in plunging into the wars of Europe.'

This was a delicte way of saying that More knew very well that while making peace with France, Henry was about to declare war against the Emperor.

'What!' cried the King. 'Would you not now punish the Emperor for his vile sacking of Rome and his imprisonment of the Pope? Would you not have us appear as His Holiness' protector, we who are named Defender of the Faith?'

More hesitated how to answer. Like Bishop Fisher, he still thought of the King as led astray by the forceful Wolsey and infected with Wolsey's insane ambition. And he was perfectly aware that the hand of Wolsey was to be seen in this new policy; having failed to get elected Pope,

Wolsey was to be, not Clement VII's protector, but his supplanter.

'With your Grace's favour I must remind you,' said More at length, 'that it was not the Emperor but his mercenary troops under the traitor Bourbon who were responsible for the sack of Rome and the Pope's imprisonment. And being of the City, born and bred, I cannot but deplore hostilities with the Empire; our trade depends upon peace with the Emperor's dominions. Moreover I can never forget that his Imperial Majesty us the secular head of Christendom and our champion against the Turk.'

They walked in silence for a while. Then, abruptly:

'We have good reason, as you know,' said the King, 'to make this new treaty with our brother of France. It is our bounden duty to provide for the Succession, and if we lay aside our present unlawful marriage, and repent thereof (as we do with tears), with the blessing of God we may unite England and France by an alliance with the French King's sister, and our children shall rule over these two great realms.'

More's cheerful face was troubled. He had hoped against hope that this subject would not be mentioned.

'You have consulted with our Bishops upon our great matter, as we bade you?' rather sharply enquired the King.

'I have, Sire.'

'And we will warrant you found only old Bishop Fisher speaking for the validity of our present marriage.'

'To be plain with your Grace,' answered More, evading this direct challenge, 'though I know these your Bishops to be learned and wise, yet in my judgement they are not meet counsellors for your Grace in so weighty a matter.'

'Not meet counsellors! Then whom should we consult?'

'Why, if your Grace would understand the truth, such counsellors might you have as neither for respect of their own worldly commodity, nor fear of your princely anger, will be inclined to deceive you. I mean St Jerome, St Austin, and the other Fathers of the Church.'

Henry snorted impatiently, and withdrew his arm from about his companion's neck.

'Now is it not true, Master More,' he cried, 'that in your *Utopia* you make it lawful for a marriage to be dissolved even for incompatibility? Now we, on the other hand, have lived in perfect accord with the illustrious princess, our wife, and would not for anything in the world part from her were it not that our conscience informs us that we are living in mortal sin. Ay, we now perceive that our marriage is not only against the written law of God and the positive law of the Church, but also in suchwise against the law of Nature that it could never be dispensed by any Pope.'

'I am no theologian, and therefore am unmeet to meddle with such matters,' pleaded More. 'But as for my *Utopia*, your Grace must be pleased to understand that this "not place" is a state guided by the unaided human reason, knowing nothing of Christian revelation. The book, Sire, was designed to provoke discussion upon the problems of society. My underlying thought was if my Utopians, with only the Four Cardinal Virtues to guide them, could achieve so happy a Commonwealth, surely, we, who have the blessing of the Three Christian Virtues, must do better. I did not intend, your Grace, to imply that Heathendom is better that Christendom, but only that some Christians are worse than heathens.'

He paused. There were times when he wished he had never written this book which had made him so famous; he had tried to make it plain that he was only repeating what so many of the great medieval writers, in particular Dante and Langland, had said before him; he had taken care to write in his own character at the end of the book:

'Many things came to my mind which seemed very absurd in the manners and laws of these people.'

But several of his friends persisted in believing that *Utopia* was his ideal; and here was the King trying to use Utopian customs as a means for prosecuting his 'great matter', a matter so odious and painful to More.

'My heathen Utopians,' he said deliberately, 'allow a man to put away his wife for adultery or incompatibility only with the consent of both parties. But, Sire for the husband to put away his wife for no fault, but that for some mishap is fallen to her body, this by no means will they suffer. For they judge it a great point of cruelty that anybody in their most need of help and comfort should be cast off and forsaken, and that old age, which both brings sickness with it, and is a sickness itself, should unkindly and unfaithfully be dealt with.'

It was a brave appeal to Henry's better self. To More, this "great matter" had two root causes; the King was wary of his sickly, middle-aged wife; and as usual he was being enticed by Wolsey to a grandiose scheme of adding France to his dominions by a marriage, since the conquest of France had proved impossible. And More wanted to evoke in his Grace the memory of the long years when he and Catherine had been happy; he was appealing to the real kindness of heart he believed the King to possess.

But there was no response. Henry said abruptly that he must be gone; and there was more than a little frostiness in the farewell he took of his host.

More was still walking slowly up and down beside the river when, a good half-hour later, his wife came to find him.

'Why, there you are, man!' cried she. 'Upon my soul I thought his Grace must have carried you back to Greenwich with him, or that you were gone into your New Building where you are wont to stay as long at your devotions as any monk. By the Mass, Mr More, this has been a wondrous evening! Though bless me, I was right glad to loosen my gown at the waist and to take off my best shoes which pinch me cruelly. Yet they became me well, so said his Highness.'

'Mrs Alice,' remarked her husband, 'if God gives you not Hell for your portion, He will do you great wrong, for you buy it very dear here on earth.'

'Tilly vally, man what things you say! But by God, Mr More, how honoured you have been to walk so familiarly with his Grace, his royal arm about your neck, which is a favour he never has bestowed, so son Roper tells me, save upon my Lord Cardinal himself.'

'I thank God, wife,' said More gravely, 'that I find his Grace my very good lord indeed, and I believe he does me as singular favour as any subject within his realm. Yet I may tell you I have no cause to be puffed up with pride, for if my head could win him a castle in France or a skirmish with the Emperor, its should not fail to go.'

She was silent with astonishment. No man had a greater reverence for authority than her husband; if there were certain things of which he disapproved in his Sovereign, he was most strict in keeping his opinions to himself. Thus while he had sympathized with the apprentices when they had risen on Evil May Day ten years previously, he had made an impassioned appeal to them to respect the King's authority. Something must have moved him deeply to have spoken as he had just now. She tried to soothe him by remarking upon the beauty of the night, and upon the happiness they all enjoyed here at Chelsea. But he burst out stronger than ever:

'Now I would to Our Lord, Alice, upon condition that three kings were well established in Christendom, I were put in a sack and cast yonder into the Thames.'

'What great things are these, man.' Alice asked fearfully, 'that should move you to wish for anything so dreadful?'

'The first is, that where the most part of Christian princes are at mortal war, or will soon be so against the Emperor, they were all at a universal peace. The second, that where the Church of Christ is at this present sore afflicted with detestable heresies, it were settled in a perfect uniformity of religion.'

He paused a moment, and then added in so low a tone that she could scarcely hear him:

'And the third, that where the King's matter of marriage is now come in question, it were to the glory of God and quietness of all parties, brought to a good conclusion.'

Chapter Two

It was publicly announced that King Henry, Defender of the Faith, had sworn to avenge the insults offered to the Pope by the Emperor's armies, and that the Cardinal was going upon an 'embassy extraordinary' to concert with the King of France the necessary measures. But a rumour had got round that the real reason for Wolsey's visit was to negotiate a new marriage for his master, and among the common folk there was a good deal of murmuring and discontent.

It irked Henry, who at the beginning of his reign had been the most popular of kings and whose vanity demanded that whatever he did he should remain the idol of his subjects; but to Wolsey it meant nothing, for he was his vigorous, confident self as he prepared to go to France in semi-royal state and with practically unlimited powers; there was only one incident which ruffled his good humour, and it was so trifling an incident that he forgot about it ten minutes later.

He came into the Great Chamber at Greenwich one evening to speak to the King, and found his Grace engaged in the childish game of hunt-the-slipper with some of the younger courtiers and ladies. Henry was the hunter, and at the moment when Wolsey entered had discovered the slipper hidden under the skirts of Mistress Anne Boleyn. He was kneeling at her feet, her black head bent down to him as she whispered something which, from his expression, was plainly a lascivious jest; raising her head, and seeing Wolsey standing there, she burst into her high laugh which had always an edge of hysteria. His dignity offended, Wolsey demanded sharply:

'Is there anything about me that amuses you, mistress?'

The black eyes drooped demurely.

'The Lord Cardinal must pardon me. You know I am but a foolish girl, as once you told Lord Henry Percy.'

He shrugged, and dismissed her from his mind. He was fully expecting the King to tire of this singularly unattractive hussy; and when that happened no doubt he would be required to find some complacent husband to make an honest woman of her, as he had done for her sister and other light o'loves.

Had you told him that a new hand held the reins of the King's immature will, and that as once had taken Henry to France to remove him from the Queen's influence, so he was being sent to France to get him away from Henry, he would have laughed in your face.

Before starting on his embassy, he went down to his new palace of Hampton Court to have a word with the man who had come to be known as 'Councillor to my Lord Cardinal,' Thomas Cromwell. Wolsey being entirely occupied with high politics, of late he had left more and more of his domestic matters in the hands of this clever lawyer, whose capacity for work was second only to his own, who had an intimate knowledge of law especially as it related to lands and property, and who seemed designed by Nature for those less savoury matters with which great men are reluctant to stain their fingers.

It was typical of Wolsey that he should wish to perpetuate his name in gorgeous buildings, and it was of the better side of his character that he should desire not only gorgeous palaces for himself but colleges for Oxford, his Alma Mater, and for Ipswich, his native town. But his affection for these places stopped short of paying for their enrichment out of his own pocket; and he had commissioned Thomas Cromwell to survey certain of the smaller monasteries and convents in which the communities had shrunk so far that the Rule could not be properly maintained therein, and to sell or lease their lands for the purpose of paying for his new colleges.

At Hampton Court he found Mr Cromwell busy as usual, his table piled with deeds of sale, valuations, inventories, reports, receipts, and petitions. Also as usual, Mr Cromwell's manner towards his master was humble to the point of servility; his awkward, uncouth gait, his large, dull, pasty face, his commonplace expression, all gave the air of a plodding and rather stupid man. His grey eyes, set close together, flickered restlessly under sharply arched brows.

He regaled his master with the progress of his work. He had surveyed the monasteries at Tiptree, and Medmenham, and Romford Priory in Suffolk, a cell of St Mary's Abbey in York. The first two he had found in a very bad state; in each the community had shrunk to below a dozen religious who were half starving and who were unable to carry out the divine service in a fitting manner. He had, therefore, suppressed them, and according to his orders had transferred the monks to larger monasteries. But the Romford Priory he had found in such good order that, though its revenue was under three hundred ducats a year, a sum scarcely sufficient to maintain it and the poor who depended on its charity, he had taken upon himself to spare it; he hoped he had done right.

Wolsey heartily approved. He honestly believed he had the welfare of monasticism at heart, and that in suppressing the smaller monasteries he was doing a service to holy religion.

When the majestic crimson figure had swept out again, Mr Cromwell smiled roguishly to himself, and his commonplace expression gave way to one most cunning and subtle. There were certain little transactions he had not seen fit to lay before his master this morning. For instance a pitiful letter from the Abbot of York, offering him three hundred marks sterling if the Romford Priory might be spared. And there were valuables from the houses at Tiptree and Medmenham which did not appear on his inventories.

He had visited the former monastery in time for Benediction, and he had seen enthroned above the altar its one treasure, given to it by some wealthy pilgrim four hundred years previously: a great golden sunflower of a monstrance. He had marked well the golden sunflower; he had ignored the plain white Heart which it enshrined, the central mystery of the Christian religion. In an age when all men worshipped, and sometimes abused worship by turning it into superstition, Thomas Cromwell was a complete materialist. He had no interest in religion, no belief in the supernatural.

That golden sunflower was but a trifle compared with the valuables he saw upon his master's cupboards; but Thomas did not despise trifles. All his youth he had had to fight with his wits to make a bare living. And moreover that particular trifle was a reminder of treasures which would make even Wolsey's wealth seem modest, the treasures contained in some eight hundred religious houses strewn over the face of little England. From the dawn of Christianity, emperors and kings, warriors and merchants, had loved to adorn these hallowed places, lavishing upon them lands and revenues, gold, silver, jewels, rich vestments. At Henry's Coronation Mr Cromwell had heard folk say it was the beginning of a golden age; they would have spoken more truly than they knew if the wealth of the Church were to fall into lay hands.

(ii)

On a mule jangling with gold-plated harness, his crimson boots thrust into solid gold stirrups, with his mounted gentlemen in their tawny velvet, his maces, his crosses, and his huge baggage train, Wolsey set for France. He met King Francis at Amiens. Since his crushing defeat by the Emperor at Pavia two years previously, Francis' obvious necessity was to buy England's friendship at all costs, and he listened sympathetically to the sad tale of his Grace of England's troubled conscience, promising that if Henry's present marriage could be annulled, he should have Francis' sister Marguerite for his bride.

But the object for which Wolsey had really come to France, and which he had expected to carry with a high hand, met with a decided check. He sent a summons to the members of the Sacred College who were not prisoners in Rome to meet him at Avignon, even drafting a form of delegation of the Papal powers to himself while the Pope remained a captive. All save the French Cardinals bluntly refused the summons, nor could lavish bribes nor the pressure exerted on them by both Henry and Francis persuade them to change their minds.

Mortified though he was at finding that he had exaggerated his power in Europe, Wolsey was still resourceful. He drafted a bull and sent it to the imprisoned Clement for his signature; in this bull Clement was to delegate all the Papal functions, even to the extent of dispensing with the divine law, to "some suitable person" during the time while the Pope remained in his present plight. Wolsey had little humour, and he saw nothing

amusing in the fact that his objection to Pope Julius'
dispensation for the marriage of Henry and Catherine
turned upon this very point – that the Pope could not
dispense with the divine law.

He wrote triumphantly to Henry:

'If the purport of that bull be well studied, it will be
found that nothing could be better suited to your Grace's
purpose, with less disclosing of the matter, for that I shall
have the power to appoint judges to enquire into your
Grace's marriage without informing the Pope of it; and if
the Queen shall appeal, the said appeal must be to me.'

Never had Wolsey felt more confident. Never had King
Francis appeared more co-operative. The French Ministers,
coached beforehand, received with assumed meekness the
Cardinal's boast that 'he had all the heads under his girdle,
so that he could rule them as he did the Council in
England'; and unable to wait for the Papal powers he had
demanded, on the last morning of his stay in France he
ordered the French Chancellor, whom the Pope had
promised to create a Cardinal, to assume the title and the
Hat.

It was at the end of September that he returned to
England. The King was at Richmond, the homely red-brick
palace built by the first Henry Tudor and called after his
native place. To emphasize his undoubted right to the
throne, Henry VII had caused to be set up everywhere here
the badges and emblems of the royal houses from whom
he claimed descent. The leopards and the lions, the falcons
and the dragons, the greyhounds and the black bulls,
seemed to grin slyly at one another as the pompous
procession of the Cardinal entered the courtyard, with
trumpets sounding and the stout, crimson-mantled figure
riding his mule under a cloth of gold canopy.

Ever since that day, early in the reign, when Wolsey had
talked himself into the young King's confidence, all

through his years of glory when he had been Henry's *alter ego,* a custom had been maintained whenever the Cardinal desired private audience with his master. He followed that custom today. He pulled from his finger a turquoise ring engraved with the Tudor Rose, and gave it to one of his gentlemen. Ordinarily no despatches or messengers could be brought to the King's presence unless accompanied by an Esquire of the Body; when the turquoise ring was shown, the bearer of it had free access to his Grace.

Wolsey had already dismounted and was walking towards the King's apartments through the ranks of his genuflecting attendants, when the gentleman he had sent in with the ring returned to him, agitated and pale.

'May it please you, my Lord Cardinal,' faltered the gentleman, 'it is his Grace's pleasure that you come to the Great Chamber.'

The Great Chamber! Wolsey felt he must be dreaming. It was the place where the King was in the midst of his courtiers, where he disported himself with dancing and gambling, where every Tom, Dick, and Harry might have access to him after they had been checked by the ushers at the door. There must be some mistake, but it would save time, Wolsey decided, to find out for himself what it was. Along the innumerable galleries and passages he swept majestically like a great red galleon, past bowing pages and saluting Yeomen of the Guard, who eyed him curiously – but he did not notice that. He sailed into the Great Chamber, and stopped dead, his mouth falling open with astonishment.

Henry and his boon companions were engaged in the children's game of Hoodman Blind. The huge figure, rapidly coarsening these last few years, groped its way over the floor rushes, the little mouth a round O of laughter under the silken napkin tied about the eyes. Rings flashed and glittered as the thick fingers clawed the air; and, as

Wolsey looked, they caught the great leopard-skin cuff of a lady. As, with peals of high laughter, she wriggled in the royal embrace, the lady looked full at Wolsey; and as she looked at him, there fell a silence.

She spoke. Her husky voice was insolent.

'Where else would my Lord Cardinal expect to find his Grace except here among his court?' asked Anne Boleyn.

Wolsey knew nothing of the secret power a woman might exert over a man. He had had a mistress himself, but one, a Miss Lark, with whom, on the threshold of middle age, he had settled down soberly and privately, marrying her later to a substantial landowner. It had been a very discreet, almost dispassionate affair, quite different from the brief amatory episodes in the life of his royal master. It had never occurred to him that any woman could possess the same sustained and driving ambition which was the secret of his own power, and which had enabled him to dominate Henry for over twenty years.

It occurred to him now. He was driven to it. While he had been in France (for so brief an absence!) his master had changed towards him, had been changed by someone. Later in the day Henry granted him a private audience, and Wolsey at once sensed that change. The tale of his reception in France, of which he made the very most, Henry received in impatient silence; and when Wolsey described King Francis' eagerness for a matrimonial alliance, his Grace interrupted sharply:

'We will make a new marriage for ourselves. And we may tell you that your zeal for the annulment of our present marriage appears to us less on account of our troubled conscience than on that of your personal ambition.'

For once Wolsey was stricken dumb. Someone had been coaching Henry, sowing seeds of discord.

'We are resolved,' the King continued, fidgeting about the room, 'to be no longer under any man's tutelage. You yourself have said, and so likewise have the majority of our Bishops, that our marriage with our late brother's wife is invalid. Our conscience tells us the same; and this being so we are resolved to wed in a way most probable to settle the vexed question of the Succession. In a word, we have chosen the Lady Anne Boleyn.'

Again Wolsey could find no words. He could not point out to this strange new master that if it really were a question of the Succession, it was odd, to say the least of it, that Henry should propose to marry a woman who would not be acceptable to the nation at large, nor to possible claimants to the throne of whom Henry was always in dread.

'While you were in France,' continued the King, with the air of a schoolboy caught in some prank and determined to bluff it out,' we despatched our secretary, Dr Knight, to Rome, to ask the Pope for a dispensation for us to marry the Lady Anne.'

'A dispensation to commit bigamy!' gasped the Cardinal, before he knew what he would say.

Then, seeing the flat eyes reddening with anger, he flung himself upon his knees.

'I implore your Grace's pardon, but consider, Sire, how dangerous such action must be for your cause. It will seem clear proof to the Pope that your Grace's scruples of conscience have their origin in carnal desire. And it will lose us the friendship of France; it will make havoc of all high affairs of state. As for the Emperor, the Queen's own nephew...'

His voice petered out. Opposition was only inflaming that primitive will, that will already passing from his domination to that of a ruthless and ambitious woman. The realization that far from the annulment of Henry's marriage being an instrument in strengthening his own international policy, it was to be a means of satisfying Henry's lust, was a bitter pill to swallow; but swallow it he must – for the present. He must make an alliance with this scheming hussy who threatened to be his rival, hoping that his Grace would tire of her and return to his senses.

He was ignorant of the weapon Anne held. She was still steadily refusing to give her lover full satisfaction until she had attained her goal, the Crown.

(iii)

Anne was at Hever. She had scored a vital point in the game she was playing, and she could afford to rest on her laurels for a few weeks, at the same time making Henry's heart grow fonder by her temporary absence from Court. While Wolsey had been in France, she had consolidated her power over her lover, who thought of himself as a man of strong will, while in fact he was always glad to abandon the initiative to others; and she had been busy poisoning his mind against his favourite.

'Alas,' she had lamented, 'I fear my Lord Cardinal does not approve of me, which seems strange, seeing that your Grace has been pleased to love me. But then it is said that of late he begins to fancy himself as your Grace's *alter ego,* and that while once upon a time he was wont to say, "The King commands such and such a thing," it soon became, "The King and I command it," until of late it has grown to be, "I command it." It seems we have now two king's in England.'

And Wolsey, on his return, had accepted defeat. He had given a splendid banquet in her honour at York Place; and now, the Pope having just escaped from his imprisonment, Wolsey himself had proposed that Clement should set up a Legatine Court in England, in which court the two judges,

Wolsey and the Cardinal Protector, Laurence Campeggio, should have full powers to give a verdict upon the validity of the King's marriage; and this though Wolsey knew now that Henry wanted to get free from Catherine that he might marry Anne.

Early in the new year, 1528, there called at Hever Wolsey's principal secretary, Stephen Gardiner, and the King's Almoner, Edward Foxe. They were on their way to the Pope, and by Henry's orders showed Anne the draft of a bull for setting up the Legatine Court. They gave her also a letter from Henry.

'Darling,' he wrote, 'these shall be only to advertise you that this bearer and his fellow be despatched with as many things' (thus vaguely and delicately did he refer to bribes) 'to compass our matter and to bring it to pass, as our wits could devise; which brought to pass, as I trust by their diligence it shall be shortly, you and I shall have our desired end; which would be more to my heart's ease than any other thing in the world, as with God's grace shortly I trust shall be proved, though not so soon as I would it were.'

She smiled drily at that last sentence. She thought she knew Henry thoroughly by this time; he still hoped she might yield and become his mistress, thus relieving him from a possible quarrel with the Pope and a lowering of himself in the eyes of his own subjects.

With the letter he had sent a rich girdle, its clasp engraved with a device such as any rustic lover might cut upon a tree; there were her initials within a heart encircled by the words, 'H Rex seeks no other.'

A letter to the Pope, shown her by Gardiner, pleased her more than the girdle. It contained a description of herself drawn up by Wolsey (who once had called her a foolish girl and a chit); Wolsey now informed the Pope that she was of regal descent, and dilated on 'the purity of her life, her

119

constant virginity, her soberness, chasteness, meekness, humility, wisdom, her maidenly and womanly pudicity, her apparent aptness to the procreation of children, with her other infinite good qualities.' She could just imagine Wolsey writing that eulogy, hating her, frightened by her, in terror for his power.

She had returned to Henry's side when, at the beginning of May, Foxe arrived home in the highest of spirits, having left his colleague with the Pope at Orvieto. He spoke with spiteful relish of Clement's condition there.

'He is living almost alone in a ruined episcopal palace, most of the Cardinals having returned to their homes after the sack of Rome. We passed through rooms unfurnished and almost unroofed to his Holiness' bedchamber, the furniture of which, bed and all, was not worth twenty nobles. His throne was only a bench covered with a piece of an old counterpane. Dr Gardiner spoke roundly to him, telling him plainly that if in the manner and form of obtaining justice, no more respect was shown to your Grace's person and the weight of your cause than to those of the inferior people, he did not doubt but that your Grace would seek a remedy at home from your own subjects. This moved the Pope sore; he is more in fear of schism even than of the Emperor's wrath.'

And it was this fear, of losing England from the unity of Christendom, which, Foxe admitted, was the reason why he and his colleague had at last, after three weeks' bullying and arguing, obtained from the harassed Clement the required commission to set up the Legatine Court. The King and Anne read the commission together; yes, there it was, wrapped up in tortuous legal Latin indeed, but there could be no mistake. It invested in Wolsey and Campeggio (Clement promising to send the latter to England for the purpose) full powers to hear the case of the King's marriage, to proceed summarily, and if either or both were satisfied that Pope Julius' dispensation were invalid, then to declare the marriage with Catherine void, and the parties in it free to marry again.

Wolsey was staying at the Episcopal Inn of Durham in the Strand. He had retired early that night, for lately he had suddenly begun to feel old and ill, when he was awakened by a gentleman who informed him that Dr Foxe was sent to him from the King. Groaning a little, the Cardinal arose, and being attired in his nightgown of figured velvet and his buskins lined with black lambswool, ordered candles to be brought to his Chamber of Presence; and there, dismissing his attendants, received the jubilant Foxe.

Foxe was surprised to notice that the Cardinal seemed to grow more and more preoccupied as he read through the commission. A faint doubt pricked Foxe's heart; he remembered belatedly that Clement VII, though a good man sincerely concerned for the unity of Christendom, had a reputation for intrigue and for indecision. Also that when menaced he was wont to defend himself, not by direct action but by an outward semblance of friendship coupled with a secret alliance with his attacker's enemies. Yet surely...

'His Grace is delighted with this commission,' Foxe said at length, unable to bear any longer the silence broken only by the crackle of parchment. 'I trust, my Lord Cardinal, that you are likewise.'

'I am perfectly satisfied, perfectly,' Wolsey answered; then abruptly stretched out his hand as a sign of dismissal.

But when Foxe had kissed the great amethyst, had made his genuflections, and departed, the Cardinal crashed his hand upon the precious document, and cursed. For he had seen how the Pope's canonists had duped Foxe and Gardiner; tied up in this mass of words was the fact that

121

the right of making the final decision was left to Clement. For Henry's purpose, the commission was useless.

He rose and paced the room, this gorgeous room hung with tapestries designed by Raphael, with the chair of estate, fringed with Venice silk, on an alabaster dais, with the scented rushes on the floor and the cupboards displaying mazers and salts set with pearl and enriched with enamel, with his emblems and initials in the classical medallions set in the gold embossed roof. The magnificence without which he could not live, the display more and more necessary to him as he grew older.

What was he to do? He dared not tell Henry how the Pope had fooled him; already his hold upon that unstable will was shaken; Henry would turn and rend him, blaming him for it all.

He gathered his intelligence, an intelligence so keen in dealing with problems immediately under his hand, so lacking in vision. At the back of his mind the voice of conscience nagged at him; but it was too late now to think of the perilous position in which, as usual reducing all things to a personal issue, he had placed the Church, the kingdom, and his own soul. He was committed to a course of action; Henry wanted an annulment of his marriage, wanted it at any price; and if he did not get it from Wolsey, Wolsey was finished.

He sat down presently and with his own hand wrote in cipher a letter to Gardiner at Orvieto. Since it was impossible to ask for a redraft of the commission, Gardiner must obtain from the Pope a Decretal Bull. He paused and thought furiously, biting his nails; yes, a Decretal Bull could yet save the situation, in fact it was the only thing that could save it. It was a document issued by the Pope giving a Decree upon a point of law, in this case that if Catherine's former marriage to Arthur had been consummated, no Papal dispensation for a marriage to Arthur's brother could be valid.

Wolsey knew well the enormity of what he was doing. He was demanding from the spiritual Head of Christendom something which would prejudice the whole case, would make a mockery of the supreme court of Rome, and would destroy the essential right of appeal to it from a lower court. Under the veiled threat of England's seceding from the unity of Christendom, he was asking Clement to create a situation in canon law such that, upon Wolsey's declaration that the first marriage had been consummated, as a necessary consequence Henry should be pronounced not married to Catherine and free to marry again. Any such judgement given by the Pope would be binding on Christians for ever, and would change the existing law of the Church.

Wolsey knew all this, but he was desperate. His sole aim now must be to get the power of giving final judgement into his own hands, so that he might pronounce sentence according to his master's desire. The alternative was to lose that master's favour, and perhaps his own head.

(iv)

In June he received cheering news.

His ruse had succeeded; the Pope had signed the Decretal Bull and was sending it over with the Cardinal Protector of England, Laurence Campeggio. In his relief, Wolsey found himself thinking kindly of Clement; weak and tortuous though that Medici had shown himself to be, it was obvious that his real fear was of losing England through schism. France had recently threatened the same thing; whole districts of the Germanies were infected with Lutherism; the Turk advancing everywhere.

At Greenwich, meanwhile, Henry and Anne were passing their time in a round of merriment marred only by the perpetual skeleton at the feast, the Queen. No hints, no persuasions, no petty persecution would induce Catherine to depart from Court; she had sent her young daughter away because she would not have the girl hurt, but she herself remained, and Henry, for form's sake, accepted her presence on all official occasions, behaved to her in public as became his Consort, and referred to her proper title.

But her presence not only irritated Anne; it made her uneasy. Though aware that for years Henry and Catherine had not been living as man and wife, she was intelligent enough to realize that a partnership of twenty years' standing is bound by small but strong threads, early memories, shared tastes, and above all, habit. And Catherine, she thought, was cunning; she had made Henry dependent on her for those domestic comforts which grew more necessary to him as he approached his forties.

'My favourite pourpoint is torn,' he would say. 'I must ask the Queen to mend it.' Or, 'The Queen and I stayed at this manor of mine before our daughter Mary was born, and her Grace planted that myrtle hedge yonder.' Or again, 'I need some more shirts; reminds me to ask the Queen to make some. I like better than any other that Spanish-work of hers.'

If only the fat old cow would die, though Anne. Her own nerves were beginning to fray after these long years of holding Henry off and at the same time keeping alight his passion for her; and things were not made any easier by her growing unpopularity. Wherever she rode with Henry the common people insulted her; occasionally her overwrought nerves caused her to quarrel with Henry, and to quarrel with Henry was extremely dangerous.

It was during this summer that she received a warning of her lover's instability of character. News came from

London that the dreaded sweating-sickness had broken out in the City. Henry, while alarmed, remarked that the Court was safe enough at Greenwich, but took care to give strict orders that on petitioners or visitors form the infected capital be admitted to Placentia. A few days later, one of Anne's maids fell ill; she mentioned it casually to the King, quite unprepared for his violent reaction. This huge tough man so devoted to rough sports, turned white with terror; the Court must move at once and Anne must go to Hever, he cried; he would write every day to his beloved, but she must go, go!

He fled from palace to palace, changing his residence almost nightly as though pursued by a human foe. Hunting and pageants were forsaken, even thoughts of the annulment of his marriage were laid aside. He occupied his days in drawing up will after will, no less than thirty-nine of them, in inditing stern letters to his sister, Margaret of Scotland, reproving her for her immoral life, and in making up pills and potions with his doctors. He heard five masses every morning instead of his usual three, confessed every day, and sent lavish gifts to shrines in return for prayers for the safety of his person. At night he returned to the connubial bed, and everyone remarked on his new kindness towards the Queen.

Even though he was at the same time sending grossly passionate love-letters to Anne, he succeeded in reassuring himself by his extreme moral punctilio. He tested himself; yes, he retained a real devotion to the Blessed Sacrament, he actually shed tears during his daily confession, he was ready to go on pilgrimage to any shrine where there was no infection in the neighbourhood. How could the intentions and desires of a man living so piously be anything but impeccable? And none but a morally righteous man would have possessed so tender a conscience. It was only because of the scruples of that conscience that he desired an

125

annulment of his marriage with dear Catherine – that and his duty of providing for the Succession.

'It is a strange thing to me, my lord,' Catherine remarked unkindly, 'that you were but thirty when you that I could bear you no more children, yet for some seven years afterwards this question of the Succession did not trouble you.'

Henry was about to make a furious retort, but remembered in time his new piety which alone could avert God's judgement in the shape of the sweating-sickness. Meanwhile he waited impatiently for the coming of the Cardinal Protector, who had embarked at Genoa for Marseilles on June 13th, and for the opening of the Legatine Court.

What Henry did not know was that Cardinal Campeggio had orders from the Pope to make every possible delay upon his journey, and that when at length he arrived, according to his instructions 'you are to do your utmost to restore mutual affections between the King and Queen. And you are not to pronounce any opinion without a new and express commission from Us.' For Clement, always hoping that something would turn up to get him round an awkward corner, was still optimistically believing that Henry would tire of the woman whom, along with everyone else, the Pope took to be his Grace of England's concubine.

Laurence Campeggio was a man of high integrity, now advanced in years, and crippled with gout. His calm and steadfast face commanded the respect of all who came in contact with him, as did his high intelligence and his equable temper. But in fact he was two persons; the man and the legist. As the latter he never allowed personal feelings to influence him; he was always ready to doubt human evidence, however sincere, always concerned with abstract principles of law. By his profession he was bound to work for the Papal government throughout Europe; and as Cardinal Protector of England it was his duty to make out the best presentation that could be made for the demands of the English Crown.

With extreme slowness he progressed through France; it was not until mid-September that he arrived in Paris. Here he fund Clerk, Bishop of Bath, who had been sent by the impatient Henry to discover what could have happened to him. Primed by Wolsey, who still thought that all men had their price, Clerk offered the Cardinal Protector a large sum of money 'to defray his expenses', to which Campeggio replied with dignity that it was not poverty but gout that was delaying him. Clerk promptly ordered a litter, and by October had got the sick man to England; to Henry's extreme annoyance Campeggio, at his first audience, made it plain that his main object in coming over was to persuade his grace to return to his wife.

Concealing his fury, Henry dilated on his conscience, and having been primed by his tame theologians, argued learnedly for four hours. He appeared so sincerely troubled on the one hand, and so absolutely determined to proceed with the case on the other, that Campeggio saw nothing for it but to appeal to the Queen. He opened his interview with her by saying that the King had told him she was willing and even eager to enter a convent, and that in his, Campeggio's, opinion, this would be a most happy solution to the dilemma.

She looked such a homely, placid little woman that he was taken aback by the passion with which she answered him.

'A convent? Never! I know this idea had been spread abroad, and to show the falsity of it I have been for some time past unusually frivolous, so much so that his Grace has rebuked me for it, saying that my cheerfulness shows I do not love him.'

There was a trace of dry bitterness in her voice, and it was clear that the rebuke had stung. Henry always expected everyone to love him, no matter how he treated them.

'I am, my lords,' she continued vigorously, 'resolved to die a wife, as God had made me. Neither the whole realm, nor, on the other hand, the greatest punishments, even being torn limb from limb, shall alter me in this; and if after death I were to return to life, I would die again, and yet again, rather than I would give way!'

'I must inform your Highness,' interposed Wolsey, 'that we are about to hold a court of inquiry into your marriage, wherein many matters must be sifted which will be offensive to your Highness' womanhood and will put you to the blush.'

She ignored this mean threat, and said with dignity:

'Alas, my lords, is it now a question whether I be the King's lawful wife or not, when I have been married to him almost twenty years, and no objection made before? Divers prelates and lords, Privy Councillors of the King, are yet alive who judged our marriage good and lawful; and now to say it is detestable is a great marvel to me, especially when I consider what a wise prince the King's father was, and also the natural love and affection my father, King Ferdinand, bore me. I think that neither of our fathers was so weak in judgement as now you imply they were. As for my former marriage with the Prince Arthur, I swear most solemnly, here with my hand upon the Holy Gospel, that it was never consummated; though I need not to do this, for the dispensation allowed for it.'

The again her calm broke. Her fair skin flushed crimson, and her southern passion burst through the rigid self-control she exercised upon it.

'But of this trouble I may only thank you, my Lord of York,' she cried at Wolsey. 'Because I ever wondered at your pride and vainglory and abhorred your voluptuous life, and little cared for your presumption and tyranny, therefore of malice have you kindled this fire; especially for the great grudge you bear my nephew, the Emperor, whom you hate worse than a scorpion because he would not gratify your ambition by making you Pope by force, and therefore you have said, more than once, that you would trouble him and his friends – and you have kept your true promise! As for me, his poor kinswoman, what anguish you put me to, whom am a lone woman without friends or advisers in this country, by this new-found doubt, God only knoweth, to whom I commit my cause.'

Campeggio glanced sideways at his companion as they left the apartment. He said gravely:

'She is indeed the daughter of the heroic Isabella. You will not move her, my lord.'

'I shall not need to move her,' said Wolsey stiffly. 'I shall bring in evidence to show that her former marriage was consummated, and then we will produce the Decretal Bull.'

Campeggio stopped short in his tracks. He said briskly:

'My lord, it seems you are labouring under a misapprehension. I must tell you now at once that I am under the strictest orders from His Holiness that this Decretal is not to pass out of my possession. I am given permission to show it to yourself, and to his Grace, but to none other, and certainly it cannot be produced in court.'

Wolsey stared at him in angry bewilderment, while his quick mind sought the reason for so strange an order. It did not take him long to find it. A document which was not to pass out of Campeggio's possession could be of no use to the advocates in the King's case; and the tortuous Clement would not consider himself bound by it. But he must get hold of it; at all costs he must get hold of it, and thus defeat the Pope's vacillations.

Campeggio seemed to guess something of what was passing in his mind, for he said drily:

'So weighty a document, my lord, must be preserved with the greatest care. And I, to whom it was entrusted, shall see that it is so.'

It was not, in fact, preserved, in the sense that Campeggio intended then. Before the opening of the Legatine Court, the Pope, in sudden panic, sent his most confidential secretary, Campana, to England, with an order to destroy the Decretal Bull at once, which order Campeggio obeyed by committing it to the flames.

Chapter Three

(i)

On the south-west corner of the walled City, with the great stone fortress called Baynard's Castle to the east of it, and to the west, across the Fleet River, the royal palace of Bridewell, was the house of the Black Friars. It was a great priory, enriched by former Kings of England who had always favoured the Dominicans. Here Edward I had buried the heart of his Queen; and in its Great Hall with its open timbered roof the few Parliaments called in national emergencies were wont to sit.

It was in this Hall that the drama of the Legatine Court was to be played, and the vast place had been specially prepared for the purpose. In the midst, upon a raised platform, sat the two judges, Wolsey magnificent in crimson silk cassock and snowy rochet, Campeggio a shabby and somewhat pathetic figure, his gouty feet propped upon a cushion. On their left was a throne and canopy emblazoned with the Royal Arms, and on the opposite side, but lower down, a chair of estate for the Queen. At the judges' feet sat the Clerks of the Court; and beyond, on the opposite side, where the King's advocates, and on the other the Queen's, the latter having been chosen for her by her husband. Old Warham, Archbishop of Canterbury, with the Bishops, sat on benches facing the judges.

Henry was staying at Greenwich and arrived in the royal barge; he was in his full state. Heralds proclaiming him, trumpets sounding, his Cap of Maintenance borne before him on a cushion. His Collar of the Garter flashed in the sunlight over the deep revers of marten which adorned his surcote; beneath the short skirts of his tunic the legs of which he was still so proud stumped purposefully towards his throne.

From without there sounded a sudden spontaneous roar of welcome, causing Henry to frown; and a moment or two later the stout little figure of the Queen, with her ladies behind her, appeared through the entrance from the bridge which connected Blackfriars with Bridewell. A murmur ran round the Great Hall as it was seen that she wore her long russet hair loose in the manner of a suppliant, and that her gown above her Spanish verdingale was dead black.

'Henry, King of England, come into the court!' rang out the tremulous voice of the Usher.

'Here, my lords!' responded Henry. His cheerfulness sounded slightly forced; Anne had told him roundly before he parted from her at Greenwich this morning, that this trial was a pompous farce and would achieve nothing. Besides he was irritated by the roar of welcome which testified anew to his wife's popularity.

'Catherine, Queen of England, come into the court!'

She did not answer. She rose, and signing to her ladies to remain where they were, she walked steadily across the width of the Hall, every eye following her, bowed low to the judges as she passed, and sank on her knees at Henry's feet. The silence was electric as she began to speak, in the French which she found so much easier than English when she wished to speak from her heart. I was as if only she and her husband were present.

'Sir, I beseech you, for all the love that has been between us, and for the love of God, let me have some right and justice. Take of me pity and compassion, for I am a poor stranger born out of your dominions; I have here no unprejudiced counsellor, and I flee to you, as to the head of justice within your realm.'

The tears welled out of her china-blue eyes, and she stretched out her hands imploringly.

'Alas! Alas! wherein have I offended you? I take God and all the world to witness that I have been to you a true, humble and obedient wife, ever conformable to your will and pleasure. I have been pleased with all things in which you found delight, and have loved all whom you loved, only for your sake, whether they were my friends or my enemies. This twenty years I have been your true wife, and by me you have had many children, though it has pleased God to call all save one of them out of this world, which was no fault of mine. And I put it to your conscience' – her voice rose suddenly – 'whether I came not to you a maid.'

The court hung upon his reply to this challenge. But he sat silent, frowning, his great jowl nursed in one heavily ringed hand.

'It,' continued Catherine, 'You have since found any dishonour in my conduct, then am I content to depart; but if none there be, I beseech you, thus lowlily, to let me remain in my proper state. You cause me to stand in the judgement of this new court, wherein you do me much wrong, for you may condemn me for lack of sufficient answer, since your subjects cannot be impartial counsellors for me, daring not, for fear of your wrath, to disobey your will.'

His flat eyes narrowed at this thrust, but still he said nothing.

'Therefore do I most humbly require you, in the name of charity and for the love of God, to spare me the sentence of this court until I am advised by my friends in Spain what way I must take. But if you will not give me this favour, I here and now do appeal to the Pope, the common Father of all Christians, to judge and defend my cause.'

She rose. Stout and homely though she was, and now with her long hair dishevelled and her face blotched with tears, she had tremendous dignity. Making a low curtsy to the King, she walked across the Hall, but instead of returning to her seat, she signalled to her attendants and went towards the door by which she had entered. At this sight, Henry recovered his tongue.

'Usher!' he barked. 'Order the Queen's Grace to return.'

The usher obeyed in ringing tones, and the gentleman on whose arm Catherine was leaning said unnecessarily:

'Madam, you are called.'

'I hear it well enough,' said Catherine. 'But on! On! This is no impartial court for me, and I will go my ways.'

'The Queen has said she is an obedient wife,' sneered Wolsey, quick to take advantage of the situation, 'yet here she publicly disregards his Grace's command.'

But Henry was concerned to take off the impression made by his wife's touching appeal to him, and to appear morally superior.

'Forasmuch as the Queen is gone,' he said emotionally, 'we will in her absence declare unto you all that she has been to us as true, as conformable, and as obedient a wife as we in our fancy could desire. And if it be adjudged that she is our lawful wife, nothing will be more pleasant or more acceptable to us; for we assure you all, my lords, that besides her noble parentage, she is a woman of great gentleness and humility, yea, and of all good qualities pertaining to nobility she is without comparison. So that if we were to marry again, we would choose her above all women.'

The ghost of Anne, with her penetrating black eyes and her sharp tongue, seemed suddenly to confront him, and he reverted to his conscience.

'But if it be determined in judgement that our marriage is against God's law, then must we with sorrow part from so loving a lady and sweet companion. These are the sorrows which vex our mind, these be the pangs which torment our conscience, because learned and godly men have told us that we have been living for twenty years in detestable incest and fornication.'

'May it please your Grace,' said Wolsey, after a suitable pause for reverence, 'it is commonly mooted about the town that it was I who, for my own ends, first suggested to your Grace an annulment of your marriage. I pray you do me justice; was this so?'

'It was not,' Henry replied majestically. 'Our conscience was first pricked by chancing upon the passage in Leviticus wherein is forbidden the marrying of a brother's wife; and after much disquiet we desired my Lord of Canterbury to consult with the Bishops, all of whom confirmed our fears, putting their hand and seal to their opinion.'

'That is true,' quavered Warham. At his age, and with his fundamentally honest character, this business was killing him. 'I have no doubt my venerable brethren will confirm the same.'

A voice spoke unexpectedly from among the Bishops.

'No, my lord, not so. Under your favour, all the Bishops were not so far agreed, for to that instrument you have neither my hand nor my seal.'

A gasp ran round the court, and every eye was turned on Fisher of Rochester. The King lost his temper.

'God's body!' he roared. 'Set the paper before him – so – is that not your hand and seal?'

'No, your Grace, it is not,' emphatically replied Fisher.

'How say you to that?' the King rapped out to the agitated Warham.

'Sire, it is his hand and seal.'

'No, my lord.' Fisher's warm brown eyes, so large in his gaunt face, looked reproachfully at the Archbishop. 'Indeed, my Lord of Canterbury, you were often pressing me for my hand and seal, as other of the Bishops have given you; but then I ever said to you I would in no wise consent to any such act, for it is much against my conscience to have this matter so much as once called in question; and therefore, said I, my hand and seal should never be put to any such instrument, God willing, if you remember.'

'Indeed,' the Archbishop said hurriedly, his eyes avoiding the other's, 'true it is that such words you had with me; but after our talk ended, you were at last resolved and content that I should – should subscribe your name and put to your seal, and you would allow the same as if it had been done by yourself.'

Fisher's voice answered very distinctly:

'Under your favour, my Lord Archbishop, all this that you have said of me is untrue. My name upon this instrument is a – '

Before he could utter the dreadful word 'forgery', Henry blustered into the breach.

'God's body, God's body, my Lord of Rochester, it makes no great matter; we will not stand in argument with you about this business, for you are but one man against the rest, if the worst fall.'

'It may be so, your Grace,' Fisher replied gravely, 'But this I must say upon my conscience; I implore my lords the judges to take heed what they do in so weighty a matter, and to think upon the dangers which may ensue to the whole of Christendom if the validity of his Grace's marriage be called in question; for of its validity there can be not the shadow of a doubt.'

(ii)

It was not an auspicious beginning to the trial.

It was all very well to pronounce Catherine guilty of contumacy because she had refused to return to the court, and to continue the sittings without her. The forgery of Fisher's hand and seal could not be kept secret; attendants and officials talked; and what the old Bishop had said, he so famed for learning and holiness, would do the King's cause much harm in Europe. Besides him there were other men of standing who while they lacked his courage, were known to be of his opinion; Bishop Tunstall, now of London, presented to Campeggio a scholarly treatise he had written in defence of the marriage, and asked to be allowed to read it in court. As in duty bound, Compeggio mentioned this to Henry who, nursing his wrath against such malcontents, sent Tunstall off on an embassy to Cambrai, where France and the Empire were negotiating a peace.

With the Bishop the King sent Sir Thomas More, whose steady refusal to give an opinion on the 'great matter' argued that he was the same mind as Tunstall.

Day after day the court debated the delicate question, had the marriage between Catherine and the boy Arthur been consummated? Forty noble witnesses stood up and maintained, some of them from their personal experience, that Prince Arthur's tender age would not have prevented consummation. In the midst of this appallingly gross and presumptive evidence, Campeggio said impatiently:

'No one can know the truth of this except her Grace.'

But again rang forth that bell-like voice from the bench of Bishops.

'I know the truth.'

'How do you know, my Lord of Rochester?' snapped Wolsey.

'I know that God is truth. He says, *Quod Deus conjunxit homo non separet.* Forasmuch then as his Grace's marriage was made by God, it cannot be broken by the power of man for any pretended reason.'

'All faithful men know as much,' Wolsey retorted contemptuously, 'but the King's counsel bring forth presumptive evidence that the marriage was not good from the beginning, and that it was not made by God. You must therefore go further than that text. You must disprove the presumptions.'

'The truth of his Grace's marriage was plain to be proved good and lawful from the beginning,' persisted Fisher, 'whether there was carnal communication in the former marriage or not. For the case was thoroughly scanned and debated by many great learned divines and lawyers, whereof I myself remember the time, and am not altogether ignorant of the manner of dealing therein; and being afterwards ratified and approved by the authority of the See Apostolic so amply and so largely, I think it now a hard matter to call it again in question before any judge.'

There were one or two low murmurs of assent.

'As his Grace,' continued Fisher, 'has said that his only object is to have justice done, and has invited us his Bishops to throw light upon it, I will not be unfaithful to God or his Grace. I will not incur the damnation of my soul, by refraining from declaring publicly the result of two years' study into this great matter. I affirm therefore that this marriage cannot be dissolved by any power human or divine, and in support of this opinion I am willing to lay down my life. As St John the Baptist thought it glorious to die in defence of Christian marriage (and marriage was not then so holy as it has since become through the shedding of Christ's blood), so I encourage myself more confidently to dare the same peril for the same cause.'

His fearless eyes looked direct at Henry as he spoke, and when he ceased there was a portentous silence. For suddenly it was clear to all men present that this was indeed a struggle to the death.

The case dragged on, the King's advocates using every art to procure a sentence in his favour. At Greenwich Anne was pressing Henry hard; she was losing her youth, she cried; all this legal business was to no purpose; Wolsey was a broken reed. Why could not the King burn his boats, marry her, and explain it to the Pope afterwards? Always wavering, always shrinking from making a decision, Henry put her off with excuses; and all the while he was accumulating in his heart a store of hate. Though he did not know it, his 'great matter' had become for him, not so much the annulment of his marriage and the gaining of Anne, but a desire to show that he was master, to bend all men to his will.

At last his lawyers called for judgement; but before Wolsey could speak, Campeggio said gravely in Latin:

'No, not so; I will give no sentence until I have made relation to His Holiness of all our doings, whose command I will observe in this case. I have been one of the twelve judges of the Rota for many years, and I have never known such hurry, even in matters of little moment, much less in a case of such weight as this, which involves the hasty dissolution of a marriage held valid for twenty years, the bastardising of a royal issue, the sowing of discord among Christians, and contempt of the Papal powers of dispensation.'

Wolsey stared at him in consternation; such plain speaking was not used in the royal presence.

'Remember,' Campeggio went on, 'whose commissioners we are, my Lord Cardinal, and under whose authority we sit. I came not hither to please, for favour or dread of any person alive, be he king or subject, neither have I any such regard to the person, that I would violate my own conscience or displease God. I am now an old man, weak and sickly, and daily look for death. And should I now put my soul in peril for fear or favour of any prince in the world?'

There was an angry growl from the throne, but Campeggio disregarded it. He gathered up his papers and said distinctly:

'And forasmuch as I understand by the allegations the matter to be doubtful, and also that the party defendant will make no answer here, but does rather appeal from us to Rome, considering the King's high authority within this his own realm where she thinks we dare not do her justice for fear of his displeasure – I say, that in consideration of these things, I intend not to wade any further in this matter till I have the just opinion and assent of His Holiness. Wherefore I do here adjourn this court for the time of the summer vacation, according to the custom of the Court of Rome, whence our authority is derived, which if we should transgress, might be accounted in us great folly and rashness, and redound to our discredit and blame.'

Long before he had finished speaking, the King, his eyes dark with anger, had risen and stalked out of the Hall; and as Campeggio ended, the nobles burst into passionate denunciation. But it was not against Campeggio they raged, their venom turned upon Wolsey, sitting there stricken, Wolsey the butcher's son. Wolsey the richest man in England after the King, Wolsey who had lorded it over them, ordered them about at the Council-board, annexed the great offices they regarded as their exclusive right.

'Now by the Blessed Virgin!' shouted the Duke of Suffolk, 'it was never merry in England whilst we had Cardinals among us!'

Wolsey roused himself for a moment. Long ago, when Suffolk had married Henry's sister without seeking the royal permission, Wolsey had pleaded for him and had shielded him from the King's wrath.

'Sir,' said he quietly, 'of all men in this realm you have least excuse to disparage Cardinals. For if I, a simple Cardinal, had not been, you would not have had at this time a head upon your shoulders wherein to have a tongue to speak thus of me.'

(iii)

But though he showed a bold front, he knew his peril.

Throughout the remainder of the summer, excuse after excuse was made for keeping him from Court. Whispers against him became open words, even secretly printed ones. He had chosen with skill the men who worked for him, but there was not one who was devoted to him save those too lowly to affect his course. Especially did he fear "the night crow", as he called Anne; it was plain that she had never forgiven him for his part in preventing her match with young Percy. And she, like himself before her, sought complete dominance over the vain and fickle King; what would happen to him depended entirely upon Henry, who was warped by his disease and obsessed with a clever and ruthless woman. But though he feared greatly, Wolsey was not the man to give up without a struggle.

At about the same time as Campeggio adjourned the Legatine Court, the Pope had published a bull removing the case to Rome, and citing Henry and Catherine to plead there in person or by proxy, under pain of excommunication. In August copies of the bull arrived in

England, and Wolsey acted with his old vigour, he wrote to his agent in Rome: 'If the King be cited to appear, and his prerogative be interfered with, none of subjects will tolerate it; and if he appears in Italy it will be at the head of an army.' That should suffice to make the weak and now extremely sick Clement think again. Wolsey then went to the Queen, and using all his powers of persuasion induced her not to publish the bull, though she still insisted that the cause be carried on in Rome.

With these little advances made, Wolsey wrote humbly to the King begging to be allowed to come to Court with Campeggio when the latter took his leave on September 19th. Not only did Henry give permission, but he kept his old favourite to dinner with him afterwards, talking kindly to him. Pathetically eager to please, really troubled in his conscience at last, Wolsey turned the conversation to the reform of abuses.

'I intend, with your Grace's permission, to make an order for all Bishops to reside in their own Sees. And I will set an example, if it please your Grace, by going into residence at Winchester.'

'Nay, rather at York,' broke in Norfolk, before the King could reply. 'For after all, my Lord Cardinal,' he added blandly, 'your Archbishopric is the principal of your two Sees.'

But what he really meant, and knew that Wolsey knew he meant, was that York was two hundred miles away.

Wolsey had one more card up his sleeve, and it was a desperate one.

When Campeggio started for the coast, Wolsey summoned one of his most confidential agents and gave him orders. He was to follow Campeggio, and he was to find means to search the old Cardinal's baggage. What Wolsey wanted was the Decretal Bull; he did not know that it had been destroyed months before, and if he could get hold of it, it would save him. He could reopen the Legatine Court, silence Catherine's protests by producing the Decretal, and proceed to give judgement against her.

He waited in an agony of suspense. On October 9th, the very day on which Campeggio set sail from Dover, the messenger returned to his master, stammering a woeful tale. He had been obliged to enlist the help of the custom-house officers, who had demanded the Cardinal Protector's keys to examine his luggage. The Cardinal Protector indignantly refusing, they had broken the locks and searched; whereat Campeggio, very wroth, had sworn he would write to the King and protest against this violation of an Ambassador's privilege.

And of the Decretal there was no trace.

Next day was the first of the Michaelmas Term, when the courts opened, the Chancery among them. Wolsey went to Westminster Hall in his customary state, and took his seat as Lord Chancellor; many curious eyes were upon him, for here the courts functioned in public, following the ancient tradition that the law should be administered where all could see and hear.

The eyes made him nervous, so that he could not concentrate upon his business. Sniffing at an orange stuffed with sweet herbs, he thought belatedly of the powers he had misused, those powers to which he had desired no limit. Especially did he think of his extraordinary demand, seconded by the King, when, only just come into the public eye as Bishop of Lincoln, he had intrigued for and presently had obtained from Leo X a Legacy a *Latere* and, clean contrary to custom, for life. He had told himself that only by being in effect Pope in England could he reform abuses, enforce residency, restore the prestige of the clergy, root out the superstitions which encrusted the pure Faith. But he had been working for

143

himself, only for himself; throughout his career he had reduced all things to a personal issue.

Yet surely it was not too late to make amends. He was still but fifty-six, and though the recent crisis had told on him, he had a vigorous constitution. His failure to get hold of the Decretal meant that he had lost all chance of re-establishing himself as Henry's favourite; undoubtedly his secular offices would be taken from him, but he did not think for a moment that Henry would deprive him of his spiritual ones. And he would use them better now; he would do all he could to combat the pernicious heresies of his man Tyndale, whose unauthorized New Testament, with its craftily mistranslated key-words, was being smuggled into England along the trade routes from Germany. He would give his whole-hearted support to Thomas More, who had perceived from the beginning that Tyndale's pretended desire for reform was a threat to the unity of the Church, and who was throwing himself so zealously into the work of counter-propaganda...

Someone was speaking to him, handing him something, looking at him curiously. He took the document and read it.

It was a Bill of Indictment against him, newly filed in the King's Bench opposite, for having, in the fifteenth year of King Henry's reign, accepted form the Pope a Legacy a *Latere*, thereby incurring the penalties of *Praemunire* which deprived him of all his possessions, and of his liberty during the King's pleasure.

(iv)

The stark injustice of it took his breath away. Out of his personal vanity, Henry had badgered Pope Leo to give Wolsey a Legacy, and now was indicting him under a Statute of 1392 which had been enacted to provide a weapon for the Crown against fiscal and other encroachments of the Papacy upon its rights. Wolsey had Henry's own licence under his Grace's hand and seal confirming his Legatine authority. But now, when he searched for that precious licence, he could not find it; mysteriously it had disappeared.

But the threat to Christendom was far more serious than his personal danger; a Papal Legate was being indicted by the civil power. It Wolsey gave way, the Church's independence for which St Thomas of Canterbury had died would be so shaken that it might be lost for ever.

Wolsey knew this. But he knew also the alternative; if he resisted, the aristocratic clique who hated him would demand his head. Yet if he so resisted at least he would have left a precedent, and possibly some later chance of a restoration of the Church's rights. Thus he swayed to and fro in an agony; he seemed broken in spirit, talking incoherently, refusing to eat. He wrote a tearful, cringing letter to Henry, begging for mercy, and received in reply permission to appeal to the Parliament about to be summoned, if he would prefer that to a trial in a court of law. The hand of Norfolk, his most bitter enemy, was plainly to be seen; Parliament would make short work of the Cardinal.

He gave in, accepted the jurisdiction of those lay courts which had no just authority over a cleric, pleaded guilty, and submitted himself to the King's mercy. At York Place he ordered all his riches to be set out, hoping to appease Henry's wrath by the sight of so much booty; the October sun flashed upon the gold and silver, the jewels, and the rich stuffs, heaped on tables and cupboards. On Monday the 18th he went down to his barge, rocking at the water-gate; from a mass of boats, backing their oars against the flood to keep in place, the citizens feasted their eyes on fallen greatness.

His oarsmen rowed him upstream, for he was going into exile at Esher, one of the houses of his Winchester diocese. At Putney he landed; his mule and his gentlemen's horses were waiting here to carry them the rest of the way by road. Scarcely had he mounted when a young man came riding hard down the main street of the little town: Sir Harry Norris, one of the King's boon companions. Wolsey watched him come, fearing the worst; but the King, it seemed, was still as wavering as ever, still torn between natural affection for a man who had served him all too faithfully, and the new influence which was tightening its grip upon his will.

'His Grace had sent me to say, my Lord Cardinal, that you are not to think you have lost his royal favour. He is compelled to act thus by others; but in proof of his regard for you he sends you this ring, which is one, says he, you will know right well.'

Wolsey gazed with blurred eyes at that familiar turquoise engraved with the Tudor Rose. Then he struggled out of the saddle, the tears streaming down his fleshy face, and knelt in the mud.

'I – I – I am so overwhelmed,' he stammered, 'that I must needs give thanks to God in this very place. And to the King, my Sovereign Lord and master – '

As he said the words he made to pull off his velvet cap in reverence, and because the knot fastened under his chin would not yield to his trembling fingers, he tore the laces apart in his eagerness. When he would have mounted again, his emotion had so exhausted him that he had to be half lifted into the saddle. Yet he talked animatedly to Norris all the way up the hill till they came to the heath at the summit where the road to London branched off eastwards by Wandsworth. Here Norris took his leave, but not before the Cardinal had unfastened from about his neck his greatest treasure, a little gold reliquary containing

146

a relic of the Cross. Pressing the gift upon the embarrassed Norris, he murmured:

'When I was in prosperity I would not have parted with this for a thousand pounds, but now I beseech you take it and wear it about your neck for my sake.'

He sat slumped upon his mule, watching Norris ride off along the road to London. Then suddenly he roused himself, and called urgently to the young man, and when he came cantering back again, the Cardinal said with tears:

'Alas, I have no token to send my Sovereign Lord in exchange for the ring he sent me, for I am altogether despoiled.'

He looked about him in a sort of desperation, and his eyes lighted upon Master Patch, his Fool. Patch, thinking to cheer his master, immediately began his antics, pulling comical faces under his hood with its ass' ears.

'Take this Fool!' Wolsey cried to Norris. 'He is such a good fool that a rich man would pay a thousand pounds for him, so admirable is his folly.'

Even yet his mind ran upon money and saw all things in the light of it.

But Master Patch was one of those poor men who alone were devoted to Wolsey, and falling on his knees he begged most earnestly that he should not be sent to the King. It took six strong yeomen to drag him to Norris; they fastened a rope about his parti-coloured tunic, and bore him away captive, the bells on his garments ringing an accompaniment to his dismal howls.

Chapter Four

There was one member of Wolsey's household who wished he were in Master Patch's shoes, for he would have gone most willingly. But for the first time in his life, Thomas Cromwell found himself in a cleft stick.

For a good many years now he had been known as the Cardinal's right-hand man whenever there was some less reputable business to be transacted, and as such he had got himself heartily hated. But on the other hand to desert Wolsey in the hour of his disgrace would make him more detested than ever. Thus did Cromwell commune with himself as he rode in the Cardinal's train towards Esher; he confided his dilemma to no man, for it was his habit to watch all men silently and to open himself to none. He was one of those rare characters who have no personal feeling of love or hate; his personality consisted in different manifestations of one fundamental trait, a strict attention to business – his own.

And so, like the worldly-wise steward in the parable, he was not long in arriving at a solution to his problem. He must keep up an appearance of doing everything he could for his fallen master, and at the same time he must insinuate himself into the good graces of that master's enemies.

On the morning of the feast of All Hallows, simple, honest Mr Cavendish, Wolsey's Usher, came into the Great Chamber at Esher to fetch something and was mightily surprised to see Mr Cromwell leaning against a mullion of the window, with a Primer in his hand and the tears trickling down his large dull face. It was not often one saw Mr Cromwell with a prayer-book, and the emotion was still more unusual; touched by the sight, Cavendish asked gently:

'Why, sir, what means this dole? Is my lord in any danger that you lament for him?'

'I have done my master most diligent service all the days of my life,' blubbered Cromwell, who in fact had been in Wolsey's service less than nine years, 'and am disdained now for his sake, as all those are who serve him. An evil name once gotten will not lightly be put off.'

'If his Grace but knew,' sighed Cavendish, 'how broken in spirit my lord is, ay, and in health likewise,'

The little piggy eyes flickered at him under the light, arched brows.

'I am but a humble servant,' murmured Cromwell, 'yet there are some I know at Court might listen to me if I pleaded my master's cause. Yes, this very afternoon, with my lord's permission, I will ride to London, where I will either make or mar or ever I come again.'

He was called in by his master after dinner to assist Wolsey in discharging those servants whom the Cardinal could no longer afford to retain. In return for the numerous benefices his chaplains had received through the years of his greatness, he bade them pay part of these servants' wages; and he was very much touched when Cromwell, whom he had never thought of as a particularly generous man, and who was not a cleric, begged to be allowed to set an example by contributing five pounds. Wolsey was still more impressed when this man whom he had used for his more unsavoury business, suggested that he go to London to see what he could do for his master's cause. The tears which came so readily to the Cardinal's eyes nowadays burst forth; to discover that he had a true friend where he had thought he had only a business agent, moved him deeply.

Humbly he begged Cromwell to do whatever he could to persuade the King to pardon his old favourite; for himself, he was ready to do anything Cromwell advised. But he had little hope, he moaned, that he would be reinstated; his enemies were great and numerous and were determined to destroy him. And the King was so easily swayed by those who had his ear.

'Therefore, Cromwell, if ever you chance hereafter to be of his Council, I warn you to be well advised what matter you put into his head, for you shall never put it out again.'

Having replied suitably, Mr Cromwell rode off in the rain towards London. His commonplace, heavy expression gave no hint of his thoughts as he went to "make or mar" his own future career.

(ii)

Several years previously, Mr Cromwell had built for himself a spacious house on the west side of the huge friary of the Austin Friars. He was fond of this house, especially of the view from his study window of the friary church, with its fine spired steeple; often when he sat there at his desk, he thought about the riches which pious benefactors had lavished upon the Austin Friars since they had settled in London in the thirteenth century.

He was a man who liked to be private, for he still kept up his trade of money-lender, and he had many visitors who shrank from being recognized when they called on him. And the manner in which he had obtained this privacy was very typical of Mr Cromwell. One morning his neighbours on all sides had awakened to find that during the night their palings had been uprooted, twenty-two feet measured into their gardens, a trench dug there, and the foundations of a high brick wall laid. It was not the kind of thing the independent citizens of London stomached, but stomach it in this case they found they had to; Mr Cromwell was the right-hand man of him who embodied the ecclesiastical and civil power.

Within the house, everything was in the Italian fashion, for the spirit of Italy had stamped itself on Cromwell during his youthful travels. Especially did he treasure a manuscript copy of Machiavelli's *The Prince*, with its maxim that the prime art of the politician is to penetrate through the disguise which kings throw over their real intentions, and to devise the most specious expedients whereby they may gratify their appetites without appearing to outrage morality or religion.

Here now in this house did Mr Cromwell take up permanent residence, leading a pleasant bachelor existence (for his wife had just died), and replying to all Wolsey's appeals to return to Esher by saying that he was too busy looking after his master's interests in London.

He was, in fact, very busy looking after his own. The first necessity was to ingratiate himself with the aristocrats who all along had been Wolsey's foes and who were not likely to look with any favour on Wolsey's 'Councillor'. But as Cromwell well knew, these nobles were constantly in debt; only by pawning plate and mortgaging lands could they make a good appearance at Henry's extravagant Court, and some of them had never recovered from the Field of the Cloth of Gold, when, as a wit had expressed it, they had carried on their backs their mills and forests and manors.

Cromwell wrote carefully to his master. A Bill of Attainder was preparing against the Cardinal; he would, he wrote, use what little influence he had against it, but meanwhile it would be prudent if the Cardinal tried to buy off the enmity of those who were sponsoring it. And so it came about that great men like Norfolk, and Anne's father, just created Earl of Wiltshire, found the stocky, plodding, seemingly rather stupid Mr Cromwell waiting upon them in their ante-rooms.

'My Lord Cardinal had sent me to your lordship to beg that you will accept as a little token of his esteem this gift of two hundred silver marks. By the Mass, my lord, I am half ashamed to offer it, though it was I advised my master to send it – advised, I say! Your lordship would scarcely credit the labour I had in persuading the Cardinal to part with this paltry sum.'

When Cromwell was in the presence of those he wished to conciliate, no man could be a more adroit flatterer; he could put even shrewd diplomats off their guard. Norfolk and Wiltshire and the rest, while refusing to be won over to the Cardinal by such trifling bribes, began to look with a more friendly eye upon this agent of his, who on the one hand was putting himself out to help his stricken master, and on the other was so properly respectful towards themselves. They even accepted Mr Cromwell's diffident invitations to dinner, and were gratified and amazed by his lavish hospitality and by his geniality as a host. Perhaps after all he was not quite such an uncouth person as he seemed, and it was clear that he, like his upstart master, would presume to intrigue for offices sacred to the aristocracy.

So far, so good. The next step towards 'making' himself was a piece of luck.

As soon as Wolsey had gone to Esher, the King, while writing him maudlin letters and sending him his own physician, had looted the Cardinal of his wealth. He had seized the temporal revenues of St Albans and Winchester,

the two beloved colleges at Oxford and Ipswich, the gold
and silver, the horses and the litters, the tapestry and
jewels. And because Anne wanted York Place, since there
were no apartments in it suitable for the Queen who, to
Anne's fury, persisted in remaining at her husband's side,
Henry, renaming it Whitehall, had annexed it, a fact which
was extremely interesting to Mr Cromwell. For York Place
did not belong to Wolsey; it was the property of the See of
York. Always in the past when Church lands or buildings
had been taken by the Crown they had been exchanged for
something else. Henry was setting a precedent; and
Cromwell, who had been Wolsey's agent in the dissolution
of the smaller monasteries, noted it well.

Now according to the Statutes of *Praemunire* under
which Wolsey had been indicted, the wealth taken from
him could not be retained by the King after Wolsey's death
unless he confirmed its transfer during his life. These
Statutes were most intricate, and the matter was agitating
not only the King but those favourites of his with whom he
had shared the loot. And here came Cromwell's piece of
luck. Norfolk, now the principal man on the Council,
referred his Grace to this Thomas Cromwell who, it
seemed, had the most intimate knowledge of law,
particularly of its more seamy side.

So Mr Cromwell found himself invited to Court. He had
taken care to remind his Grace via Norfolk that in the
Parliament of 1523, when he was quite unknown, he had
distinguished himself by a maiden speech in which he had
implored his fellow Members not to grant the subsidy
Wolsey was demanding for the continuance of the French
war, because he, Cromwell was overwhelmed with dread at
the thought of his Grace insisting on risking in battle his
precious person.

'I know,' he had cried, 'that his Grace is possessed of a
courage and self-sacrifice to the interests of England which

must render him impervious to any argument against personal risk. But his person is absolutely necessary for the welfare and prosperity of his realm... '

To be told that he had courage and self-sacrifice, amply had compensated Henry for Parliament's refusal to grant the subsidy.

And now here was this same Cromwell wresting by some chicanery the transfer of the wealth of the fallen Cardinal. Henry smiled upon Cromwell, though there was something about the man that jarred on the King from the first. Even when he flattered, there was an edge of cynicism; and the uncouth gait, the pasty face, the bullet head, all were so distastefully plebeian. But Cromwell gratified the royal ego, and undoubtedly was useful at the moment.

It was not for some little while that Henry began to perceive a further and much more valuable potential usefulness in this man who held no office and seemed to desire none.

(iii)

It was December, the wettest December within living memory, and Henry was in an extremely ill humour.

The ominous little lesion had appeared in his leg once more; only now it was not just a little lesion but an ulcer which sometimes closed, causing him such agony that he went black in the face. And worse than the lesion was his growing unpopularity with his subjects. Of late the hostility of the common people towards his beloved (an hostility which reflected on himself) was spreading among his courtiers. He had just given a great banquet in Anne's honour at Whitehall, and had ordered the Duchesses of Norfolk and Suffolk to sit on cushions while she had a chair. This had been fiercely resented by their respective husbands, Suffolk going as far as to tell Henry that Anne had been the mistress of her cousin, Sir Thomas Wyatt. Suffolk was ordered to leave Court in disgrace; and in a kind of reaction Henry sent Wolsey, now on his way to York, yet another ring. He missed Wolsey; there was no one to take the burden of public business off his hands.

He was pacing the Long Gallery at Greenwich one morning, glaring at the rain which had ruined a tournament he had planned, while beside him, dwarfed by him, head bent deferentially, waddled Thomas Cromwell. They had been discussing some point connected with the seizure by Henry of Cardinal College, Oxford, when suddenly the King burst out:

'This Bill of Attainder against the Cardinal; it is most violent and false and makes the inferior folk pity him.'

'I understand, Sire,' murmured the humble voice beside him, 'that my Lord of Norfolk – '

'Norfolk wants his head, and a rich slice of his revenues. Norfolk was ever a grasping man; ay, we have heard him inveigh against the Cardinal because he, a butcher's son, was grown rich, while the Howards remained impoverished. He forgets, does Norfolk, that his grandsire fought against our royal sire at Bosworth. And he is a fool; on the Council he does nought but fumble and delay.'

Cromwell made a suitable pause, and then said timidly:

'If, with the greatest respect, I might presume to suggest it, Sire, the fact that my Lord Cardinal had made a written confession of his misdeeds, a confession I can produce, might give your Grace ample pretext for exercising the royal mercy and abandoning this Bill of Attainder.'

Henry stood stock still and looked at him, legs straddled, bejewelled hands on hips.

'I think you are a knave,' said he jovially. 'I believe it was you who stole from your master my licence confirming his Legatine authority. Ay, from henceforth when I hold a knave at cards I shall call it a Cromwell. But God's body! you have the right sow by the ear there.'

They paced to the end of the gallery in silence; then Henry heaved a deep sigh.

'I am become like Job upon his dung-hill,' he said solemnly, sitting down upon his chair of estate. 'Like that great man I am sore tormented by the Eternal, and yet, examining my conscience, I can find no fault therein save for that heinous fault in marrying my brother's wife. And this sin I would forsake entirely, but no man tells me how it may be done.'

Under his reverant exterior, Cromwell metaphorically pricked his ears. He had been waiting a long while to have this subject introduced.

'I am betrayed by most trusted councillor, him whom I raised from nothing,' continued Henry. 'Evil things are spoken of me by my brother the Emperor; my subjects' loyalty cools towards me; the Pope whose rights I so staunchly upheld that he named me Defender of the Faith, now shows himself much my unfriend, albeit I impoverished myself for his sake by fighting holy wars; but most of all am I tormented in spirit. Upon my great matter I am so discouraged that I see naught for it but to abandon all attempts to secure an annulment of my marriage, and to live henceforward like a monk, trusting in God to provide for the Succession.'

Cromwell drew out his napkin and buried his face therein, his thick shoulders heaving with his sobs. To find someone partaking in his own self-pity was meat and drink to Henry, and he regarded his companion with a favourable eye. Cromwell threw himself upon his knees.

'Pardon, most gracious Sovereign, a thousand times I implore your royal pardon that I, a mere worm, should dare to offer my poor counsel; yet my devotion to your Highness will not permit me to be silent when I see your

Highness in such sorrow and dole, and your sacred conscience in such torment.'

Henry gave him a little push.

'Get up, man, get up and speak plain,' he said irritably; but it was obvious that he was both flattered and curious.

'With your royal permission, then, I will be bold,' said Cromwell. 'It appears to me that the trouble your Grace has encountered in bringing your great matter to a happy issue is due to the weakness of those who will not venture to act as they should. The wise and learned, both clerical and lay, within your realm are in favour of the annulment of your Grace's marriage; all that is wanting is Papal sanction.'

'All!' bitterly ejaculated the King.

'Last year, Sire, there came to me here in London to plead in the matter of certain rights of property pertaining to his College, a Doctor of Divinity of Cambridge. He dined with me afterwards, and the talk turning upon your Grace's great matter, this priest (Cranmer is his name, Thomas Cranmer) most humbly put forward the suggestion that it should be laid before the Universities, since these are the places wherein problems in moral theology and in Canon Law are debated. He reminded me that during the divisions of the Papacy a century ago, the decision of the Universities of Europe had been of great weight when General Councils had assumed the right to end the distractions of Christendom.'

He shot that oblique glance of his towards the King, and found the narrow eyes regarding him with interest.

'Now it is well known, Sire, that at this present time the Pope hesitates to act as he should in your Highness' great matter because he fears the vengeance of the Emperor whose troops took him prisoner not so long ago. Therefore I say that no decision be expected from His Holiness, and your Grace's conscience must continue to be tormented –

157

unless it may be relieved by the wise and learned here at home.'

There was a considerable pause. Henry sat nursing his great jowls, his face shadowed by his French bonnet with plume and gaudy ornaments. His visitor was conscious of a prick of fear; the King was incalculable, and might very well decide on the impulse of a moment to fling this nobody into jail for his impertinence. But after a while his Grace said mildly:

'This Cranmer – I do not know him. What manner of man is he?'

'In Cambridge, Sire, he has a reputation for learning and for being much concerned with the reforming of abuses – '

'Not one of these knavish Lutherans, I hope,' Henry interrupted, very sharp.

'No, no, indeed not, Sire,' Cromwell lied boldly. 'For the rest, he is a gentleman of coat-armour, has studied Greek, is a Fellow of his College, and is a man seemingly without ambition, of good address and right pretty penmanship.'

'Penmanship,' thoughtfully repeated the King. 'Think you he could write a learned treatise upon my great matter, such as would serve to answer this naughty book put out by my Lord of Rochester?'

'I have no doubt he could, Sire.'

'Then send for him, send for him,' Henry cried imperiously, flapping his hand. 'Let every man have his own doctor, but this is the doctor for me. Yet stay a moment; the opinion of learned men in the Universities would be of little use unless Convocation agreed with them. And you know well how some of my Bishops have vaunted their disapproval of the annulment of my marriage.'

Cromwell hesitated a second. For what he was going to say now might indeed make or mar him. Then he took the plunge.

'Under favour, it appears to me that your Grace's Bishops would do well to look to themselves for your Grace has them all at your mercy.'

'Eh?' snapped the King.

'Your Grace indicted my Lord Cardinal under the Statutes of *Praemunire* for accepting a Legacy, and the licence he obtained from your Grace so to accept has – er – disappeared. Now since Convocation recognized him as Papal Legate, are not all the Bishops equally guilty with him? According to the Statutes, Sire, they are his "fautors and abettors" in this matter.'

The King stared at him in silence.

'Further it appears to me, Sire,' went on Cromwell, plunging yet deeper, 'that at present England is a monster with two heads. For do not the Bishops at their consecration take two oaths, one to your Grace and the other to the Pope?'

'Why so they do,' Henry said impatiently, 'And so it has ever been.'

'But if your Grace should take upon you the supreme power, religious as well as secular (as is your Grace's right, I had almost dared to say your Grace's duty), every incongruity would cease, and clergy would realize that they were bound to obey the Supreme Head of the Church in England, and at one stroke your Grace could free yourself from Papal restrictions, secure the annulment of your marriage, and relieve your sacred conscience of an intolerable burden.'

He had said it. He had staked his all on two things: Henry's despair of getting free from Catherine, and Henry's insane vanity. Seeing there was no indignation expressed on that wide square face, he struck while the iron was hot.

'Your Grace mentioned a while since that you have impoverished yourself by fighting wars in the cause of the Pope who now shows himself much you unfriend. Sire, if you would deign to trust me, the humblest of your subjects, I could make you the richest King in Christendom.'

'God's body!' growled Henry, 'you promise large, man.' The piggy eyes looked at him, cunning and earnest.

'Out of the great love I bear your Grace, I have made it my business to discover who they are who secretly oppose your royal will in your great matter. And I have found that they are the same who throughout your reign have opposed your Grace's demands for amicable grants; they are the Religious Orders. There are traitors, Sire, behind those walls where men should confine themselves to the *Opus Dei*. Traitors whose wealth, justly forfeited, could fill your Grace's empty coffers without your Grace having to prevail on parliaments (with what sordid haggling and reluctance!) to give you the grants necessary to make you the equal in state with the other kings in Europe. The wealth of the monasteries – '

'Nay, you go too fast!' interrupted the King. 'By God's body, you go too fast!' But his anger sounded a trifle forced.

Cromwell bowed his bullet head almost to the ground.

'Pardon, my Sovereign Lord, if I have said anything amiss. Upon my salvation, it was only because I could not endure to see your Highness abused by those who should know better, and your royal conscience in such mortal anguish.'

'We will think upon all you have said,' observed the King, solemnly stretching out his hand to be kissed. 'But now keep it close, lest these matters be bruited abroad and leave a stain upon our honour.'

Cromwell's solemn expression concealed inward exultation as he left the royal presence. If all went as he hoped he had no doubt that while making Henry supreme in Church and State, he would make himself the richest and most powerful subject in England.

(iv)

Meanwhile the man who had been the richest and most powerful subject in England was moving slowly northwards towards York; and with him went Cromwell's spies.

Wolsey's heart was ill at ease; he knew full well the enormity of what he had done in submitting to secular jurisdiction, and to assuage his conscience he threw himself heart and sold into his pastoral duties, visiting every church and abbey on the way, giving Confirmation, entertaining the poor at his own table. But he could not shake off the habits of a lifetime; he borrowed so that he might keep up some shadow of his old magnificence; and he wrote secretly both to King Francis and the Emperor, begging them by fair words or by threats to bring his master back to heel. They were unwise letters, and copies of them somehow found their way into the hands of Cromwell, who showed them to Norfolk. And Norfolk decided to strike hard and fast, for Henry was still wavering, still sending messages of good-will to Wolsey, still in two minds whether or not to recall him.

It winds again when Wolsey arrived at Cawood Castle whither he summoned all the neighbouring clergy and gentry to escort him to York where he was to be enthroned on November 6th. Ill health and mental strain had

161

increased that superstition which had always been one of his weaknesses; and when his physician accidentally knocked down his great silver cross which had been propped against the wall, the Cardinal brooded over the trifling mishap, regarding it as an ill omen.

He was sitting at supper on the day preceding his entry into York, when the Earl of Northumberland was announced, and there entered the spindly, weak-chinned man who, as Lord Henry Percy, had wooed Anne Boleyn. Expecting yet another message of good-will from his master, Wolsey welcomed him kindly; but Northumberland, having kissed the great amethyst, raised a face that was deathly pale, and faltered:

'My Lord Cardinal, I arrest you for high treason.'

They brought him south to Sheffield Park where the Earl of Shrewsbury, by orders of the capricious King, gave him a magnificent reception. But all his native vigour and assurance had forsaken him; he was now without hope. A fortnight passed; he heard the bustle of some cavalcade arriving, and when he asked who it was, they told him that Sir William Kingston, Constable of the Tower, had come to conduct him to London.

Ever since he was a young man he had a violent and irrational fear of the name Kingston, so much so that when going from London to his palace of Hampton Court he had been accustomed to make a long detour in order to avoid the town of that name.

His failing health broke under the shock, and he had to lean heavily on the arms of his attendants as they led him out to begin his fatal journey. So slowly did he travel that it was not until the 26th that he reached Leicester, where he chose to lie at the great Augustinian Abbey. It was night, and the monks came out with torches to meet him; half falling as he dismounted from his mule, he whispered to the dim figure into whose arms he swayed:

'Father Abbot, I have come to leave my bones among you.' They helped him to bed, and brought him a cup of broth to revive him. He took a spoonful, then asked of what the soup was made, and when they told him of a chicken, he set it aside saying:

'It is Friday; I will eat no more.'

He would have slept, but Kingston began to press him about a matter of fifteen hundred pounds which the King thought he had concealed when his Grace had plundered him of all his wealth.

'I implore you that you leave me in peace,' said Wolsey. 'This money of which you speak is none of mine, but I borrowed it from divers friends and servants that I might make my entrance into York.'

'I will take my leave now,' said Kingston, 'but we must speak further on the matter tomorrow morning, for such are my orders.'

The Cardinal smiled and murmured:

'Tomorrow morning I shall die upon the stroke of eight.'

He slept fitfully, and his faithful Cavendish, who lay on a mattress in his chamber, heard him muttering to himself; the King was out of hand, heresies were mounting everywhere, the lay power was encroaching on the rights of the Church. He beat his breast and moaned that it was his fault, his most grievous fault. At five he asked for the Abbot and began his shriving; for a full hour his attendants waited outside the door of the little bare monastic room in which he lay. Presently they were joined by Kingston who, directly the Abbot opened the door and beckoned, began again to interrogate the dying man about the money. A feeble hand from the bed waved aside the matter, and the voice, so changed from the confident, resonant tones they knew, spoke with a last rallying of the failing powers.

'Oh Kingston! If I had served my God as diligently as I have served my King, He would not have given me over in my grey hairs. Howbeit this is the just reward that I must receive for my worldly diligence and pains that I have had to do him service, only to satisfy his pleasure, not regarding my godly duty. He is sure a prince of royal courage, and hath a princely heart; but rather than he will miss any part of his will or appetite he will put the half of his realm in danger. For I assure you I have often kneeled in his Privy Chamber the space of an hour to persuade him from indulging some appetite, but all in vain. Say to his Grace from me that with my dying breath I implore him in God's name to have a vigilant eye to repress this new pernicious sect of Lutherans, that it do not increase within his dominions through his negligence.'

Exhausted by his long speech, he fell back upon the pillows, murmuring:

'Master Kingston, farewell. I can no more, for my time draws on fast. But forget not, I pray you, what I have charged you withal, for peradventure when I am dead you will have cause to remember my words'.

He turned his face from Kingston, and from the world, as his Mother the Church, whom he had served so ill, began preparing him for his last journey. The eyes that had worshipped gold, the ears that had loved flattery, the mouth that had intrigued and had urged a vain young King to dream of empty renown, the hands that had been lavish with bribes, the feet that had been shod in white silk slippers and thrust into stirrups of gold all were anointed with the sign of the Cross. The mysterious Food for the journey was given; and the Abbot had begun to recite the Commendation of a Departing soul, when the great bell of the Abbey rang out the hour of eight.

When those solemn shocks had ceased to reverberate, they saw that Thomas Wolsey had gone to his account.

PART THREE

The Deluge

Chapter One

Sir Thomas More, Lord Chancellor of England, came up-stream in his great state barge, with trumpets sounding and the busy traffic of the river respectfully making way for him. There was a waving of caps and some cheering as he was recognized, this most popular man; he raised his hand in acknowledgement, but his expression was heavy and his right shoulder raised higher than the other, a mannerism of his when he was ill at ease.

At his own water-gate in Chelsea he found his favourite daughter Meg looking out for his return. He put his arm about her waist and walked slowly with her through the gardens.

'You are sorrowful today, Father,' she said. 'More sorrowful than I have seen you since, with such reluctance, you accepted this great honour of the Chancellorship.'

'It is true,' said More. 'For I witnessed this day the sorriest sight I ever saw in my life.'

He sat down on the built-up bank which surrounded his garden, a bank on which the old-fashioned flowers he loved, columbine and larkspur, sops-in-wine and bachelor's buttons, grew haphazardly among the grass.

'You know,' he went on, 'that the Queen has steadfastly refused to leave her husband's side, even to see their daughter, lest it be said she willingly forsook him. This morning the King moved to Woodstock for his hunting; I was there in the courtyard when he mounted, and there came one of her Highness' gentlemen to him with a message regretting that he had not taken his leave of her and enquiring after his health. He fell into such a rage, Meg, that it was terrible to see; and before all his Court he cried that he did not want his wife's farewells, and that his health was no concern of hers, for she was not his wife at all. Then he sent back a formal order that she was to be gone from Greenwich ere he returned thither, and to move to the More, a house belonging to the late Cardinal Wolsey.'

Meg gave an indignant exclamation.

'Her Highness sent for me thereafter,' her father went on. 'She had been weeping sore, yet was she calm and dignified. She said to me, "Go where I may, I remain his wife, and for him I will pray." (I was a truer prophet than I knew, Meg, when at her Coronation I compared her to Alcestis and Penelope.) Then she asked of me what she should do, pleasing to call me her true friend. I could answer her nothing but that she must observe his Grace's command.'

He was silent for a moment, and then burst out:

'Well did Erasmus make a play upon my name in his *Praise of Folly*, for I think your father is the veriest. When his Grace pressed the Great Seal upon me I accepted because I had his solemn promise that I should not be troubled in my conscience. He has known from the beginning my private opinion of his great matter; I will not debate it with any man, for it is not my business; but now I perceive that my silence vexes him, and that he will not rest until he has won me over to his side. And likewise – '

'And likewise, Father?' she prompted anxiously, as he paused.

'I should have known that as Chancellor I would needs be the King's mouthpiece in whatsoever he chooses to decree. Indeed I did know it, but I believed it was the late Cardinal (God assoil his soul) who had put into his Grace's head vain-glorious notions and doubts upon his marriage, and that Wolsey being gone, all would be well again. But now I see that it is not so; for though his Grace has all the accomplishments of a great prince, yet *quid quid vult, valde vult –* '

He glanced quizzically at this learned daughter of his to see if she recognized the quotation. She answered immediately:

'It is a comment in one of Cicero's letters. I would translate it as, "It matters little what this man wants, but whatever he wants, he wants intensely." '

'And so it is with his Grace. It is not for me to speak evil of my King, yet I cannot but perceive that he has changed greatly these past few years, and is unable to master himself or to curb his appetites. And though the Cardinal is gone, I much fear me that worse councillors have come in his place, though they are yet behind the curtain. I will not believe it was the King's notion, but was suggested by some knave,' cried More, beating his hands together, 'that his Grace should take upon him the title Supreme Head of the Church, nor will I believe that he is behind all these late attacks upon the clergy.'

'But, Father,' said Meg, seeking to comfort him, 'Convocation agreed to acknowledge his Grace Supreme Head, *quantum per Christi legem licit.* Surely here is a saving clause, safe-guarding the Pope's authority?'

'I suspect there be some councillors who will tell his Grace that no one knows better than he what the Law of Christ allows,' More murmured, shaking his head.

She could not bear to see him so distressed, and said gently:

'You remember, sir, what you wrote in *Utopia,* that what we cannot turn to good we must make as little bad as possible. Since his Grace has made you his Chancellor, it needs must be that he values highly your counsel.'

He smiled absently, then pulled a paper from his pouch.

'The King gave me this this morning, requiring me to study it and let him know my opinion. It is a thesis to be debated by the Universities, writ by a Dar Cranmer, of whom I know little, but that little likes me not at all. It is said, I know not how truly, that at Cambridge he is of that revolutionary group who favour the detestable heresies of Luther and Tyndale, who use the New Learning to dispute the origin of our most sacred beliefs, and who, under colour of reforming abuses, desire to abolish what is abused. However that may be, what he has writ here is very damnable.'

He spread the paper out on his knee.

'Here, Meg, is in truth a prejudgement of the whole case of his Grace's marriage. There mere thought of a man marrying his brother's wife is an abomination, says Dr Cranmer: "I marvel that Christian men do not tremble to hear it, and much more fear wittingly to do it." And upon the Pope's threat of excommunicating the King if his Grace will not answer the summons to plead his cause at Rome, Dr Cranmer writes thus: "If a man be excommunicated because he doth that which is good, or will not do that which is ill, the sentence of excommunication is none." '

He turned a page.

'But here, Meg, here is the worst or all: "Methinketh the King's Highness and his Parliament should earnestly press the Metropolitans of this realm (*their unjust oath to the Pope notwithstanding*) to set an end shortly to his great matter, and to take a greater regard to the quieting of his Grace's conscience and this realm, than to the ceremonies of the Pope's law; for by God's law they be bound to the obedience of their prince. Rather ought we to obey God than men." '

'But the Bishops,' cried the bewildered Meg, 'would never consent to violate their oath to His Holiness – '

'The Bishops,' sighed More, interrupting her, 'are much demoralized by the fall of Wolsey and by his acceptance of the jurisdiction of the lay courts. Some profess to believe that his Grace's new title of *Supremum Caput* has reference to temporal matters only; among them all there is only one who is clear-sighted and bold enough to speak out, our saintly Bishop of Rochester, who, for his plain speaking, already has received a sharp rebuke from the King.'

He put his head into his hands, drawing a heavy breath or two. His daughter had never seen him so disturbed.

'My Lord of Rochester, speaking of all these attacks upon the clergy, cried that in his ears they sounded to this effect, that our Holy Mother the Church, being left unto us by the great liberality and diligence of our forefathers in most perfect and peaceable freedom, shall now by us be brought into servile thraldom like a bondmaid, or rather by little and little be driven out of our dwelling-places.'

From the square tower of the church beyond the house there sounded the evening Angelus, sweet and solemn in the summer air. Father and daughter rose, he doffing his cap, and they said the prayers together. Then, putting her arms around his neck, noticing with passionate pity the silver hairs which had begun to shine among the brown on his temples of late, Meg said very softly:

'Father, do you remember when my husband, through consorting with the Lutheran merchants of the Steelyard, became a zealous heretic? How often and how wisely did you debate with him, but he would not listen; and so one day, walking here in the garden with me, you said, "Meg, I have borne a long time with your husband, but I perceive that nothing I can say will call him home. And therefore I

171

will no longer dispute with him, but get me to God and pray for him." And a little while thereafter, I found him burning Luther's books.'

He took her head in his hands and kissed her brow.

'My dearly beloved daughter,' said he, 'no counsel was ever more needed nor more timely offered than this that you have given me. I write too much, and talk too much, and consider myself a wise man, whereas, as I told you at the beginning, I am the veriest fool. Ay, Meg, I will even get me to God and pray.'

She stood looking after him as he went slowly towards his New Building. Her heart bled for him, for this father who had always been so full of fun, so cheerful, and so tranquil, and who now looked suddenly old, and wore his great gold chain of office as though it were a halter.

(ii)

When More has said that new councillors were come in place of the dead Wolsey, he would have been more accurate if he had said 'a councillor'. But neither he nor anyone else had as yet taken into serious account the man who for the present chose to stay 'behind the curtain', the seemingly rather full and plodding man named Thomas Cromwell.

Wolsey had had in him the potentialities of greatness, and though he had never felt the perilious contradiction between his worldliness and his sacred calling, his religion had not been mere convention. Cromwell on the other hand had no interest in any sort of religion; he used religious troubles as pawns in his game, just as he had used the fall of his master. To him the justice or morality of any action was to be disregarded; its utility was its morality and created its justification. And it was he who now, by appealing to the King's cupidity, vanity, and self-will, was driving Henry along a path which must end in a complete break from the unity of Christendom.

While keeping himself behind the scenes, Cromwell stage-managed the drama, received the reports of his innumerable spies, and drew more and more of the domestic administration of the realm into his pudgy hands. He was cunning enough not to accept any high office until the break with Rome and the annulment of the King's marriage were accomplished facts, for to the outside world they must seem the King's measures; the exaggerated respect of the age for kingship would be enough to cow opposition and prevent revolt – or so Cromwell believed. And these measures too were but pawns in his own game; what he was after, what he had been after from the beginning, was to get his hands upon the wealth of the Church.

As he walked the narrow streets of London, he whetted his appetite by viewing the material evidence of that wealth. His stocky figure was often to be seen at High Mass at the great Priory of the Holy Trinity near Aldgate, at St Bartholomew's in Smithfield, at the huge Carmelite church in Fleet Street, or at any of the other numerous religious houses which were the pride of London. And these were but a handful compared with the monasteries and abbeys and convents scattered up and down England, all of them endowed, not a friary so poor but had crucifix, chalice, and candlesticks of silver, while many were vast treasure-houses, besides possessing lands and cattle.

He opened his attack modestly and with his usual cunning. The King, it seemed, had been put to such great charges in setting up the Legatine Court, which had come to nothing only through the double-dealing of the Pope, that to recompense his Grace it would be fit to grant him all the abbeys and monasteries whose revenues did not exceed two hundred pounds. The Bishops, who had been in a panic ever since they had found themselves accused of partaking in Wolsey's guilt, were ready to agree, when there arose the tall gaunt figure of Fisher of Rochester.

'My lords,' said he in his clear voice, 'I pray you take heed what you do in haste, granting the King's demand in this matter. For it puts me in mind of a fable, how an axe, that lacked a handle, came to a wood; and making his moan to the great trees how for lack of a handle he was fain to sit idle, he desired them to grant him some small sapling to make him one. They, suspecting no guile, forthwith granted him a small young tree, whereof he shaped himself a handle, and being now a perfect axe in all parts, he fell to work and so laboured that in process of time he left in that wood neither great tree nor small standing. And so, my lords, if you grant to the King the small monasteries, you do but make him a handle and so give him occasion to demand the rest ere it be long after. Whereof cannot but ensue the displeasure of Almighty God in that you take upon you to give that which is none of your own.'

The other Bishops, shamed by this spirited speech, plucked up courage to refuse the King's demand; and Cromwell felt it was time to deal drastically with this tiresome Bishop Fisher who had a most uncomfortable knack of seeing through his little devices, and who, during Cromwell's attack in Parliament upon the evil living of the clergy, had said:

'There be some men now among us who seem to reprove the life and doings of the clergy, but if the truth were known, ye shall find that they rather hunger and thirst after the riches and possessions of the clergy, than after amendment of their faults.'

During his youth in Italy, Mr Cromwell had learnt something about rare poisons; and while he had been in Wolsey's service he had learnt also how to pick humble agents who were desperate enough to do whatever they were told however risky to themselves. To such an agent he now gave certain orders.

Fisher was staying at this time at his Episcopal Inn of Lambeth Marsh. One day there called there a man named Richard Rose, who had struck up a friendship with the Bishop's cook. While the cook prepared dinner, Mr Rose mentioned that he had a great thirst, whereupon his friend went into the buttery to fetch him a can of ale. Mr Rose, it seemed, could not stay to partake of dinner in the kitchen; and it chanced also that the Bishop, who had been overworking that morning, had lost his appetite and sent his dinner back untasted. His household, immediately after the meal, were stricken suddenly and violently ill. Two died that same day; and the story spread all over the town. It was obvious enough who the culprit was, and Mr Rose paid for his crime by being boiled alive in oil.

Cromwell, while naturally annoyed at the failure of his little plot, felt that on the whole he could afford to ignore Fisher. The majority of the great Bishops were in terror for their offices, and the lesser ones, following their example, did not dare deny the King anything. Moreover, Cromwell had great hopes that honest though timid old Warham, Archbishop of Canterbury, would die very soon; and when that even happened, Mr Cromwell knew just the man to replace him.

(iii)

'Well, Master More,' said the King crossly, 'we will take you at your word at last. For near upon a twelvemonth you have been petitioning us to accept your resignation from the great office we bestowed upon you; we would not, for you are dear to us, but it seems that we are not dear to you.'

He regarded in angry reproach the man upon his knees before him. While the question of his 'great matter' was

175

still undecided, it was very useful to Henry to have as Chancellor a man of such strict integrity; it quietened opponents with the hope that wiser counsels would prevail. Moreover, Henry really liked Sir Thomas; he had a genuine respect for the man's learning and a delight in his quaint humour. On the other hand, Henry's megalomania had now reached the stage when any criticism appeared to him in the nature of blasphemy; and More's silence was in itself a criticism. It was preposterous, he thought, scowling down upon the kneeling figure, that he should not be able to bend More to his will. Sir Thomas had always shown so great a reverence for authority; he had never spoken openly against the 'great matter' as the Bishop of Rochester had done. Yes, and as that wicked Father Peto, Provincial of the Friars Observant, had just spoken openly, here at Greenwich.

'The unbounded affection of princes and their false counsellors deprive them of the knowledge of the truth,' Father Peto had raged. 'Your Grace is endangering your crown by your determination to put away your lawful wife, for great and humble men are murmuring against it.'

Father Peto had been promptly arrested; and Henry had listened willingly to Cromwell when the latter had suggested that if there were any more of such insolence the Friars Observant should be suppressed.

'My infirmities, Sire,' said More in a low voice, 'make me useless in your Grace's service. I have a humour in my chest – and a heavy heart therein likewise.'

'A man that used to be so cheerful!' exclaimed Henry. 'And one we have so honoured. Well, we may tell you that we also have a heavy heart, for we have just discovered an abominable thing.'

He paused for effect.

'We thought that the clergy of our realm had been our subjects wholly, but now we have well perceived that they be but half our subjects, yea, and scarce our subjects. For all the prelates at their consecration make an oath to the Pope clean contrary to the oath they make to us, so that they seem to be his subjects and not ours.'

More could find nothing to say. It was indeed a very extraordinary discovery for Henry to have made in the twenty-third year of his reign.

'Well, Mr More, what say you to that?' sharply demanded his Grace.

'I cannot but remember, Sire,' More replied with an effort, 'how your Grace cried up the Pope's authority in your book against Luther.'

'A book which received but little praise from you,' cried the King childishly. It was the kind of little slight he never forgot; his turning against people he loved had always as its cause an accumulated memory of little slights, Wolsey's momentary smile at his mishap at the Field of the Cloth of Gold, Catherine's tactless remark, and her equally tactless letter after Flodden.

'And how will you employ yourself,' he asked, choosing to ignore More's awkward comment, 'now that you will leave our service?'

'I intend, Sire,' answered Sir Thomas, 'to take up my pen again and write against the heresies of Luther and Tyndale, for the peril of heresy must concern us all most nearly when the Infidel is at the very gates of Vienna. And in particular am I concerned to answer the pestilent outcries of this Fish, who so spits out his venom that he would have all the property of the Church confiscated. And he demands that the clergy be married even against their will; by which your Grace may perceive,' he added drily, 'what opinion he has of marriage, for if he thought it good he would not wish it them.'

'Ay, you will do well to write upon such matters,' said the King, 'for heresy we do detest. But we would not have you too hard on Master Tyndale. For notwithstanding he is wrong in many of his opinions (whereof we have ordered his books to be burnt), he is in the right when he maintains that the King is outside the law and shall give account to God only. Such a work is for us, and for all kings, to read.'

This was an obvious challenge, but once again More was silent. His growing silence during the past year whenever the King had sought his opinion upon controversial matters had so irritated Henry that he felt now he would be glad not to see that once cheerful face at Court. When pressed hard, all More would do was to remind his Grace of the promise made when first Sir Thomas had entered the royal service, that his conscience should be respected. Always talking about his own conscience, Henry had little time for those of other people.

'Well, well, go your ways, then, Mr More,' said Henry, thrusting out his thick fingers to be kissed. 'And for your previous services we promise you that in any suit you shall have to us that either concerns your honour or appertains to your profit, you shall find us your good and gracious lord.'

More's barge awaited him at the public stairs of the Palace, not the eight-oared barge of the Lord Chancellor with its trailing draperies and rich gilding, but a modest boat rowed by two of his sons-in-law. Inspecting it was the short, powerful figure of Thomas Cromwell who, though still having only a subordinate place on the Council, was now known by all to be the King's chief confidant.

'Alack, this is a melancholy occasion, Mr More,' said Cromwell, with that oblique, roguish glance of his. 'We shall miss your quaint wit at Court. But doubtless you know your own business best, and, like the wise man that you are, have made provision so that you may live at ease for the rest of your life in your fine house at Chelsea.'

More ignored this insinuation that he had feathered his nest during his public service. He said gravely:

'Master Cromwell, you are now high in favour with a most noble and liberal prince. If you will follow my poor advice, you will never give his Grace counsel as to what he is able to do, but what he ought to do. For if the lion knew his strength, hard were it for any man to rule him.'

'My late Master, the Cardinal,' said Cromwell, 'gave me much the same advice. God assoil his soul,' he added piously, making the sign of the Cross.

More's expression, so heavy of late, lightened as he approached his home. He was free. Here was the quiet river with its backwaters and the meadows on either side, the fishermen catching lampreys and roach, the snowy flocks of swans. And here was his own water-gate with eager faces watching for his home-coming; over the roof of his New Building the tower of his parish church rose up, that church in which he had built a tomb for himself, and in which he loved to serve Mass. In this quiet retreat he would be content to live forgotten by the great world, and to forget it, save for his writings against heresy.

'Mother is at Benediction,' Meg told him, adding: 'I have not seen you look so cheerful for a long while, sir.'

'I thank Our Lord I am very cheerful,' he said, making a pick-a-back for one of his grandchildren. 'Come, we'll go make our thanksgiving.'

Benediction was ending when they entered the church. It had been the custom while he was Chancellor for one of his gentlemen to approach his wife's pew, and with great ceremony to inform her that my Lord Chancellor had left the velvet fald-stool where he sat beneath a canopy. This afternoon More came up to where she sat, and making her a low obeisance, said mischievously:

'Madam, my lord is gone.'

179

'How you can jest about it, man,' his wife chided him, when they were come out into the churchyard, 'is more than I can tell. To be content to lose this great honour for a whim! And I must lose half my servants, I suppose.'

'Now tell me the truth, Dame Alice, did you not often complain of the great vexations you had in ruling so many servants?'

'The Fool must go. Good Master Patenson who cheered me when I was out of humour.'

'You must make do with your fool of a husband,' said More, linking her arm in his.

After supper he sat down on the flat roof of the water-gate with all his family about him, and addressed them with his old charming cheerfulness.

'It is my dearest wish that we all continue to live here together. Having discharged my gentlemen and yeomen and yielded up the Chancellor's barge to Master Audley, my successor, I have quite put off my state, and you likewise must put off yours. For now all my fees and perquisites are gone, though his Grace of his goodness allows me still to retain my salary as a Councillor. Tell me, then, how would you advise it so that we may yet continue here to live together, for now I am not able to bear the whole charges, and you, my sons, have but little.'

They looked at one another, but were silent.

'Then,' continued More, solemn-faced but with his eyes a-twinkle, 'will I show my poor mind to you. I have been brought up at Oxford, at New Inn, at an Inn of Chancery, and at the King's Court, and so from the lowest degree to the highest; yet have I in yearly revenues at this present left me little above one hundred pounds. So now must we hereafter, if we like to live together, be contributories together.'

There was a chorus of assent. They would be content to eat dry bread, they cried, so long as they could be with him.

'That is very well,' said he, 'but by my counsel, it shall not be best for us to fall to the lowest fare first. We will not therefore descend to Oxford fare, nor to the fare of New Inn, but we will begin with Lincoln's Inn diet, where many right worshipful do live full well; which if we find not ourselves the first year able to maintain, then will we next year go one step down to New Inn fare, wherewith many an honest man is well contented. If that exceed our ability too, then will we the next year after descend to Oxford fare, with which many grave, learned, and ancient fathers are conversant.'

'And then what next, I pray you?' demanded his wife.

He was silent a moment. One of the great brown-sailed barges was passing slowly upstream, and across the water came the ancient sunset hymn of the seamen to the Mother of God.

'Why,' said More, smiling tranquilly, 'if our power stretch not to maintain that neither, then may we yet, with bags and wallets, go a-begging together, hoping that for pity some good folk will give us of their charity, at every man's door to sing *Salve Regina,* and so still keep company and be merry together.'

Chapter Two

(i)

Thomas Cromwell, Master of the Jewels, Clerk of the Hanaper, Chancellor of the Exchequer, and Master of the King's Wards, sat at his table in his house near Austin Friars, busy as usual with a multitude of affairs. There were plans for the building of a new palace at Westminster, inventories of the royal plate and jewels, lists of wages for the men working on the fortifications at Calais, even patterns for his Grace's robes of state.

He was decoding a letter from one of the innumerable spies whom he insinuated into the houses of all public men, and especially into the monasteries, and had just noted the interesting report that some monk had remarked to another in the shaving-house that 'None of us shall do well as long as we forsake our Head of the Church, the Pope', when there was a discreet tap on the door, and a servant entered.

'The Reverend Master Archdeacon Cranmer is here, sir,' said he.

Cromwell immediately dismissed his secretary, and hurried forward with his awkward gait to greet his visitor, his pasty face beaming. Had Dr Cranmer supped? Was he much fatigued by his long journey? Would he wish some rest before they had their little talk?

'Yes – no – yes, I mean,' stammered Cranmer, peering with short-sighted eyes at his host. 'I am not fatigued, but in great distress of mind, sir; this sudden recall from abroad – I fear his Grace's displeasure.'

He sank down gratefully upon the chair on which Cromwell had hastened to tie a cushion, and stared unseeingly into the cup of wine placed before him.

'I do assure you, Master Cromwell,' he burst out, 'I have done all that any man could do. I did persuade the University of Orleans to give a decision in favour of the annulment of his Grace's marriage, but those of Poitiers and Orleans I could in no wise move, though I was lavish with my – my presents to them. And now that the Pope has forbidden all persons to write upon the subject while the cause is pending in Rome – '

'We have the favourable opinions of our Universities at home,' soothed Cromwell, 'that is sufficient.'

He did not see fit to mention that the commissioners sent down to obtain this favourable verdict at Oxford and Cambridge had been pelted by the townsfolk with stones.

'And then,' went on Cranmer, full of his own troubles, 'I have met with ill success in conciliating the Emperor and in persuading the Lutheran Princes to accept some aid form his Grace in their revolt against his Imperial Majesty. They have never forgiven his Grace for his book against Luther, and they are at one in deeming his marriage good and valid. And the Emperor, when at last I was able to come at him, was very short with me. He was not prepared to sell his aunt, the Queen, said he, when I offered him his Grace's handsome present. But indeed I did my best; I followed his Imperial Majesty over half Europe, over such roads! – full of the soldiery he has gathered against the Infidel, and – '

'You do not drink your wine,' gently interrupted Cromwell. 'Is beer more to your taste? I remember to have heard that in your youth you had a great partiality for beer.'

For some reason this seemingly innocent remark upset Cranmer. He swallowed audibly, sat on the edge of his chair, and was silent.

'I cannot endure,' said Cromwell very softly, 'to see my Lord Archbishop in such distress.'

Cranmer goggled at him.

'My Lord Archbishop? I heard that he was newly dead.'

'He is, God assoil his soul. And far from being displeased with you; his Grace has appointed you our beloved Archbishop Warham's successor.'

'*Me*?' cried Cranmer in a little squeak.

He was forty-two years old, completely without worldly ambition, timid, at home only among his books. At Cambridge, where he had passed the greater part of his life, his interest had centred on the New Learning, and while his dislike of anything risky had made him shrink from allying himself with the revolutionaries there, secretly for years he had leant towards Lutherism. When thrust despite himself into the King's service, made chaplain to the Boleyns, and sent off on embassies connected with the King's 'great matter', he had done what he was told, not only because that was his nature, but because the question of the marriage interested him professionally; his foundation at Cambridge was confined by statute to the study of theology. And, as he had just told Cromwell, he had honestly done his best, though he knew nothing of the art of diplomacy and shrank from the risks of travel; he had done it without hope or desire of reward.

And now that reward was being thrust upon him. At one leap he was to be kicked upstairs from archdeacon to Archbishop of Canterbury.

'You appeared perfectly stunned by your good fortune, my Lord Archbishop,' the voice of Cromwell broke in upon his thoughts. 'I cannot believe it is displeasing to you; I hope it is not, for I may tell you it was I who recommended your appointment.'

'Most kind, most kind,' mumured Cranmer.

The other put his bullet head on one side.

'I must be mistaken in thinking that your Grace seems – how shall I put it? – troubled in your mind, more troubled than when we first began our little talk.'

Cranmer gulped and said no, no, of course not.

'Tell me about your travels,' said Cromwell genially. 'I believe it was your first experience of foreign parts. Let me see, you followed the Emperor from Ratisbon to Nuremberg, did you not? Nuremberg is a fine city; I knew it well in my youth.'

Such well-meant attempts to put the new Archbishop at his ease seemed only to increase his agitation. The short-sighted eyes blinked rapidly, the scholarly face was pale.

'A fine city,' he echoed like a parrot. Then in a rush: 'And Florence too; I admired there the great gnomon set up in the cathedral by the astronomer Toscanelli, who marked how the rays of the sun at high noon on the day of the summer solstice – '

But again Cromwell interrupted. He was not interested in astronomy, it seemed.

'But the Nuremberg inns are poor,' said he reminiscently. 'I trust that my Lord Archbishop was accommodated with some private citizen? Bless me, I am sure you do not like this wine, for you have not touched it. I should have remembered that Cambridge men prefer beer, and especially a certain famous beer which is to be had at an inn named the Dolphin.'

Like a rabbit mesmerized by a stoat, Cranmer stared at him.

'The Dolphin,' repeated Cromwell, sipping his own wine and gazing into space. 'Strange what trivial things stick in one's memory. The host had a niece or a daughter called Black Joan; a rare one for the men, I have heard. (Folk love to gossip!) And she caught a young fellow and obliged him to marry her, whereupon he was forced to forfeit his Fellowship and support her and himself as best he could by lecturing on theology. Did you ever hear this idle tale, my Lord Archbishop?'

Dead silence.

'Now by the Mass, it seems I am but distressing you with my stories when I hoped they might serve to entertain you. Let us return to Nuremberg. Now there is a city breeds handsome wenches – I cannot remember if your grace informed me where you lodged?'

'With a man of – of the name of Andrew Hosmer,' the white lips told him. 'He calls himself Osiander, a semi-classical name, you understand.' A ghastly smile. 'But I must not keep you, sir – '

'Nay, nay, I have all the time in the world, and am so very honoured by your Grace's company. Osiander. Yes, I have heard of him, and not, I am afraid, to his advantage. A fierce Lutheran; a priest who broke his vows and married five years after his ordination. The King's Highness would not be pleased to hear you lodged with such a man, for his Highness detests Lutherans; no man is more orthodox. And as for married priests – my Lord Archbishop, are you sick? I will call my apothecary – '

'No!' squeaked Cranmer, the sweat shining on his forehead. He continued in a shaking voice: 'I do not know, sir, in what way I have offended you that you seek to torment me thus, you who, so you say, recommended me to his Grace for this great honour whereof I am unworthy and – and ineligible.

'Ineligible?' Cromwell repeated in feigned surprise.

Then his lips began to tremble, his stocky figure shook, and he exploded into mirth.

'Your Grace must pardon me, but to think you brought the lady over with you in a tub – a tub! – and my man who fetched you says a clumsy sailor knocked it over during the voyage, whereat a female voice shrieked from within. Of course you were not to know that you were named Archbishop, but even so, as a cleric and already in his Grace's service, to go and commit bigamy – '

'I did no such thing!' the wretched Cranmer shouted, goaded into indignation. 'Black Joan died in childbed near twenty years ago, and my marriage with Osiander's niece was perfectly valid – what am I saying! And what are you, sir, a sorcerer that you know these things concerning my private life?'

'No sorcerer,' said Cromwell, reverting to his contemptuous and masterful self, 'but one who finds it essential to discover all about the private lives of those whom he would use in his Grace's service. Ay, I know of your two marriages, and I cannot but warn you that if they came to the King's ears he would be very wroth. His clerical servants may have what amatory affairs they please, but to go through an official ceremony he would regard as an act of open rebellion.'

'I desire nothing,' whimpered Cranmer, 'but to return to Cambridge and to pursue my studies there.'

'We cannot have, sir, all that we desire in this world,' Cromwell said sententiously. 'You are appointed Archbishop; there will be no difficulty in obtaining the necessary bulls from the Pope, since he is only too anxious to oblige his Highness in what he deems small matters, hoping by this to wean him from his great one. And as for this inconvenient Mrs Cranmer, Lambeth Palace has back regions, and there she must be kept; no one will be the wiser that my Lord Archbishop has a wife – except myself.'

His cruel little mouth twisted into a smile.

'But unless I take the oath of allegiance to the Pope, the bulls for my appointment will not be obtained from Rome,' objected Cranmer. He had given up the struggle. He was simply being pushed and shoved by a stronger will, just as he had been forced into marriage by Black Joan and now twenty years later by the Lutheran's niece, Anne Hosmer.

'I had not overlooked that point,' Cromwell told him briskly. 'But before you take your public oath of allegiance to the Pope, there will be a little private ceremony wherein you will declare that you do not regard this oath as binding if it fits not with the King's just authority.'

He leaned back in his chair and regarded his guest and victim with a sunny smile.

'You see, I have arranged it all. You will have the honour and glory, and I the hard work. And we shall work very well together, my Lord Archbishop, now that we have had this little talk.'

(ii)

They worked as happily together as the jackal and the lion.

In the Chapter House of St Stephen's at Westminster, the new Archbishop made a declaration before four witnesses and a notary, that the public oath of obedience to the Pope which he must take at his consecration he privately regarded as not binding. A fortnight later he sat down and wrote a very solemn epistle to Henry (at Henry's orders), begging leave to do that for which he had been nominated Archbishop, namely to hold a court to pronounce the King's marriage invalid.

It was a letter of great length, without a single full-stop, and it was abject in the extreme. But it was not abject enough to satisfy Henry. His Grace sent it back with alterations; instead of 'upon my knees I beseech your

Highness', Cranmer must write 'prostrate at the feet of your Majesty.' Also Henry added a paragraph in which Cranmer was to take Jesus Christ to witness that his only motive in asking the King's leave to do something arranged between them weeks before, was his zeal to try the case truly and impartially. Henry's vanity and peculiar conscience being mollified, he replied graciously, but took occasion to remind his new Archbishop that he, Henry, was not 'subject to the laws of any earthly creature.'

Affairs progressed with startling rapidity. It was in January, 1533, that Cranmer had returned to England; early in May he opened his Archiepiscopal Court at Dunstable, and on the 17th he gave the verdict dictated to him by Henry: the King's marriage with the Queen (henceforth to be known as 'the Princess Dowager') had been null and void from the beginning. The farce was played out with all due solemnity; reports were sent by Cromwell's agents for his private eye that 'My Lord of Canterbury held himself very well, without any suspicion of him by the counsel for then Princess Dowager, if she had had any present' – which of course she had not. And to round it off neatly, Cranmer wrote another letter to his Sovereign, imploring him to cut short his evil and incestuous intercourse with his brother's wife. Hard though it be, wrote Cranmer, his Grace must submit himself to the decrees of his Creator, and remember what punishments were threatened for disregarding them.

It was, in fact, two years since Henry had even seen his wife. During that time he had done everything possible to break her spirit, forbidding her to see their daughter Mary, though the girl was ill with grief, moving her from one dank and isolated manor to another, and continually sending deputations of nobles and prelates to badger her into conforming to his will. The latest of these, headed by Norfolk, visited her at Ampthill immediately after the closing of Cranmer's court. They found her in bed with one of her heavy colds, but though ill she remained her sturdy and heroic self.

'The King's plea of conscience is not honest,' she said roundly. 'He is acting on passion pure and simple, and the English judges at his bidding would say black was white. I mean to abide by no decision but that of the Pope.'

'What your Highness says or does now matters little,' Norfolk told her brutally. 'You need not trouble any more about the King, for he has taken my niece to wife.'

She turned very pale, but she did not flinch.

'If you will not submit, his Grace will no longer support you.'

'All I need,' replied Catherine, unmoved, 'is a confessor, a physician, and two of my women. And if that is too much to ask, I will go out and beg my bread for the love of God.'

The deputation looked at one another uneasily. She was perfectly capable of carrying out her threat, and though it might not move her selfish nephew the Emperor to take strong measures, it might well blow into revolt the smouldering anger of the people.

They thrust a paper at her, telling her they had orders from the King that she should sign this declaration that she was Princess Dowager and not the Queen. She called for a pen, and heavily scored through the words 'Princess Dowager' each time they occurred.

'I am the Queen,' she cried at them, 'and the King's lawful wife. I was crowned and annointed, and therefore the name of Queen I will vindicate, challenge, and so call myself during my lifetime.'

'This is from a vain desire and appetite for glory,' sneered the Earl of Wiltshire, Anne's father.

'To be the daughter of the King of Spain who drove out the Infidel,' the daughter of Ferdinand and Isabella answered the plebeian, 'is greater than to be Queen of England. As for any vainglory, it is not true that I desire the name of a queen, but only the discharge of my conscience to declare myself the King's true wife, and not his harlot, for the last four and twenty years.'

Norfolk reddened. Aristocrat that he was, he understood how this suggestion must wound a woman of her breeding and character. But Wiltshire tried another mean threat. Her obstinacy, he said, would cause the King to withdraw his fatherly affection from their daughter.

'Neither for my daughter,' Catherine replied vigorously, 'my servants, my possessions, nor any world adversity, nor for the King's displeasure, will I yield in this cause to put my soul into danger. Not for a thousand deaths will I consent to damn my soul and that of the King, my husband.'

'Well, now I must tell you this, Madam,' said Norfolk. 'His Grace's marriage already has been blessed; Queen Anne is with child. And it is his Grace's pleasure that you send to her the christening robe you made of stuff you brought with you from Spain. You will have no further use for it,' he added, vicious because the demand outraged his own feelings.

She looked at him with a touch of horror.

'God forbid that I should ever help or countenance in a case so abominable as this!'

'Why then we must search your chests.'

One of the ladies attending her began to curse Anne Boleyn, but the Queen said quietly:

'Nay, rather pray for her than curse her. For even now is the time fast coming when you shall have reason to pity her and lament her case.' She, who knew her Henry, added half to herself: 'He will turn against her shortly, for so he has always been wont to do against those to whom he abandons his will.'

191

There was, it seemed, a further reason why the deputation had been sent to her. By the King's command she was to move again, this time either to Somersham or Fotheringhay.

'The two most unhealthy houses in England!' exclaimed Catherine. 'I will not go to either unless you drag me, for if I went freely I should be guilty of suicide.'

'Then we have orders to carry you away by force; and in the meantime those servants of yours who will not name you Princess Dowager must be removed from you.'

And without giving her time to argue further, the deputation left her apartments.

During the next few days they packed her baggage and household stuff, and a litter was prepared to carry her to Fotheringhay. Her servants refusing to call her anything but Queen were committed to the porter's lodge, though for decency's sake they left the sick lady two of her women and her physician. On the morning appointed for the move, Norfolk came to fetch her; and found himself confronted by the locked doors of her bedchamber. He tapped, gently at first, them more loudly; her voice rang out from within.

'Break down the door if you would come at me! If I go, it shall be so forced that all the world shall know it.'

As he stood there cursing, not knowing what to do, a gentleman of his bustled up in a state of great agitation.

'The countryfolk, my lord, are gathering about the house, armed with pitchforks and long-bows. They are crying out for the Queen, and swear that if you take her away they will attack you.

Later that morning Norfolk and his colleagues rode off alone, through a crowd of peasants who yelled rustic maledictions.

'By her looks she is in a consumption,' said Wiltshire, trying to cheer himself and his companions. 'She will not trouble us long, I think.'

(iii)

While Queen Catherine lay neglected and insulted at Ampthill, in London Queen Anne was entering upon her triumph.

She had won her game by sheer fixity of purpose. Not until Archbishop Warham's death, when the pliable Cranmer, her family chaplain, had been nominated to succeed him, and Cromwell whom she believed her zealous partisan, had become the power behind the throne, had she yielded to the lover she had held at bay for so many years. Even then she had been cautious; she had insisted that in the patent creating her Lady Marquis of Pembroke with remainder to the heirs male of her body, the customary words 'lawfully begotten' should be omitted. For though all the obstacles to her marriage seemed to have been removed, he had not forgotten the adage about the slip between cup and lip, and in case that slip happened she was going to have a title and estates which could be handed on to her son, whether legitimate or bastard. She was not going to be another Elizabeth Blount.

But though cautious where her material future was concerned, she was not clever enough to conceal her arrogance now that her goal was in sight. The iron resolution and self-command which had enabled her to keep Henry fast bound in his infatuation with her while she refused to become his mistress, were overwhelmed now by her vanity and exultation. She offended all the Court by the airs she gave herself, and there were occasions when she betrayed to Henry her secret contempt for him. Her own father warned her to have a care; his Grace had complained to him that Anne did not behave like Catherine, who never in her life had given her husband ill words. Anne laughed it away, so sure was she of the man she had twisted round her finger for all these years; had he not given her Catherine's jewels when she demanded them, together with those of his sister Mary, Suffolk's wife and Queen Dowager of France?

And three months after becoming his mistress, she was able to bind him closer by telling him that she was pregnant. It would be, of course, a son; the astrologers, wise women, and physicians he and she consulted assured them of this; and resolved that the boy should be a legitimate Prince of Wales, Henry had married her on January 25th, but in extreme secrecy, for if the news reached the Pope he would refuse to send the bulls for Cranmer's consecration as Archbishop. The bulls having safely arrived, and Cranmer having done what he was told in declaring the marriage with Catherine null and void, it now became necessary to present the Pope, the Emperor, and the English people with an accomplished fact. Hence there was to be a Coronation which, surpassing anything in the way of splendour ever seen in England, would impress upon the King's subjects that his will was now their only law.

So the day came for which Anne Boleyn had schemed and waited for nearly ten years.

On Thursday, May 19th, the Mayor of London, in a gown of crimson velvet and a collar of Esses, was rowed solemnly down to Greenwich, followed by the barge of his own Company, the Haberdashers, with the rest of the Crafts in due order of precedence. Leading the procession were two rafts; on one a huge pasteboard dragon, moved by men inside it, continually turned its neck and spat wild-fire from its jaws; on the other, upon an artificial mount a white falcon, crowned, perched on a tree of gold decorated with red and white roses, holding in one claw a sceptre. This was the device Anne had chosen for herself, with the significant motto, *Mihi et Meae*, 'To Me and Mine.'

About the mount maidens sang, but this music, together with that of the innumerable little bells sewn on the ends of pennons floating from the barges, could not quite drown the undercurrent of hissing which issued from the crowds on the river banks as the gaudy fleet sailed downstream.

At three o'clock Anne appeared at the privy stairs of the Palace, and entered the barge which had belonged to Queen Catherine. Even Henry had demurred at this, offering to have a new one specially built for her; he did not understand that no barge but Catherine's would have meant the same to Anne Boleyn. She had given orders that all Catherine's emblems be hacked off and the apocryphal coats manufactured by the Heralds for the Boleyns substituted; in the stern floated a huge banner, in the centre of which were the letters H and A for Henry and Anne.

'Ha! Ha!' yelled a wag from the crowded bank; but fortunately his voice was lost in the peals of ordnance shot off by the ships which had been ordered to lie by.

The vast walls of the Tower came in sight, its moat stinking evilly in the summer warmth, chains creaking where pirates hung in Execution Dock, the Traitors' Gate yawning for prey, the beasts in the royal menagerie roaring an ominous accompaniment to the trumpets in the barges. As she landed at the Queen's Stairs, one great cannon spoke from the ramparts high over her head; she started slightly as though she found something menacing in that great voice; but here was Henry waiting to receive her, to kiss her lips in front of his resplendent Court, to conduct her through the postern of the Byward Tower to the State Apartments.

195

On Saturday the 21st, a gorgeous procession wound its way across the drawbridge, under the Bulwark Gate, where, on very different occasions, the Constable handed over to the Sheriffs prisoners for execution on Tower Hill, down the short street lined by almshouses of the Priory of Holy Trinity and by a convent of Poor Clares, and so through the Ald Gate into the City.

First came twelve French merchants in violet velvet, wearing Anne's colours of red and white; and immediately from the crowds there came a titter. For it had got round that his Grace's attempt to induce King Francis to send over a galaxy of French noblemen had been coldly refused. The Judges followed, then the Knights of the Bath in hoods powdered with miniver, then the mitred Abbots and Bishops, the earls and marquises weighed down by their robes, the Lord Chancellor Audley, the Archbishop of York with the Venetian Envoy, the Archbishop of Canterbury with the French Ambasador who looked harassed, the Mayor with his mace, Garter King-at-Arms in his tabard, Lord William Howard with the Marshal's rod, deputising for his brother Norfolk who had been sent to France to try to dissuade King Francis from his proposed meeting with the Pope.

Preceded by the Duke of Suffolk, made for that day High Constable of England, came the new Queen. She was in a litter of white silk drawn by two palfreys entirely masked in the same costly stuff and led by footmen in her livery; her plentiful but coarse black hair was loose under a circlet of precious stones; over her, borne by knights, was a cloth of gold canopy with gilded staves. The bells upon it tinkled prettily; church bells pealed out and trumpets blared; but these sounds of triumph only emphasized the silence of the crowds in the streets and at the windows. London was wont to cheer any procession so long as it was colourful and meant a holiday and free wine; but there was not one solitary cheer for Queen Anne Boleyn.

Her poppy mouth smiled, but her black eyes were angry as she marked that silence, encountered the stony faces which lined the route, saw how many men kept their caps upon their heads. The City had carried out the King's orders; streets were gravelled and refuse cleared away, carpets and arras hung from windows, the Companies stood in all the glory of their parti-coloured gowns and hoods behind the rails, the conduits on Cornhill and in Cheapside ran red and white wine, the great Standard in Chepe had been freshly painted, the Children of St Paul's School recited long orations, the Recorder presented her in the name of the City with a thousand gold marks in a purse of the same precious metal, musicians welcomed her with a concert from the leads of St Martin's, priests censed her from the steps of churches, and from the turrets of a tower contrived on the Fleet Street conduit the Cardinal Virtues promised never to forsake her.

But beneath all this official rejoicing she could not miss the deep, sullen hostility with which the common folk had regarded her ever since she had become a public figure. She was Queen Anne, but to them she remained 'that naughty whore, Nan Bullen.' She told herself she did not care, that the rude inferior people were beneath her contempt, that she had the infatuated Henry and the all-powerful Cromwell and the pliant Cranmer to support her against all her foes. Yet her vanity was wounded to the quick, and especially when she perceived that even in its official welcome the City had contrived to convey subtle insults.

In Gracechurch Street St Anne sat enthroned, and in flowery verse declaimed that from herself had sprung a fruitful tree; the same, she promised, would prove true of her name-sake. But St Anne had borne only Our Lady, and all knew that Queen Anne was confident of a son. On the landward side of their great warehouses, the merchants of the Steelyard had fashioned Mount Parnassus, and upon it sat Apollo and the Muses who, while the fountain of Helicon spouted Rhenish wine, addressed Anne in complimentary verse. But she did not hear a word of it. For upon the top of the Mount, above the Arms of England and the sham coat made for the Boleyns, was a great Imperial Eagle, bearing on its breast the emblems of Aragon and Castile.

'Well, let them wait, these impudent low creatures; she would punish them. And she would punish this so famous scholar, Thomas More, and this dreary ascetic, Bishop Fisher, for refusing to be present at her triumph. So she told herself; but all the while a strange little childhood memory nagged at her; she was sitting at the window of her grandfather's house, watching King Henry's Coronation, watching a young and radiant Queen ride by on her Spanish mule, while the Londoners shouted themselves hoarse in acclaiming her.

Next day came the climax of her achievement when, with the old Duchess of Norfolk bearing her long train, she descended from her chair of estate in the Abbey and went up to the High Altar, where Cranmer, having annointed her, placed the Crown of St Edward upon her black hair, a sceptre of gold in her right hand, and a rod of ivory with a dove in her left. The Crown was heavy, yet for her it was replaced all too soon by a lighter one made for her little head. When Mass was done, she was led out by her father and by Lord Talbot who was deputising for his father, the Earl of Shrewsbury, Shewsbury whose daughter had been married and discarded by Lord Henry Percy, Anne's old suitor. At the banquet in Westminster Hall, another old suitor, Sir Thomas Wyatt, held her ewer, the Earl of Essex carved for her, the Earl of Derby on his knees presented her with wine; and there was Archbishop Cranmer humbly standing until she had been served with two courses.

In a little closet contrived in St Stephen's Cloisters, the King and Thomas Cromwell watched her triumph. Glancing obliquely at his master, Cromwell thought: Certainly he is in love, but I wonder whether it is with Queen Anne? I wonder if it is not rather with his own will, whether that beaming is the result of his having got his own way in spite of the Pope, rather than because he has got this woman for his Queen.

Cromwell was also smiling, remembering the monks singing the *Te Deum* in the Abbey just now. You were singing your own doom, my friends, did you but know it, he thought. I have freed the King from his wife; I shall keep my vow, ere it be long, of making him the richest king in Christendom.

Chapter Three

(i)

King Henry came walking through the gardens of Greenwich from the direction of the Franciscan Friary next door. His vast face fringed with auburn hair was solemn, and he held a rosary in his hands, the beads slipping through his ringed fingers as he walked.

Cromwell, now his Secretary, waited for him in an alley lined with the fruit trees planted by Queen Catherine's Spanish gardener, and as he waited he observed his master. Henry seemed to be growing more corpulent every day, and more frighteningly incalculable in mood. Having boasted to everyone that he had begotten a son, his rage had been really alarming when Anne's child turned out to be a girl; yet a few days later he had been all smiles again, standing at a window with the infant Princess Elizabeth in his arms to show her to the people, carrying her round his courtiers, just as he had been used to carrying the Princess Mary, assuring himself and all the world that at least he had begotten a healthy daughter who no doubt would have brothers.

Today he appeared to be sober and slightly uneasy; the little mouth was pursed, the flat eyes held in them a hint of awe.

'Well, I have seen the Holy Maid in her ecstasy,' said he, as he came level with the Secretary. 'And God's body, it was an awesome sight. Her tongue lay out upon her cheek, and her eyes had naught but the whites showing. And Mother of God! The things she spoke!'

'Things which I fear have discomposed your Grace,' Cromwell murmured anxiously. 'Yet this simple, ignorant woman – '

Henry interrupted by boxing his ears.

'Am I not right in calling the knave in playing-cards a Cromwell? You have no reverence for holy matters, you rogue. I tell you it is impossible for a simple dame to speak so of Heaven and Hell unless it were revealed to her from above. And was she not miraculously cured of the falling-sickness when she was a serving wench? You understand no more of visions and revelations than does a dog.'

'Like the dog, I desire only to serve my master,' fawned Cromwell. 'I see him distressed, and is it my blame that I would bite those who distress him?'

'Every day the Sacred Host wafts Itself from Calais to her lips,' Henry went on, ignoring this. 'And albeit she has eaten no mortal food for the space of a year, and has practised the most rigorous mortifications ever since she was professed at the Priory of St Sepulchre, she is hale in her body. I mind me how impressed by her was the late Archbishop Warham, and I hear my Lord of Rochester regards her as a saint. To hear her speak of shrift and of the Blessed Sacrament made me plentifully to weep, so blessed were her words and look.'

He groped in his pouch for his napkin, and wiped his white-lashed eyes.

'And then she spoke of Hell, and I swear I felt the dreadful heat and heard the cries of the Damned in their torment. After a while I bade the reverend fathers present to tell her to look at me and to speak comfortable words.

But though she looked, her eyes saw something behind me' – he shuddered – 'and she began to weep, begging me for the preservation of my soul and the good of my realm to take back the Princess Dowager. Then she cried out as if in agony, and fell into a swoon.'

He sank his great bulk on to a bench, waving back his attendants who had been following at a respectful distance, and looked challengingly at Cromwell. But the piggy eyes of the Secretary perceived behind that challenge a veiled plea for reassurance.

'Your Grace says right,' observed Cromwell humbly, 'that I understand no more visions and supernatural revelations than does a dog. But I understand treason, Sire; ay, I am a good watch-dog there, and can smell out a traitor under any guise.'

'What mean you by that?' growled his master.

'Your Grace has said it is impossible for a simple maid to speak such things as your Grace has heard her speak, unless they were revealed to her from above. With the greatest submission, I too think it impossible unless she were prompted; but not, I would venture to say, by any supernatural agency. For some while now I have feared that this Maid of Kent is an agent of your Grace's enemies.'

He gave Henry his oblique glance. Yes, that shot had gone home. With the loss of his popularity as a result of his marriage with Anne, Henry had fallen into a permanently suspicious state.

'During the past few years,' went on Cromwell, 'this woman's name has become a household word and the pulpits have rung with her praises. And I have noted that those who so cry her up are those who show or have shown resistance to your Grace's will. The late Archbishop Warham protested on his death-bed his allegiance to the Pope; my Lord of Rochester has ever spoken openly against the annulment of your Grace's marriage with the Princess

Dowager; and the Carthusians and the Friars Observant, the two Orders most loud in their devotion to this Maid of Kent, have shown themselves the most obstinate in their resistance to your Grace's just claim to be Supreme Head of the Church in England.'

Henry muttered something, and began to gnaw his nails.

'So long as she confined her – er – revelations to holy matters, I would let her alone. But now, Sire, when she presumes to meddle in affairs of state, and even to incite your Grace to the sin of returning to an unlawful marriage – '

He broke off for a moment in apparent horror.

'Your Grace's affairs gossiped over in ale-houses, oafs and country housewives venturing to decide your Grace's business at the direction of a probably fraudulent visionary – it is intolerable! To put it blunt, Sire, I fear this is a traitorous conspiracy to undermine the loyalty of the inferior folk, which may even lead to armed rebellion.'

The King stared at him, the vast face paling. Cromwell flung himself upon his knees on the flagstones.

'I would sooner cut out my tongue, Sire, than to be obliged to tell your Grace what I have heard. Yet for your Grace's preservations I must and I will.' He pulled some papers from his pouch. 'Here are reports I have received from justices of the peace in several parts of your realm, if your Grace would please to read them.'

Henry took the papers, and his pallor changed to flaming crimson as he read.

The notes were the results of Cromwell's most efficient espionage; it had become impossible now for anyone to tell who his spies were, and the most intimate conversations were mysteriously reported to a justice. Some old husbandman walking home from market had remarked to his neighbour that 'there was never good weather since the

King put away the Queen'; a village housewife, taking a glass of ale at the inn, had called Queen Anne 'a goggle-eyed strumpet.' Sir William Hoo, vicar of Eastbourne, had told his sexton that some people round the King could make his Grace sign whatever they chose. Another priest, Sir James Harrison, had declared, 'I will take none for Queen but Queen Catherine; who the devil made that whore, Nan Bullen, Queen?' A rural squire at a hawking-match had said that 'The King's Grace first kept the mother and afterwards the two daughters, and now lives in open adultery with one of them, who may be his own daughter as well as his concubine.'

Noting the clenched fingers and the mouth gibbering with rage, Cromwell played his trump card.

'Being so sore uneasy in my mind, I sent to my Lord Archbishop of Canterbury, begging him to see this Nun of Kent, and while making her believe he deemed her holy and inspired, to lead her to betray her real character. And indeed, Sire, she did. She said to my lord (I scarce dare repeat the abominable thing) that if your Grace would not put away Queen Anne, you would not be King six months hence.'

'Body of God!' bellowed Henry, springing to his feet. 'Then why is not this she-devil under arrest?'

'I feared to give the order for it. Sire, because I have understood that your Grace believes her to be of God. But if I have your Grace's permission to uncover this vile conspiracy – '

Henry interrupted by cuffing him again.

'Permission, you rogue! You have our order. We will have a public confession from this witch of her lying prophesies. And we will have the blood of those who dare name her a holy woman.'

Cromwell smiled to himself as he watched his master stride away through the gardens. For some while now he had been seeking for a pretext either to win over by terror or to destroy certain persons known to be hostile to the King's new marriage and to his new title of Supreme Head of the Church. There was disaffection among the common people, and it would continue while they were set an example by the Religious Orders, and by men like Fisher and More.

(ii)

The first thing to do was publicly to discredit the Maid of Kent. This proved comparatively easy. Wrested from her convent, closely confined in the Tower, and subjected to rigorous interrogations in the Star Chamber, the good but simple woman was tricked into something which, suitably embellished, could be used as a confession of fraud. On November 23rd, this confession was read to the people from Paul's Cross by Dr Capon, Bishop-elect of Bangor, while the Maid did public penance on a scaffold erected near the Cross. Dr Capon was at pains to point out to the crowds that this traitorous impostor had been encouraged by Benedictine monks and Friars Observant to maintain the 'false opinion and wicked quarrel of the Princess Dowager against the King.'

So far, so good. But now Cromwell met with an unexpected check. In the list of names of all those who had conferred with her, a list extracted by Cromwell, the Maid steadily refused to include those of Queen Catherine and her daughter. Moreover, a consultation with the Judges revealed the fact the they could not be depended upon to convict the Maid and her associates if there were a trial in the ordinary courts of law.

Early in the new year, 1534, Cromwell received a visit from Sir Thomas More. He had been half expecting it; ever

205

since the arrest of the Maid, all who had had any dealings with her had been in a state of acute anxiety, which was precisely what Cromwell had hoped. More, however, was his brisk and cheerful self when he entered the Secretary's chamber; and wasting no time in small-talk, said he wished to give a full account of his own relations with her who was called the Holy Maid of Kent.

'It was eight or nine years past,' said he, 'when I first heard of the housewife from the late Archbishop, who asked me to see her and to give him my poor opinion. Now, sir, I have ever believed that certain superstitions which have crept in under the guise of religion have been largely invented by cranky knaves and heretics in order to diminish the authority of the true Christian doctrines by associating them with fables. You remember St Austin observes that where there is the least scent of a lie, the authority of truth is immediately weakened.'

Cromwell gave him a sharp glance, but for the life of him he could not tell from that open face whether 'crafty knaves' was a hit at himself.

'I saw the Maid,' continued More, thrusting his hands into the sleeves of his unfashionably long surcote, 'and I reported to my Lord Archbishop (God assoil his soul) that I found in her revelations nothing but what a right simple woman might speak of her own wit. This tale of her receiving the Sacred Host miraculously from Calais; why from Calais, when Our Blessed Lord is present upon the altar in her convent? Nevertheless, in view of her reputation for sanctity among right holy and learned men, I durst not, nor would not, be bold in judging the matter.'

'By "right holy and learned men" I take it you mean my Lord of Rochester, Mr More?' Cromwell inquired ingenuously.

'There was one Father Rich, a Friar Observant of Richmond,' said More, not replying to this catching question, 'since imprisoned with the Maid, was singing her praises one day at my table. I spoke thus to him: "Father Rich, that she is a good virtuous woman I hear so many folk so to report her that verily I think it true, and deem it well likely that God worketh some good and great things by her – " '

'Does God work the sowing of treason?'

" – but wot you well," More continued quoting, again ignoring a provocative question, ' "these strange tales be no part of our creed, and therefore before you see them surely proved, you shall have my poor counsel not to wed yourself so far north to the credence of them as to report them surely for true, lest that, if it should hap that afterwards they were proved fake, it might diminish folks' estimation of your preaching, whereof would grow great loss." '

He crossed one leg over the other and nursed his knee.

'This is what I said to Father Rich, of which doubtless he will give you an account when he comes to his trial. But when of late this Maid began to speak of the affairs of the realm, then did I refuse to hear any more of her from any man.'

'You have proof of this, I suppose?' sneered Cromwell.

'It so happens that I have,' replied his tiresomely serene visitor. 'As soon as I heard she was speaking of the King's matters I wrote to her, of which writing I kept a copy, warning her to forbear to touch on such things. Now I desire you, Master Secretary, that I may be permitted to appear before his Grace and his Council and defend my poor character.'

Cromwell regarded him for a moment in silence. Then he exploded his mine.

'You will have an opportunity to explain, Mr More, why you have been in communication with this traitress, not only to his Grace but to Parliament. For I must inform you that a Bill of Attainder is preparing, wherein the Nun of Kent and six priests, her associates, are indicted for high treason, and yourself and the Bishop of Rochester for misprision of treason.'

He was exceedingly mortified to observe that his shot had fizzled like a damp squib. Without any change of expression, More said musingly:

'A Bill of Attainder? Is it, I wonder, that you doubt whether the Judges would give the required verdict if the case were tried in the ordinary courts of law?'

He had hit the nail so exactly on the head that Cromwell's pasty face flamed.

'And misprision of treason,' went on More; for all the world as though they were discussing a matter of merely academic interest. 'How may that be, when the Maid said to the King himself that his soul was in danger while he would not put away Queen Anne?'

Crashing his fist on the table, Cromwell cried:

'By the Mass, Master More, it is perilous striving with princes! The King's wrath is exceedingly inflamed against you; and while it is now but misprision of treason, with loss of your goods and liberty if you are convicted, who knows but, if you remain so obstinate, it may soon be high treason, and your head shall fly for it.'

'Is that all?' mildly inquired More. 'Then in good faith, Master Secretary, there is little difference between you and me, except that I shall die today and you tomorrow.'

He stood up, and shrugged himself into his old patched gown.

'I know my innocence, and I will not mistrust my King's justice. When I resigned the Great Seal, he promised that he would abide my good and gracious lord, and I am sure he will be.'

(iii)

When Cromwell had told More that a Bill of Attainder was being prepared, naturally he had not thought fit to add that he was having as much difficulty in managing even this carefully packed Parliament as he had had with the Judges.

They were ready enough to condemn the Maid of Kent and the six priests, her associates, for high treason; and they were equally content to decide a case which had been examined, not by them but by 'the King's most honourable Council.' But they were not ready to condemn for misprision of treason the universally respected Bishop of Rochester and Sir Thomas More; despite Henry's threat to come in person to the House and force the Bill through, they insisted that, unlike the unfortunate Maid and her companions, Fisher and More be heard in their own defence.

A few days before the Bill was due to come up for its final reading, Cromwell sent for More, who found himself ushered into the presence of a committee composed of Cromwell himself, Lord Chancellor Audley, Archbishop Cranmer, and the Duke of Norfolk.

'Why here be we, five Thomases,' he exclaimed gaily. 'But let us hope there is not a doubting one amongst us.'

Cranmer smiled at the little joke, but Cromwell said gravely:

'Let us hope we are five good subjects of the King, Mr More; which is more to the matter.'

'I intend to prove myself so for my part,' said Sir Thomas. 'I have brought a copy of the letter I wrote to this Maid of Kent, warning her not to meddle in the King's matters. And with your kind permission, I will call witnesses to the conversations I had with Father Rich and Father Risby, wherein I – '

'Nay, then,' Cranmer interrupted soothingly, 'you need not so trouble yourself. All that is desired is that you prove yourself a loyal subject of his Grace; and if you do, you can ask no profit nor worldly honour at his hands that is likely to be denied you.'

There was a short silence. More laid down his papers and glanced uncomprehendingly from one to the other of the committee.

'And see,' Cranmer continued in a wheedling tone, 'how easily you may convince his Highness of your loyalty, despite your indiscreet communing with the Maid of Kent. All his Grace requires of you is this: that you give your hearty consent to that which the Parliament, the Bishops, and the Universities have approved. I mean that the marriage of his Grace with the Princess Dowager was unlawful and invalid from the beginning.'

More rose and began to walk up and down, one shoulder hunched.

'Now I verily believed that I should never have heard of this matter again!' he burst out presently, 'Considering that I have, from time to time, always from the beginning so plainly and truly declared my mind unto His Highness, which he, like a most gracious prince, ever seemed very well to accept, never intending, as he said, to molest me therein, for he knew I spake only according to my conscience.'

'And will you not speak to us, then, according to your conscience?' coaxed Cromwell.

'Master Secretary, that will I not,' flatly replied More. 'As I am ready to leave every man to his conscience, so it seems just to leave me to mine. And in this matter I would never meddle, seeing that I am no theologian, but only when his

Grace pressed me for my poor opinion, then did I speak of it, but to none other.'

'Now I tell you what, Master More,' barked Cromwell laying aside his geniality. 'The King has given us in commandment that if we can by no gentleness move you, we are in his name to charge you with great ingratitude, and to tell you that in his Grace's view never was there a servant so faithless to his master, no subject so traitorous to his prince, as you.'

'I cannot understand what you say,' observed More, shaking his head. 'I am no longer in his Grace's service, but am living quite retired as a private person. And as for treason, I have offered to prove that I would have no more to do with the Maid of Kent when she began to meddle with – '

'Your treason has nothing to do with the Maid of Kent,' interrupted Cromwell, 'but with other matters I believe you will find hard to disprove.'

'In fact, the Maid of Kent was but a pretext,' More said drily.

'Your treason consists, Mr More, in your allegiance to the Pope who encroaches upon his Grace's just prerogative. Dare you deny that when his Grace was writing his book against Luther, you villainously and traitorously provoked his Grace to maintain the Pope's authority, and thereby, to his Grace's dishonour throughout Christendom, did put a sword into the Pope's hands against your King and master?'

More smiled broadly.

'Mr Secretary,' said he, 'these be arguments for children, not for men.'

'You have leave to go home, Mr More,' said Cromwell, very cold and distant. 'But you have not heard the last of these matters, I warrant you.'

Standing at the window, he watched More enter his barge; as it made its way through the busy traffic of river, More's shabby figure was recognized, and hands waved a greeting from tall ships, from tilt-boats, and from wherries.

'God damn him!' Cromwell muttered to Audley who watched with him. 'London has not forgot him, retired though he lives now; and he has not forgot his old shrewdness. He is not to be moved by aught we can attempt *in terrorem*; and it is certain Parliament will acquit him if, as they insist, he be heard in his own defence. His name will have to be taken out of the Bill of Attainder if it is to pass; but we shall catch him, wary fox though he us, over the new Oath.'

(iv)

The very next day, More's son-in-law, Will Roper, who was a Burgess of Parliament, came hastening home to Chelsea in high good humour.

'Your name is withdrawn from the Bill, sir!' he cried.

But More did not seem particularly elated.

'What is put off is not laid aside,' he observed. 'And I verily believe that they have withdrawn my name, not to save me but to save the Bill.'

On March 12th the Bill of Attainder was read a fourth time and accepted by the Peers, none of those accused being heard in their own defence. Fisher was too ill to attend, a circumstance Cromwell found agreeable, for otherwise Parliament would have insisted that he be allowed to speak; as it was they pardoned him in return for a year's revenue of his bishopric. The Maid of Kent, with two monks, two Friars Observant, and two secular priests, were condemned to suffer the penalties for high treason; but Cromwell delayed their execution, still hoping to induce the priests to accept the Royal Supremacy in return for their lives.

Ten days later, Will Roper, returning from Parliament, sought out his father-in-law, whom he found tranquilly working in his garden.

'There is an Act of Succession brought in,' he said uneasily, 'which bastardizes the Princess Mary and fixes the Succession upon the heirs of his Grace and Queen Anne.'

More sighed, but went on working as he said:

'I pity from my heart, son, our sweet Princess; yet it is within the right of his Grace and the Parliament to settle the Succession as they please.'

'But it is noised abroad, I know not how truly, that the Pope has at last given his sentence upon the question of his Grace's marriage with Queen Catherine; she is, says His Holiness, his Grace's true and lawful wife.'

More made no comment.

'And there was something else I do not well understand which passed in the Parliament House,' Roper went on with a frown. 'To this Act of Succession there it to be added, without debate or vote but by order of the King himself, an Oath – '

'An Oath?' sharply interrupted his father-in-law, laying down his spade.

'It is to be framed separately from the Act, and may be offered to all the King's subjects. Those who refuse it are to suffer the penalties of misprision of treason; but the nature of it I could not well discover.'

More said nothing, but he seemed very much disturbed.

The Act of Succession was made law on March 30th, but the Oath, which was contained in the preamble to it, was being hotly debated by the Lords. So far as the rather simple Roper could make out, all that was required was for everyone to swear to be true and obedient to the heirs of Henry and Anne; and since Parliament has passed the Act of Succession, he did not understand why there should be this pother. At the beginning of April, all London was startled by the news that Bishop Fisher, who had been too ill to attend his session of Parliament, had been summoned to Lambeth Palace, had refused the Oath, and straightway had been committed to the Tower.

On Low Sunday, April 12th, More, accompanied by Roper and his wife Meg, went into London to hear the sermon at St Paul's purposing afterwards to dine at their old home in Bucklersbury with Meg's foster-sister, Margaret Clement. It was a sweet spring morning, and More, who had been so heavy of late recovered his cheerfulness; there was time before dinner to revisit some of their old haunts, he said, and he had a particular desire to see again the great Charterhouse of the Salutation near Barbican. In its mortuary chapel, built after the Black Death, he prayed for a long space; and when they came out into the sunlight once more, he said softly, taking an arm of each of his young companions:

'I thought never to tell you this, and yet today, I know not why, I have a great wish to tell you. When I was a young man first starting to read law, I was much drawn to the religious life, and especially to that of these same Carthusians. So much was I drawn (to the great disgust of my father) that for near upon four years I lodged in the guest-house yonder, with freedom to come and go as my studies required, but sharing as far as possible in the life of the good monks.'

They looked at him in astonishment; no one seemed less fitted for enclosure and silence than this man whose greatest joy was to be surrounded by his family and friends, and who took such delight in good conversation.

'At that time,' continued More, 'the Prior was Master Tynbygh, he who was captured by the Saracens in his youth while on pilgrimage to the Holy Land, a very saintly

214

man. And in the end of it, said to me, "You are a man of strong passions, my son; rather be a chaste husband than an impure monk.' (Would Luther had said the same; but because he doubted of himself, he went by the proverb, "Doubt makes a monk".) Yet this at least I learned while I was at the Charterhouse, that those whom God calls to spend all their lives in a straight, hard, penitential way, praying ever for the souls of others, are the most blessed men upon this earth.'

They had come by this time into Bucklersbury, and here, above the intermittent ringing of the many bells of London, the squawking of the kites and crows which, protected by law, helped to diminish the piles of refuse in the streets, and the singing of clerks in some parish procession, the waterfalls between the starlings of the Bridge made such a thunder that conversation was impossible. They were nearing the Barge, when they saw a man dismounting from his horse there; and he at the same time noticing them, paused as he was about to knock upon the door.

'That is the livery of my Lord Archbishop,' Roper exclaimed in surprise.

His father-in-law answered nothing, but hastened forward. The horseman, bowing, and raising his voice above the din, said with a trace of hesitation.

'I have been seeking you, Master More, and was told at Chelsea that you were come into London. My master, the Lord Archbishop, has bidden me serve this summons on you.'

More took the paper and read it in silence. It cited him to appear next day at Lambeth Palace to swear to the Act of Succession and to the separate Oath which appeared in the preamble.

*   *   *

He returned at once to Chelsea. His family did not see him for the remainder of that day, for he was closeted with his confessor; far into the night the anxious Meg saw a taper burning in his New Building, and now and again past the windows of the gallery there paced the figure she loved, the right shoulder raised, the head bent, hands clasped behind him. She knew that some lonely conflict was being fought out there, and she who loved him better than husband or child was powerless to help him. Next morning he went early to his parish church and received the Sacrament; then, refusing bite or sup, returned to his retreat, his face pinched and grey.

At ten o'clock Roper came to tell him that it was time to row down to Lambeth. He nodded, still not speaking. As always when he took the boat, his family was at the water-gate to wave to him as long as he was in sight, but this morning he pulled-to the wicket quickly, almost harshly, shutting out the view of those loving, anxious faces. As they rowed down-river, still there was that heavy silence, nor did he once look back to wave, nor lift his hand to acknowledge the greetings of the fishermen and the bargemen who loved him. But just as the tall brick battlements of Lambeth came in sight upon the southern shore, he turned suddenly to Roper who was sitting behind him and whispered so that the oarsmen should not hear:

'Son Roper, I thank Our Lord the field is won.'

The simple Roper, bewildered but not liking to appear so, replied:

'Sir, I am very glad thereof.'

'It was strange,' murmured More, half to himself, 'what great desire was on me to revisit the Charterhouse. It minded me how longed I once to be straight shut up.'

He squared his shoulders, and became the familiar Thomas More, brisk and cheerful.

'How well I remember that fine gatehouse yonder, when it was a building,' said he, pointing to Lambeth Palace. 'For you know that when I was a lad I was sent to learn the ways of the great in the service of Cardinal Morton, and it was while I was here with him at Lambeth that he built the gate. And here he would feed the poor with his own hands, for he was a great good man, God rest him, a friend of learning and marvellous concerned for the welfare of the Church.'

They landed, doffing their caps to the image of St Thomas of Canterbury in the water-tower, and were conducted through the outer courtyard which was full of clerics dismounting from their mules or walking to and fro in the April sunshine, their heads together as they conversed.

'A poor layman feels he intrudes among so many reverend fathers,' More observed humorously. Roper was astonished at the change in him; he had the air of one who has come victorious through some great ordeal.

A fellow in livery conducted More at once to a downstairs parlour where Cromwell, Chancellor Audley, the Abbot of Westminster, and Archbishop Cranmer were sitting at one side of a board which had been set up on trestles. They greeted More courteously, though Cromwell's little eyes were watchful, and the Abbot seemed nervous.

'You live much retired, Mr More,' began Cranmer, 'and therefore it may be you know little of this Act of Succession lately passed by Parliament for the love they bear his Grace. Well, then, here it is – ' he pushed a printed roll across the table ' – and here likewise is the Oath which goes with it, as you see under the Great Seal. Pray read them, Master More, and then we shall desire you to swear to them. And I may tell you you are honoured, for save for the Lords Temporal, you are the first layman to be desired so to swear.

217

He took the documents to a window embrasure and sat down. They whispered together, watching him, but he was unaware of them. He was reading and re-reading, not the Act of Succession, but the Oath framed separately in the preamble, thoroughly digesting its implications.

'...No man henceforth is to swear faith, truth and obedience to any other but the King's Grace and the heirs of his Grace and Queen Anne, begotten or to be begotten, within this realm, nor to any foreign authority or potentate. And in case any oath hath been taken by you to any person or persons, that then you repute the same as vain and annihilate; and that to your uttermost power ye shall observe, keep, maintain, and defend the same Act of Succession, and all the whole effects and contents thereof, and all other Acts and Statutes made in confirmation and for execution of the same or of anything therein contained. And this ye shall do against all manner of persons of what estate, degree, dignity, or condition soever they be.'

'Well, Master More?' sharply inquired Cromwell at last.

He came slowly back to the table and laid the papers down.

'My lords, to the Act of Succession I am ready to swear; but I cannot swear to the Oath without the jeopardizing of my soul to perpetual damnation.'

'Why, what quibble is this?' demanded Cranmer. 'Here is a splitting of hairs that you will take the one and not the other, when they are both – '

'Come, Mr More,' interposed Cromwell, 'so weighty a matter needs further deliberation. We have many to swear this morning, many holy and learned men; do you please to go out into the garden, and you shall give us your opinion presently.'

But when a servant had conducted him to the garden door, he stopped abruptly, putting his hand before his eyes, and seeing another garden, dear figures busy in it, his grandchildren at their games, his strange pets in dens and hutches, the quiet river flowing past. He asked the man to show him some room where he might be private while he waited; and in a little bare chamber looking out on to the gardens, he sat down in the window and faced the situation.

To simple men that Oath, framed in tedious official jargon, would seem harmless, and was intended so to seem. The subjects of the King were required to swear truth and obedience to their natural lord and not to any foreign potentate; it would never enter the heads of ordinary folk that by 'foreign potentate' was meant the Pope, for to them he was the common Father of Christendom. But to More the implication of the Oath was all too plain.

No man in England was less blind to the Papal scandals of his age than Thomas More; on the other hand, no man saw more clearly that if, as he himself had once written, the vices of men were to be imputed to the offices they hold, it would be the end of all authority and order. Moreover, while all save sycophants and heroes held fast to the hope that the quarrel between King Henry and Pope Clement would be made up again, as had happened so many times before in history, More was too honest and too clear-sighted to pin his faith on such a sheet-anchor. This was no quarrel between two temporal rulers; it was a severing of the chain which linked England with the rest of Christendom.

Ever since Roper had first mentioned to him that some Oath was to be taken, he had been troubled. In his *Utopia* he had contended that no man was to be coerced into saying that he believed what he did not believe; and vigorously as More himself fought with his pen against heresy, his anger was directed only against those who disturbed the faith of others and caused sedition and strife.

219

Thus had he steadily refused to discuss the King's 'great matter', even with his own family and friends. And now he was being required to swear to a greater matter still; he who so reverenced authority, must choose between two authorities, and since the temporal was usurping the just rights of the spiritual, he knew what that choice must be.

He had made it in agony, during the past twenty-four hours, for he had foreseen the nature of this Oath. He understood also the implication of Cranmer's ironical compliment; he, a man living in retirement, holding no public office and desiring none, was yet the first layman called upon to swear, because he was beloved by the City, because he was a scholar of European reputation, and his course of action inevitably would influence others. He had told Roper the truth when he had said that the field was won; he had faced the consequences of the choice he must make and had accepted them.

But as he sat here alone in this bare chamber, pity and dread racked him sore. Pity for the King so spoiled and misled, first by the vainglorious Wolsey, now by the cold and ruthless Cromwell, the King whom More would always remember as the gallant boy riding to his Coronation. Pity for the big happy family at Chelsea, soon to be made destitute and stricken, and that by his act which some of them would regard as folly. And dread of his own future. Oh yes, he had hankered in youth after the solitary life of the Carthusians; but he was fifty-six now, set in his ways, a father and grandfather, and he did not hanker after the solitary life of a prisoner.

As he sat watching those who passed busily to and fro in the garden below him, he drew out his tablets and stylus, and seeking comfort by comforting the anxious ones at home, began to write an amusing description of the scene for Meg; it might be long before he saw that beloved daughter of his again.

'There is Master Dr Latimer just come into the garden, with other learned doctors and chaplains of my Lord Archbishop; and very merry he seems to be, for he hast just taken one or twain about the neck so handsomely, that if they had been women I would have weened he had waxen wanton. Now comes Master Dr Wilson, who once was his Grace's confessor; I fear he is one of the bad boys for whom there is a rod in pickle, for he is brought out between billmen and thrust into a barge. Here now come some of the good boys, speeding apace to their great content; and Master Phillips, the Vicar of Croydon, either for gladness or for dryness, or to show his familiarity with my Lord Archbishop, is gone into the buttery where I hear him call loudly for drink.'

It was rather forced humour, but it served; and when the servant came to fetch him to the Commissioners again, he was his merry, confident self.

'Here, now, Master More,' began Cranmer, pushing a paper towards him, 'see all these names to the Oath. All these good and learned fathers have signed, and will you stick to do the like?'

'I being neither good nor very learned.' More answered wryly,' must even stick to what I said before.'

'To which part of the Oath do you object?' asked Cromwell casually.

More smiled with slight contempt; the trap was so obvious.

'If I should open and disclose the causes, Master Secretary, I should thereby further exasperate his Highness, which I would in no wise do, but rather would I abide all the danger and harm that might come towards me, than give his Highness any occasion of further displeasure.'

'Now look you, Master More,' said Cranmer in a sweetly reasonable tone, 'since you do not condemn any who have taken this Oath, it follows that you hold the swearing or not swearing to be a thing uncertain and doubtful. But there can be no doubt that you are bound to obey the King.'

It seemed to him that he had staggered More by an argument so subtle; as indeed he had, though not in the way he thought. It astounded Sir Thomas that the successor of Augustine and Becket, of Anselm and Dunstan, seriously should advance the argument that in all matters wherein we are not prepared to condemn the consciences of others, we are bound, for ourselves, to accept the orders of the temporal power – a maxim which would put an end to all religious freedom.

'Of a truth, my Lord Archbishop,' said More, solemn faced, 'if we accept that view we have a ready way to avoid all perplexities. For in whatsoever matters the doctors stand in great doubt, the King's commandment, given upon whither side he lists, solves all the doubt. But in my conscience this is one of the cases in which I am bound – that I shall not obey my prince, since that whatsoever other folk think of the matter (whose conscience and learning I will not condemn, nor take upon me to judge), yet in my conscience the truth seems to be on the other side.'

'Now by the Mass!' cried Cromwell, bringing his hand flat down upon the table, 'out of your own mouth you have condemned yourself. You are not bounden, you say, to obey your Sovereign Lord, acknowledged by Convocation as the Supreme Head of the Church.'

' "So far as the Law of Christ allows," ' quoted More. 'Yet if there were no more than myself upon the one side, and Convocation on the other, I would be sore afraid to lean to my own mind against so many reverend fathers. But if it so be that in some things for which I refuse this Oath, I have upon my side as great a Council, and a greater too, I am not then bounden to change my conscience and conform to the Council of this realm against all the General Councils of Christendom.'

'We commit you to the charge of my Lord Abbot here,' Cranmer said glacially, 'until we know his Grace's pleasure regarding so disloyal and unnatural a subject.'

(v)

Just under a week later, the Maid of Kent and her six companions were executed at Tyburn; and on that same day, having again refused the Oath, More was sent to the Tower. As he alighted at the Bulwark Gate, and saw those grim, massive walls frowning down on him, for a moment his courage failed, and there was no real humour in the jest he made when the porter according to custom demanding his upper garment as 'garnish', More gave him instead of his gown his shabby felt cap. But by the time the Lieutenant, an old friend of his, had conducted him to the lower chamber in the Bell Tower on the south-west corner of the Inner Ward, he had recovered his wit.

'Alack, sir,' lamented the Lieutenant, looking round the cold, vaulted chamber with its eight-foot-thick walls, 'I must ask your pardon that I cannot, without risking his Grace's displeasure, make you better cheer.'

'Assure yourself, Master Lieutenant,' More answered, with extreme gravity, 'that whensoever you hear me complain of your cheer, you may thrust me out of your doors.'

It was not, indeed, so very comfortless a prison room into which Dame Alice was ushered a few days later. Straw matting and hangings kept out the draughts; he was waited on by his own servant, John Wood, he had the consolation of knowing that in the chamber above, called the Strong Room, was good old Bishop Fisher, with whom he had

223

contrived to get into communication, and piled on a little table were his books and writing materials.

'Come now, Dame Alice,' he coaxed his tearful wife, 'is it not meetly fair? Or if you will not allow so much, you must confess that it is strong enough.'

'To be locked up at night!' wailed Alice. 'By my troth, if the door should be bolted on me I am sure it would stop my breath.'

He smiled behind his hand. For at home it was one of his wife's greatest cares to see that her chamber was bolted at night and all her windows fast closed. Drying her eyes, she turned fretful; she was having to pay fifteen shillings a week for 'board lodgings' for her husband and his servant, she who was now so poor, and all because Mr More chose to play the eccentric.

'What a good year, man! I marvel that you, that have always been taken for a wise man, should be such a fool as to lie here in this close, filthy prison, and be content thus to be shut up amongst rats and mice, when you might be abroad and at your liberty, and with the favour and good-will both of the King and his Council, if you would do what all the Bishops and best learned of his realm have done. And seeing you have at Chelsea a right fair house, your library, your books, your gallery, your garden, your orchard – '

He longed to cry to her to stop, so vividly did she evoke in his mind the beloved home he had sacrificed.

' – and all other necessaries so handsome about you, where you might in the company of me your wife, your children, and household, be merry, I marvel what a' God's name you mean here thus fondly to tarry.'

He took her hands and asked gently:

'I pray you, good Mistress Alice, tell me one thing. Is not this house as nigh Heaven as my own?'

'Good God, will you never leave fooling?' she chided, twisting her hands to free them.

'It is so indeed,' he said. 'And be assured, sweetheart, that I am very tranquil here. I would not or I could not be a monk when I was young, and now God compels me to live like one. And I am at my writing again; and needing no longer to attack heresy, since it is not meet work for prisoners, I am engaged instead upon a *Dialogue of Comfort*, which shall be, I hope, a testament for my children.'

But he was destined to suffer a far greater test of endurance than the complainings of his somewhat shrewish wife. Meg wrote to him, the ink smudged with her tears, beseeching him with every loving plea she could think of, to submit to the King's will. A few days later she came to see him, and was shocked by his drawn face and hollow eyes.

'If I had not been, my dearest daughter,' he burst out, as soon as they were alone, 'by God's great mercy at a firm and fast point, your lamentable letter had abashed me above all earthly things, of which I hear divers times not a few terrible towards me. But surely they all touched me never so near as to find you, my dearest child, in such vehement piteous manner labouring to persuade me to do that which, for respect unto my own soul, I have so often refused to do.'

'It was partly a trick,' she said, clinging to him. 'I knew that all letters to you would be opened, and I hoped that Master Secretary, seeing me urge you thus, would be the better minded to give me frequent access to you. And yet in honesty I must confess it was not only that; the thought of you in prison – '

'We are all God's prisoners,' he interrupted softly; 'the world is a prison, and we are all condemned to death. I surely suppose that if we took not this figure as a fantasy, but for what it is indeed, men would bear themselves not much higher in their own esteem for any rule or authority they may have in this world, for they are but like the tapster at the Marshalsea, or at the uttermost one so put in trust with the Keeper that he is half an under-gaoler over his fellows, till the Sheriff and the cart come for him.'

She caught her breath at those last words. There were rumours abroad that a new Act was to be brought in whereby any man denying the King's title of Supreme Head of the Church should be declared a traitor. She had come here today determined to save him despite himself; and she now drew from her gown a letter, telling him that her step-sister, now the wife of Sir Giles Alington, had interceded with Chancellor Audley, who, while promising to do what he could, had marvelled that Mr More could be so obstinate in his own conceit, since everyone had taken the Oath except himself and 'one blind old Bishop.'

'What, Mistress Eve!' cried More playfully. 'Has my daughter Alington played the serpent with you, and with a letter set you at work to come tempt your father?'

But then, reading the letter, he was nettled by Audley's suggestion that his 'obstinacy' was due to Fisher's example.

'In very truth I hold my Lord of Rochester in such reverent estimation that I reckon in this world no one man, in wisdom, learning, and long approved virtue together, meet to be compared with him. Yet I never intend (God being my good Lord) to pin my soul at another man's back, not even the best man that I know this day living, for I know not whither he may hap to carry it.'

'But Father,' she persisted, 'now that this Oath is being generally administered, all your family have taken it, though with this mental reservation, "So far as the Law of Christ allows".'

'Why then it seems you are convinced that if you say one thing and think the while the contrary, God more regards your heart than your tongue, and therefore your oath goes upon what you think, and not upon what you say.'

He took her hand and tucked it under his arm as they sat together.

'Did I ever tell you the tale, Meg, of a suit between a Northerner and a Southerner which had to be settled by a jury? – or was it a per-jury?' he asked slyly. 'All upon that jury were Northerners except one, whose name was Company, and all agreed but he. "Company," said they, "play the good companion, come forth with us and pass even for good company." "But," retorted Company, "when we shall hence and come to God, and He shall send you to Heaven for doing according to your conscience, and me to the devil for doing against mine, if I shall say to you all again, Go now for good company with me, would ye go?" '

Her mouth dropped like a child's, and he gave her hand a little pat.

'How now, Mother Eve, where is your mind now? Sit not musing with some serpent in your breast, upon some new persuasion to offer Father Adam the apple yet once again.'

'Since the example of so many wise men, and of your own family, will not move you,' said Meg, between laughter and tears, 'I have but one argument left. Master Patenson, that used to be our Fool and is now in the service of the Mayor, met one day one of our own men, and when he had asked where you were and heard you were still here in the Tower, this good Fool waxed very angry with you, and said, "What ails him that he will not swear, seeing I have sworn the Oath myself?" And so Father, I can say no more than Master Patenson; why should you refuse to swear, since I have sworn myself?'

'That word was like Eve too,' chuckled her father, 'for she offered Adam no worse fruit than she had taken herself.'

Then he went on gravely:

'My most beloved daughter, though I know full well that if they could make a law to take away my life, that law could never be lawful, yet since nothing is impossible I have not forgot the counsel of Christ that ere I should begin to build this castle for the satisfaction of my soul, I should sit and reckon what the charge would be.'

She would have spoken, but he laid his hand gently on her lips.

'I reckoned, Meg, full surely many a restless night, while my wife slept and thought I slept too, what peril was possible to fall to me. And in thinking thereupon I had a full heavy heart. And yet (I thank our Lord), for all that I never thought to change, though the very uttermost should hap me that my fear ran upon.'

'You may repent it,' she sobbed, 'when it is too late.'

'Too late, Meg? I beseech Our Lord that if ever I make such a change it may be too late indeed. For well I wot that such a change, grown but by fear (there being never so frail a man as your silly father), may put my soul in danger. Mistrust God I will not, though I feel faint. And though I should feel my fear even to the point to overthrow me, yet shall I remember how St Peter with a blast of wind began to sink, and shall do as he did, call upon Christ to save me. Yes, and if He suffer me to play St Peter further, and swear and forswear too, yet after shall I trust His goodness will cast upon me His tender pitying eye, and make me confess the truth of my conscience afresh, and abide the shame and the harm of my own fault. And if He suffer me for my faults to perish, still shall I serve for a praise of His justice.'

She could find no word to say, for she knew that she was beaten.

Chapter Four

At the royal manor of Hatfield, another daughter was weeping for a very different kind of father.

Late in the previous year the Princess Mary, now a young woman of seventeen, had been visited by a deputation of nobles who had told her that by his Grace's command she was no longer to call herself Princess of Wales on pain of the King's high displeasure, and that she was to go to Hatfield as an attendant upon the true Princess of Wales, the baby Elizabeth. Mary was her mother's daughter; she had replied that the title belonged to herself and to no one else, and having registered this protest, she had obeyed. Watching in dry-eyed dignity while her devices were ripped off her servants' coats and her cloth of estate removed, she had pressed against her heart a letter she carried there, a letter from the mother who was a prisoner like herself.

'The time is come when God Almighty will prove you,' Catherine had written, 'and I am very glad of it, for I trust He doth handle you with a good love. Obey the King your father in everything, save only that you do not offend God. Speak few words and meddle nothing. And now you shall again, and by likelihood I shall follow. I set not a rush by

229

it; for when they have done the uttermost they can, then I am sure of the amendment.'

It was a warning to Mary that the King, who already had sworn that if Parliament did not rid him of his wife and daughter he would provide for this himself, might be persuaded by Anne to carry out his threat, either by public execution or by some secret means.

For the past nine years, when she ought to have been courted as the heir to the throne and to have known the delights of the Court, this lonely young creature had experienced nothing but humiliation, separation from her parents, and the bitter knowledge that her mother had been replaced in her father's affections by his concubine. All the while she had told herself that it could not be her father's fault, her father so big and jolly, who had been so proud of her as a child. No, it was Anne, whom anyone could see was a witch. It was Anne who had taken from her her dear Governess, the Countess of Salisbury; it was Anne's two aunts, Lady Shelton and Lady Clere, who, here at Hatfield, denied her the riding she loved, the walking necessary for her health, even the hearing of Mass at the parish church.

'His Grace has given order that you be kept close lest you raise a rebellion,' they told her.

She had come to the end of her money, and even lacked clothes; well, said they, she could write to the King. She did so, humbly and confidently, signing herself as a matter of course, Mary, Princess of Wales. They refused to send the letter unless she would delete the title. And when one day she was walking along an open gallery, and a group of country-folk shouted out for her as their true Princess, Anne's aunts imprisoned her in the worst room in the house, gave her a common chambermaid for her only attendant, and refused to have her food put to the Assay, so that she expected to be poisoned. And by whom but

Anne? No father, much less hers, could put to death his own daughter who loved him.

'The King is coming to visit his daughter, the Lady Elizabeth, Princess of Wales,' Lady Clere told her spitefully one summer day.

But he will ask to see me when he comes, Mary told herself. Perhaps they would walk in the garden, and she would unburden her heavy heart to him, beg him to be allowed to go to Kimbolton whither her mother had been moved, remind him of all the happy times the three of them had had together.

A prisoner in her wretched room, she heard the arrival of the royal cavalcade, and as she listened at her locked door she caught the echo of the jovial voice she loved, the tread of his strong feet. The hours went by, and still she was not fetched; there was the clatter of hoof-beats again; he was leaving. In desperation she ran out to the little balcony of her window, a pitifully thin girl in a shabby gown and coif; and as that corpulent figure rode by beneath, she cried out something and sank on to her knees.

He looked up. Instinctively his gloved hand went to his feathered cap and pulled it off; he made his daughter a little bow, half cold, half embarrassed, and then averted his face. Looking beyond him, the girl saw the prominent black eyes of Anne Boleyn, glittering with malice.

'Give that wench a box on the ear for the cursed bastard she is,' Anne said loudly to one of her aunts who was riding beside her to the verge of the estate. 'When I shall have a son, I know what then will come to her.'

But even as she said it, her heart sank. She had told Henry she was pregnant again when in fact she was not; it was a desperate feint to induce him to go without her on his forthcoming visit to France, for then he would name her Regent and while he was absent she would find means to have both Catherine and Mary put out of the way, since

231

he was to squeamish to do it himself. It was only because of them that she remained unpopular with the people; only because of their whining letters that she and Henry quarrelled. And then she shivered with rage and humiliation as she remembered the bitter public quarrel they had had only that morning.

They had been starting out for Hatfield when Anne had noticed among her train a certain very young Maid of Honour at whom she had caught Henry making eyes of late. Anne had snapped at the girl:

'It is not your spell of duty. You must stay behind.'

'It is by our order that she comes,' Henry had said immediately. And then, with one of his alarming outbursts of temper: 'As for you, you can shut your eyes, as your betters have done before you.'

The whole retinue had heard it. 'Your betters'; everyone must have known he had meant Catherine, who indeed had shut her eyes to his many infidelities. Yes, both Catherine and Mary must go. They were sickly; it could be made to seem natural death. And she could rely on Cromwell to help her in the business; he was a realist and her staunch supporter.

It was as well for her peace of mind that she could not read the thoughts of Henry as they rode away from Hatfield.

He was still obsessed by her, but his obsession was now on the perilous border-line between love and hate. A familiar process was at work in him, that process which took place with each successive abandonment of the initiative to others; first irksomeness, then resentment, then violent reaction. Behind the amiable mask he was wont to accumulate a store of hatred for those who mastered him, though he must always, to satisfy his vanity, find a plausible excuse when he wished to destroy them. And his vanity had grown in proportion to the coarsening of his mind and body. In youth his vigorous constitution had enabled him to fight off the effects of his horrible disease; but that disease had begun to move with terrible impetus, and now in his early forties it was manifesting itself in phobias, excessive coarseness, a degeneration mental, moral, and physical.

He had begun to find Anne irksome very soon after she had become his mistress. He had told himself that with her, the one great passion of this life, he would prove his virility; but it was not so. He was still defective as a lover and he had a monstrous suspicion that she laughed at him; to laugh at him was blasphemy; it was as though she laughed at God. And to present him with a daughter when he had boasted to everyone that it would be a son, was the thing he could not forgive; he had bought jousting-toys for the heir-to-be, little brass models of knights in armour on wheeled pedestals; he had ordered all priests to be ready to pray for the new little Henry the moment the bells of London proclaimed that Anne was delivered.

Brooding on his wrongs, he remembered belatedly that Anne had kept him on the end of a string year after year, steadily refusing to give him satisfaction. He remembered that it was she who had forced him into a quarrel with the Pope. He remembered that it was through her that he had lost his popularity with his own subjects, and had had ill things said about him by his brother kings. And as though he had called to it where it slept in its lair, his peculiar conscience began to stir again. Was his marriage with Anne valid? Her sister had been his mistress; surely there was an impediment of affinity arising from the unlawful intercourse of concubinage... no, that would not serve; if he repudiated Anne, he would have to take back Catherine.

He became aware presently that Archbishop Cranmer was talking to him, riding there on a mule at his side.

'I have been thinking, please your Grace, that my Lord of Rochester and Master More might be allowed to swear to the Succession only, but that this be kept secret. Then will folk believe they have subscribed to the whole Oath, which will influence those who look to them for guidance.'

'And on being freed they would immediately deny it,' said the contemptuous voice of Cromwell from the King's other hand.

Henry immediately was thrown into a new agony of indecision. As King Herod had feared John the Baptist, knowing him to be a just and holy man, and willingly had heard his preaching, so Henry in his heart feared the saintly Bishop who had been his tutor, and the great humanist in whose companionship he had found such delight. He was always seeing himself in the role of some Old or New Testament hero; and for the moment it pleased him to appear even as the very unheroic Herod, torn between his love for a new Herodias and his respect for godly men. It was impossible for him to believe that his desire to destroy them was the result of his need to assure himself that his will was supreme.

He spurred his horse and galloped on ahead of his suave Archbishop and his ruthless Secretary. He did not get enough exercise nowadays. He would not joust because, whereas a few years ago he had vanquished his opponents by true superior skill, now he suspected that he overcame them because they were afraid to incur his wrath if they did not let him win. He hunted still, but his corpulence had increased so alarmingly that he had to have a whole string of spare horses, tiring out each after an hour or so; and once or twice when his Grooms of the Stable had brought these horses from the royal mews in Holborn, he had fancied he had seen them exchanging glances.

Galloping now through a forest ride, he sought comfort in the thought of a woman; and she was not the Maid of

234

Honour with whom his dalliance had aroused Anne's wrath.

On one of his recent Progresses he had stayed a night or two with a Wiltshire family, the Seymours of Wolfhall. They, like the Boleyns, were of the new men; the two brothers, Edward and Thomas, were among the younger set at Court, and the sister, Jane, had been Queen Catherine's Maid of Honour. Now she was living at home; and on his visit there Henry had seen her as it were for the first time, a country maiden, tending her flowers, busy in her stillroom, scarcely daring to raise her mild eyes when the King of England addressed her.

Such a child, he thought reminiscently. (Actually she was twenty-five.) As pale as a primrose, the very antithesis of Anne. Virginal, submissive, pure; he turned the adjectives over in his mind. He could not imagine Jane Seymour ever resisting his will, fraying his nerves with arrogance as Anne did, causing him to alienate his people and his fellow kings. He fell into a day-dream in which Catherine and Anne were both dead, and he and the meek Jane Seymour were truly and incontestably man and wife.

(ii)

Cromwell knew very well what was passing in the King's mind, even to his thoughts of Jane Seymour. And because by indulging Henry's appetites and gratifying his egoism, Cromwell had raised himself to what he was, he was fully prepared to find some way of getting rid of Anne. At the moment, however, she could wait; she was most obligingly working for her own downfall by her conduct. Henry used her supposed pregnancy as an excuse for not going to France himself, since he was affronted by King Francis' vigorous denunciation of his conduct; and later Anne was obliged to tell him that she had been mistaken about her condition.

Meanwhile Cromwell's attention was concentrated upon two things: the catching of Fisher and More, and the forcing of the Religious Orders to declare themselves hostile to the King's measures.

In November Parliament assembled: and never had there been one more shamelessly packed. With every writ Cromwell had sent a private letter, directing the city or borough to choose the person named therein. In at least one instance, the commonalty having elected two burgesses before the King's will was known, Cromwell wrote sharply to the Mayor and bade him, notwithstanding the fact that the election had already been held, to proceed to a new one and elect the King's candidates. Through this pliant Parliament Cromwell drove a new Act of Supremacy, wherein the King was named Head of the Church in England without the saving clause, 'So far as the Law of Christ allows'; a few days later there followed an Act of Treasons which decreed that anyone who, either in words or writings, maliciously deprived the King of his title of Supreme Head was to be reputed a high traitor. The word 'maliciously' had been included only after a hot debate between Cromwell and the Parliament, packed body though they were. They had won, pathetically hoping thereby to set some limitation on the Act.

As Cromwell had expected, there immediately began to be a great coming and going between Abbots and Priors, for the new Oath was being administered throughout the kingdom. While the stricter Religious Orders had taken but little interest in the King's matrimonial affairs, unlike the Friars who were itinerant preachers and lived among the people, this new Act of Supremacy was a very different matter. Hearing that the Priors of the Charterhouses of

Axholme and Beauvale were come up to consult with their head, Prior Houghton of the London Charterhouse, Cromwell summoned them, together with a Brigittine monk of Syon, a secular priest, and Houghton's Procurator, to wait upon him and take the Oath. As he had hoped, they all refused; they were tried; the jury were about to accept their plea that they had not refused 'maliciously' as expressed in the Act, when Cromwell appeared in person and threatened the jurors with the King's wrath. All were condemned and sent to the Tower to await death.

It was a test case establishing a fatal precedent. But in Cromwell's view it was something else. It was what he needed to persuade Henry that the Religious Houses in general were hot-beds of treason and ought to be dissolved.

The day after the condemnation of the Carthusians and their companions, Cromwell went down to the Tower. With him went Sir Christopher Hale, Attorney-General, Sir Richard Rich, Solicitor-General, Thomas Bedell, and smooth-tongued archdeacon, Clerk of the Council, and Dr John Tregonwell, who had been Proctor for the King in the annulment of his marriage. The constable, warned of the coming of these great personages, had prepared for them the best apartment in his lodging; and thither presently was summoned Thomas More.

Cromwell regarded him with some curiosity. For several weeks past, More had been kept a close prisoner, which meant that his family and friends could no longer have access to him, nor was he allowed to hear Mass at either of the Tower chapels. Cromwell deliberately had refrained from giving the prisoner any reason for this change, choosing to leave him a prey to horrible suspicions that it might be the prelude to torture. The effect of all this on a man who was now in very bad health, and who, so Cromwell knew (he who could spy out the secret weaknesses of all men), feared physical pain, must surely have broken him. But, so Cromwell noticed with disgust, though More's old gown hung loose on his shrunken frame, and the hair showing under his cap was plentifully streaked with grey, his eyes were as bright as ever and his manner as brisk and cheerful.

'Doubtless, Mr More,' began the Secretary, 'you have been shown the new Statutes.'

'Yes, verily,' replied More. 'However, forasmuch as being now a close prisoner I have no conversation with any people, I redelivered the book shortly, and the effect of these Statutes I never studied to put in remembrance. I concern myself, sir, with the *Treatise on the Passion* I am writing, which appears to me a more fit occupation for a poor prisoner than in studying Statutes which cannot concern him.'

'In this you are mistaken,' said Rich. 'It is now by Act of Parliament established that his Highness and his heirs be, and ever rightly have been, Supreme Head of the Church of England under Christ; and the King's pleasure is that those of his Council here present demand your opinion and what your mind is therein.'

'I do not remember,' More said impassively, 'that the words "under Christ"; occurred in the Statute.'

Rich bit back a curse. He had slipped in those words in order to trick More, and it seemed he had failed.

'You said just now that you had not studied the Statute,' he grumbled.

'In good faith,' said More, letting this pass, 'I had well trusted that the King's Highness would not have commanded any such question to be demanded of me, considering that I have from the beginning truly declared my mind unto him. And now I will neither dispute kings' titles nor popes,' but the King's true faithful servant I am and will be, and daily pray for him and his; and otherwise than this I never intend to meddle.'

'His Grace is merciful,' purred Dr Bedell, 'and is anxious that you should have your liberty again, provided only that you will submit to his will in this matter.'

'For a very truth, I will never meddle in the world again to have the whole world given me,' More cried with vehemence. 'But my whole study shall be upon the Passion of Christ and mine own passage out of this world. I do nobody harm, I say no harm, I think no harm, but wish everybody good. And if this be not enough to keep a man alive, in good faith I long not to live.'

Cromwell signed to the warder to take him away, and the commissioners conferred together. Would it be an idea to tell him that Fisher had taken the Oath? No, it was unlikely he would believe it, or, if he did, be moved by it. Fisher had not believed them when they had told him More had taken it.

'There is one thing I think may move him,' Cromwell said meditatively. 'Or rather I should say one person. We shall see.'

It was four days later when Meg came hurrying to the Bulwark Gate and showed the man on duty there an order, signed by Cromwell himself, summoning her to visit her father on this day at the hour of noon. Even as she arrived at the gate, the many bells of London rang out mid-day Angelus, saluting the Mother of God. The warder, taking off his cap and mumbling the prayers, looked at her sideways with a faint compassion; then he beckoned to one of his fellows to conduct her to the Bell Tower.

There was no entrance to the Bell Tower from the Outer Ward, so that it was necessary to pass under the great vault of the Bloody Tower with its two portculises, into the Inner Ward and so through an entry next door to the Lieutenant's lodging. She had been so preoccupied in wondering about the reason for this sudden summons, imagining her father being taken mortally sick, that she had not noticed the number of extra guards at gateways and upon the ramparts; but now, entering the Inner Ward, she became aware that this was some special occasion. The open space before the White Tower, the heart of the fortress, was filled with horsemen, all of them in armour and some with their faces concealed by vizards. They had the air of men waiting tensely for something or somebody, and as Meg went towards the entrance to the Bell Tower she asked her conductor whether the King was visiting the fortress.

'No mistress,' he answered briefly, giving her that same odd glance with which his comrade at the gate had regarded her.

Her father was standing at the window with his back to the door, but turned sharply as he recognized her footstep. As he stared at her, there came into his eyes a horror she had never seen there before; he came quickly to her and took her in his arms.

'My Meg, why have you come here today?'

She told him, showing him the order signed by Cromwell. He muttered something which sounded like, 'God forgive him!', and then said very tenderly:

'You must be brave, my darling. Doubtless they think that your distress will shake me, for a fainter heart than your frail father has, you cannot have. But we will give them the lie. Will you come with me to the window and watch some great good men starting on their road to martyrdom?'

The blood fled from her face and her mouth was dry, but she could not fail him. She took his hand, drawing strength from it, and together they walked steadily to the window looking down upon the Outer Ward. Even as they reached it, the head of a procession began to emerge through the vaulted archway of the Bloody Tower.

It was a company of billmen, the sun glinting on their crescent-shaped blades and their polished breastplates, their mailed shoes ringing on the flagstones. Behind them, guarded by halberdiers and archers, came something which made Meg draw one sobbing breath. On a wide hurdle fastened by traces to a horse, lay two figures flat upon their backs, bound by ropes to the sled, garbed in familiar white habits, their tonsured heads bumped violently up and down by the unevenness of the ground. Behind this hurdle followed two more; then came a terrible figure in tight black hosen and tunic, bearing upon his shoulder a short-handled axe. And rattling out in their mail, the plumes on their helmets gay and colourful, the great company Meg had seen in the courtyard brought up the rear.

She had seen executions, for they were common enough in the London of her day, but this was something new, and for the first time she realized fully the absolutism of the King. That the manner of taking the Carthusians and their companions to Tyburn had been arranged by him was plain; he had sent the principal personages at his Court to represent him, and in order to impress on the people that he was indeed supreme in Church as well as State, the religious were to be executed in their habits. Even as she stared in horrified fascination, the mask covering the face of one of the horsemen slipped out of place; he shot up a hand to adjust it, but not before she had recognized the countenance of the Earl of Wiltshire, father of Anne Boleyn.

She turned to look at her father, and surprised on his face something resembling envy.

'Lo, Meg,' he murmured, 'do you not see that these blessed fathers be now as cheerfully going to their deaths as bridegrooms to their nuptials? Wherefore you may see what a great difference there is between such as have spent

241

all their days in a straight, hard, penitential life, and such as have in this world, as your poor silly father has done, consumed all their time in pleasure and ease. For God, considering their long continued life in grievous penance, will no longer suffer them to remain here in this vale of misery; whereas, not thinking your silly father worthy so soon to come to that eternal felicity, God leaves him still in this world.'

But she was not listening. She was looking at the aloof faces of the martyrs passing below, seeing them as they soon would be, befouled with the fifth and the dust of the London streets, distorted by the half strangling noose. Stately as princes they were now; in an hour they would be a collection of bloody pieces, head, arms, and legs hacked off, bowels ripped out, trunks flung into a common pit.

'Father!' she cried frantically, 'you called me brave, but I am a woman and your daughter. Tell me they could never do that to you!'

'They can do me no hurt if they do me wrong,' he said steadily. 'Which is like a riddle, a case in which a man may lose his head and have no harm. And be assured of this, Meg; I will never run heedlessly upon my death; I will not tempt God, lest for my presumption He suffer me to fall.'

(iii)

Cromwell's trick to shake More through his daughter's distress had failed, and he would have to try some new devices. While both More and Fisher steadily refused to assert that Henry *was* Supreme Head, they remained safe from the Act of Treasons which had made it a capital offence to say or to write that Henry was *not*. Cromwell had failed too in breaking the resistance of the Carthusians, even though the bloody arm of their Prior was fastened over the door of their house. With them he had recourse to torture; three of them he confined in the Tower dungeons, fastened to posts by iron collars and great fetters, never to be loosed for any natural necessity, and nine others he sent to the filthy hole called Limbo in Newgate for similar treatment.

But such methods could not be used with More and Fisher. They were public figures, the City was hot for them, especially for More, for so long its Under Sheriff. He could only hope that by rigorous and prolonged cross-examination he would induce these sick and lonely old men to slip from a refusal to acknowledge the King's supremacy to a denial of it.

Fisher was at the moment too ill to be questioned, but More was brought almost daily to the Lieutenant's lodging for interrogation.

'We demand, Master More,' said Cromwell, 'that you either acknowledge it lawful that the King is Supreme Head, or plainly utter your malignity.'

'Since I have no malignity, I cannot utter it.'

'Now I must tell you that I like you very much worse today than I did the last time I examined you. For evidence has been disclosed that you have, by secret means, held converse and communication with my Lord of Rochester, which seeing you are both close prisoners, is a heinous offence. Call Richard Wilson.'

This was Fisher's servant, who was hustled into the room and stood twisting his cap and shuffling his feet, abashed in the presence of these fine gentlemen.

'Say what you have carried between your master and the prisoner here,' he was commanded.

'Please your honours,' faltered Wilson, 'there was half a custard last Sunday. My Lord Bishop being so sick was not able to eat it, and says he to me –'

'What else have you carried?'

Wilson scratched his head.

'Well, your honours, it were a long time ago – Lammastide, I think it were, though I'd not take my Gospel oath on't – but it were a green salad I gave to George Golde, Master Lieutenant's man, to carry to Master More, for my Lord Bishop says, Master More be marvellous fond o' green stuff; he don't ever eat no meat, he says, but herbs and such-like – '

'You are amused, it seems, Mr More,' Cromwell broke in coldly. 'But I wonder what was in that custard and that salad.' He shot out an accusing finger. 'I think there were notes inside them, a hatching of treason between my Lord of Rochester and you.'

'Then I marvel they did not give me an aching belly,' said More, still smiling. 'For I assure you I ate them to the last spoonful and the last leaf.'

His own servant, John Wood, was called next; he was protesting that all he had carried from his master to the Bishop was some fruit, when Cromwell cried wrathfully:

'You lie, you knave! You carried a New Year's gift to my Lord of Rochester. Confess, or I will have you racked.'

'Nay, tell their worships, John,' said More gently. 'Speak the truth, man; never fear.'

The ashen lips whispered:

'It – it were – two thousands pounds in gold.'

One of the commissioners fairly leapt from his seat; a medley of questions and exclamations broke out. Where had Mr More contrived to hide this huge sum, when all his goods were forfeit? Audley rounded on the Lieutenant; so this was how he fulfilled his trust, was it allowing close prisoners to secrete fortunes. In the midst of the to-do More broke in, his face alight with humour.

'Pray, sirs, allow John to inform you exactly what it was he carried to my Lord Rochester.'

'It were a piece of paper,' quavered the servant, 'shaped into a bag, and on it my master wrote somewhat. I can't read, but says he to me, "These words and figures, John, signify two thousands pounds in gold, which my Lord Bishop will understand is the New Year's gift I would send him if I could, so deep is the love and reverence I bear him." '

'Your quaint humour does not desert you, I see, Mr More,' Cromwell said thinly. 'You must pardon us, his Grace's loyal subjects, if we deem such levity out of place. Now there are three questions I must put to you; and pray restrain your delight in fooling, for I warn you they touch you near. First, will you obey the King as the Supreme Head of the Church in England?'

'I regret I can make no answer.'

'Will you acknowledge the King's marriage with Queen Anne to be lawful?'

'I have never spoken against it, nor will I.'

'Lastly, since by the Statute you, the King's subject, are bound to answer my first question, what objection do you make to saying whether or not you recognize his Grace as Supreme Head?'

More replied in exactly the same words as before:

'I regret I can make no answer.'

It was all they could get out of him.

At the end of May tidings reached England that the new Pope, Paul III, had created Fisher a Cardinal, obviously hoping that this great dignity would save him. Instead it so increased the King's wrath, Henry swearing that if Fisher ever wore the Hat it should be on his shoulders, for he would have no head to put it on, that Cromwell was driven to extreme measures. A few days later Sir Richard Rich, the Solicitor-General, called to see him, plainly in the best of humours.

'At last!' he exclaimed, as soon as they were alone. 'We have caught Fisher.'

He sat down and continued complacently:

'I flatter myself no man could have carried matters with more adroitness. I told him as we arranged that the King, for the satisfaction of his own conscience, desired to know the opinion of his old tutor touching the Supremacy. He reminded me of the recent Act of Treasons; but I told him the King had willed me to assure him on the royal word that whatsoever he should say to me in secret he should abide no peril by it; no, although his words were never so directly against the Statute, seeing it was but a declaration of his mind secretly to me, as to the King's own person. And I added that his Grace, for the love and reverence he bears his lordship, was inclined to abide by his advice.'

Rich paused for effect.

'He said these words to me, and I do not think he will have the face to deny them if brought to trial: "I believe directly in my conscience, and know by my learning precisely, that the King is not, nor can be by the Law of God, Supreme Head of the Church in England." Those were his very words.'

'We have him fast,' said Cromwell. He put his hands round his neck, choked, and gave Rich a roguish wink.

'And his Grace's fury against him is much increased,' added Rich, 'by the tale sent him from Rochester. It seems the commissioners sent thither to seize the Bishop's goods came upon a coffer in his private oratory, and the chaplains making a great pother to secrete it, 'twas thought there must be some rare treasure within. But when the commissioners broke it open, all they found was a hair shirt and one or two disciplines.'

Cromwell was not attending. He said thoughtfully:

'Since you have been so successful in entrapping my Lord of Rochester, it is in my mind that you try what you can do with Mr More. But I warn you, he is as slippery as an eel. Hark you now what method you shall use with him.'

More was busy writing his *Treatise on the Passion* in his prison room; he was engaged on a description of Judas' betrayal, when his door was unlocked and two men entered, Sir John Palmer, Sheriff of Surrey, and Richard Southwell, who held some minor post at Court.

'We have orders to remove your books and papers, Master More,' Southwell abruptly informed him; and straightway both men began stuffing these articles into sacks they had brought for the purpose.

They were in the midst of this task, when the door opened again, and in strolled Sir Richard Rich, with the air of a man who has nothing to do. He greeted the prisoner in a friendly way, regretted that he now must lose his silent friends, the books he loved so much, and then blurted out that he was troubled and would be most grateful for Mr More's advice.

'Forasmuch as it is well known,' said he, 'that you are a man both wise and learned, as well in the laws of the realm as otherwise, I pray you therefore, sir, let me be so bold as to put unto you this case for the easing of my mind. Suppose there were an act of Parliament that all the realm should take me for King. Would not you, Master More, take me for King?'

'Yes, sir, that would I,' More replied tranquilly.

'I put the case further,' continued Rich, inwardly gleeful, outwardly earnest, 'that there were an Act of Parliament that all the realm should take me for Pope. Would not you, then, Master More, take me for Pope?'

More regarded him in silence for a moment, his head to one side like an intelligent terrier's, his face extra solemn. Then he said:

'For answer, sir, to your first case. The Parliament may well, Master Rich, meddle with the state of temporal princes. But to make answer to your other case: Suppose the Parliament would make a law that God was not God. Would you then, Master Rich, say that God was not God?'

Master Rich held his peace, inwardly fuming. More, meanwhile, was closing the shutters at his window.

'Why do you do that, sir?' snapped the discomfited Rich.

More flapped a hand towards the sacks of books and papers, and answered merrily:

'Now that the goods and implements are taken away, the shop must be closed.'

(iv)

Cromwell wasted no more time. Trickery had failed with More, but the royal lion was roaring for prey and Cromwell must give it him, lest perhaps he turn upon his keeper. Three of the tortured Carthusians were executed at Tyburn with the full barbarities; and on June 17th old Fisher, who was so far recovered that he was able to totter along with the aid of a stick, was brought to his trial in Westminster Hall.

There was only one witness against him, Sir Richard Rich, who repeated the private conversation in which, on the King's promise of secrecy, he had induced the Bishop to declare his mind on the title of Supreme Head. Fisher confessed that he had spoken the words, but describing the circumstances maintained that they could not have been spoken "maliciously".

'If I made the promise to you in such sort as you have declared,' said Rich, with an impudent shrug, 'I would be glad to know what discharge this is to you in law?'

The judges, very solemn, ruled that in law not even the King's command to Fisher to speak his mind made him less guilty of treason, and that the word 'malicious' in the Act was void and superfluous, seeing that any man speaking against the King's Supremacy must needs have malice in his heart.

Three days later the Court staged a great masque for his Grace's entertainment. The Beast of Apocalypse came up out of a trap-door into a tinfoil sea, the men inside him roaring lustily and the diadems upon his seven heads flashing in the torchlight; a knight, clothed for the occasion in the King's own armour, engaged the Beast in combat, and duly presented the seven heads, realistically bleeding red paint, at the feet of his Grace, who laughed savagely.

'So will we do,' roared Henry, 'to all those Bishops who presume to utter blasphemies against us who are God's Vice-regent.'

While this gruesome farce was taking place at Greenwich, old Fisher, spared the full sentence of the law because he would certainly have died on the hurdle, was being carried in a chair to Tower Hill; and when his aged neck had been severed at a blow, his emaciated corpse stripped naked and left all day on the scaffold, the halberdiers who guarded it putting a little of the bloody straw about the privities out of seemliness, the executioner put the head in a bag and was rowed upstream against the tide. He was landed at the southern end of the Bridge, under the shadow of St Mary Overie, the priory church of the Augustinian Canons. Upon the towered gate he climbed, and fixed the head to a vacant pike which stood among a little forest of these weapons, each bearing its gruesome fruit.

It was full summer. In the smokeless air the outlines of the houses which lined the Bridge were clear and sharp; the windows in the Chapel of St Thomas of Canterbury, which stood in the middle of the old stone structure, glowed like rubies in the sunset light. The Bridge had always been the busiest spot in London; strings of packhorses threaded their way through the crowding humanity on the narrow roadway; on the ground floors of the beetling wooden houses mercers and haberdashers did a brisk trade; workmen constantly repaired the dilapidations caused by fire and erosion; and there was periodic congestion when the drawbridge in the centre must be raised to allow tall ships to pass.

But now to this crowded mass of folk were added sightseers who blocked the southern gatehouse. Shading their eyes against the sun, heedless of the shouts of those who wished to pass, they stared in awe at the grim forest of heads impaled upon the pikes above, and as they stared they muttered to each other.

'He looks fresher than ever today. I never see him look so healthful in his life.'

'Look at his eyes! They're never the eyes of a dead man.'

'They say there's a kind of light shines round him in the night-time.'

The kites and crows hovered and fought over that dreadful fruit; but it was observed that they never touched the head of Bishop Fisher. In ale-house and in market the talk of a miracle increased, and the very constables sent by the Mayor to disperse the crowds lingered to stare with the rest at those large brown eyes, at the face which showed no signs of corruption, at the mouth which seemed at any moment about to speak.

'But skin and bone he was when he took off his gown on the scaffold,' London remembered, 'and yet how clear was his voice when with his dying breath he bade us pray for the King's Grace.'

All sorts of tales were recounted. Of how, when a false rumour had got round that he was to die on a certain day, his servant had brought him no dinner, and the Bishop had chided him gently.

'Well, you see me yet alive; and therefore whatsoever news you hear of me hereafter, let me not lack my dinner, but make it ready, and if you see me dead when you come, then eat it yourself.'

And when he had been waiting for the Sheriff's men to carry him to the place of execution (because he was too weak to walk), he had opened his Bible at random, asking that some comforting words might be shown him, and his eye had lighted on the last prayer of Christ for His disciples. Fisher had shut the book, exclaiming joyfully:

'Here is learning enough for me to my life's end!'

They had tumbled his headless corpse flat on its belly in a grave hastily scraped out with halberds, without sheet or shroud, as though the most learned and best loved Bishop in England had been a dog.

At last, when the tale began to creep round of how the head had been carried direct from the scaffold to the Queen, and that Anne had struck it on the mouth, thereby suffering a scratch upon her hand which would not heal, the King acted. The citizens awoke one morning to see an empty pike among that forest on the southern gateway of the Bridge; during the night, Fisher's head had been cast into the Thames.

But another head, scarcely less venerated, was soon to replace it. On July 1st Sir Thomas More was rowed the two and a half miles up the busy river to stand his trial in that Westminster Hall where he himself had administered justice when he was Lord Chancellor; and all knew what the verdict must be.

Chapter Five

(i)

Under the superb hammer-beam roof, all carved with angels, the little procession came slowly, the executioner walking in front with the axe's head turned away from the prisoner, and More hobbling along in the midst of a guard of billmen. There was a great groan of pity from the citizens who loved him as they saw the long white beard, the drawn face, the uncertain steps, the eyes dulled by long confinement. But his voice had the old firm cheerful ring when he answered to the long indictment, in which the world 'maliciously' occurred no less than eight times.

'Treason' he said, 'lies in word or deed, but not in silence. For this my silence neither your law not any law in the world is able justly and rightly to punish me. And the maxim of the civil law, *Qui tacet, consentire videtur*, would seem to construe my silence rather as ratification than as condemnation of your Statute,' he added with his irrepressible sense of humour.

'But we shall prove that you have not kept silence,' the Lord Chancellor told him.

Sir Richard Rich was called and sworn. With an air of reluctance he repeated the conversation he had had with the prisoner when he had chanced to visit him on the

252

occasion of his books and papers being removed; only now the end of that conversation was slightly different.

'And in reply to my answering his fanciful question, that no Parliament could say that God was not God, Master More said roundly: "No more can Parliament make the King Supreme Head of the Church."'

There was a sudden breathless hush. Then More spoke.

'If I were a man, my lords,' he said, his voice low but each word distinct, 'that did not regard an oath, I needed not to stand as an accused person. And if this oath of yours, Mr Rich, be true, then pray I that I never see God in the face.'

In the same quiet even tones he recounted exactly what had passed between himself and Rich on the occasion; but then suddenly he rounded on his accuser, and the nerves of all present thrilled to the passion he unleashed.

'In good faith, Mr Rich, I am sorrier for your perjury than for my peril! I, as you know, of no small while have been acquainted with you and your conversation, who have known you from your youth, for we long dwelled in one parish together, where, as yourself can tell (I am sorry you compel me so to say) you were esteemed very light of your tongue, a great dicer, and of no commendable fame. Can it therefore seem likely to your honourable lordships,' he went on, turning in contempt from Rich, 'that I would utter to such a man the secrets of my conscience, which I have refused to reveal to any of his Grace's Councillors, nay, not even to my own wife?'

'Now by the Mass!' Rich shouted furiously, 'it may well be seen how loyal a subject you are when you would name his Grace's Solicitor General a perjurer, and that in open court. But I will give you the lie in your teeth, for here be those who were witnesses to our conversation.'

Sir John Palmer and Richard Southwell were called; but though both were Court officials and now obviously in some terror, all attempts to make them swear to the truth of what Rich had said proved useless. They repeated over and over again that they had been too busy trussing up the prisoner's books and papers to hear anything that passed between him and Sir Richard Rich.

Audley was about to pronounce judgement when More very courteously but firmly interrupted him.

'When I sat where your noble lordship sits now, the manner of such case was to ask the prisoner why judgment should not be given against him.'

The judges conferred in whispers. They had been instructed by the King not to let More speak at any length for fear of the impression he would make on the spectators; yet in common decency, they decided, they could not refuse him this ancient privilege.

'You are so fond of the maxim, *Silence is golden*,' sneered Audley, 'that we did not think you would wish to break this precious silence of yours. However, say what you desire.'

More bowed without a touch of irony. Those nearest him noticed how he drew himself up, squaring his shoulders; he would speak his mind at last.

'Seeing that you are determined to condemn me (God knoweth how), I will discharge my conscience touching my Indictment and your Statute withal. And forasmuch as this Indictment is grounded upon an Act of Parliament directly repugnant to the Laws of God and His Holy Church, the supreme government of which, or of any part thereof, may no temporal prince presume by any law to take upon him, as rightfully belonging to the See of Rome – '

'Now indeed you speak plain!' exulted Audley. 'Now all the world may hear your treason proclaimed by your own mouth.'

Ignoring the interruption, and slightly raising his voice, More continued:

'– the See of Rome, which is possessed of a spiritual pre-eminence given by the mouth of Our Saviour Himself only to St Peter and his Successors, Bishops of the same See, therefore in law, among Christian men, this Indictment is insufficient to charge any man. For like as the City of London, being but one member in respect of the whole realm, may not make a law against an Act of Parliament which binds the whole realm, no more may this realm, being but one member and small part of the Church, make a particular law disagreeable with the general law of Christ's Universal Catholic Church. So also is it contrary to the rights and liberties of the Church affirmed in the first clause of Magna Carta, to the Sacred Oath taken by the King's Highness at his Coronation, and to the continuity of English Christianity.'

'Yes, indeed ye see plainly now,' said Audley, addressing the spectators, 'what malice is in this prisoner.'

'Then also do you perceive what malice was in the dead of these thousand years past,' cried More, 'of whom many be now saints in Heaven, and as such are venerated; for while they lived they thought in this case the way I think now. But as for malice, it was very and pure necessity for the discharge of my conscience that has enforced me to speak as I have done. Wherein I appeal to God, whose sight pierces to the very depths of man's heart, to be my witness.'

In a silence broken only by the weeping of the crowd, Audley pronounced the full sentence of high treason. The prisoner listened apparently unmoved; and when Audley asked him the formal question as to whether he had any more to say, he answered with that charm which had made him universally beloved:

'More have I not to say, my lords, but that like as the blessed Apostle St Paul was present and consented to the death of St Stephen, and yet they are now both twain holy saints in Heaven, and shall continue there friends together for ever, so I verily trust, and shall therefore rightly pray, that though you lordships have now here on earth been judges to my condemnation, we may hereafter in Heaven all merrily meet together, to our everlasting salvation.'

His step had been slow and hesitant when he had come up the Hall to his trail. It was brisk and confident as he turned down again in the midst of the billmen, with the axe's edge turned towards him so that on his journey to the Tower all London might read his fate.

(ii)

Upon the Wharf, which extended along the whole river frontage of the Tower, a great crowd watched for his coming.

The older men among them remembered him as a little boy at St Anthony's School in Threadneedle Street, disputing in Latin with his fellows under a great elm there. There was a man who had been with him in Cardinal Morton's household and told his fellows how when plays were acted, More would step in among the players and make a part of his own, to the great delight of his master. There were lawyers who had known and revered him at New Inn and Lincoln's Inn. Many had heard his public lecture in St Laurence Jewry; or they had listened to him speaking on behalf of the City at the Guildhall. The educated among them had read his books, especially his famous *Utopia*. They had venerated the late Bishop Fisher; but More was a citizen born and bred, a freeman of the Mercer's Company, Under Sheriff before he had entered the King's service, habitually remitting the fees of both plaintiff and defendant, as Lord Chancellor sitting in his open hall to receive suitors and settle disputes, entertaining the poor at his own table, building almshouses for them and putting them under the care of one of his daughters.

Talking thus, the crowd upon the Wharf cast compassionate glances at the little group huddled together near Traitor's Gate, at that united family who had lost all worldly honours and nearly all worldly possessions, and who were soon to lose their father.

Meg stood within her foster-sister's sheltering arm, glancing now and again at the homely face which was so strong and steadfast. Margaret Clement was one of those doggedly heroic women who shrink from nothing if it is a work of mercy; she had even penetrated to that fearful black hole in Newgate and had washed and fed the fettered Carthusians until the Keeper; terrified of the King's wrath, had forbidden her to come. Throughout these past months she had been a tower of strength to the stricken family at Chelsea; and now, as the craning of the crowd in one direction informed the sensitive Meg that her father's barge was approaching, Meg would have fallen but for that strong supporting arm.

There were whispers among the crowd as it was seen that Sir William Kingston, Constable of the Tower, was in tears, used though he was to escorting prisoners through that fatal gateway; perceiving the pathetic little family group upon the Wharf, he shouted an order to the billmen to stand back, and himself assisted More to land for a moment so that he might take farewell of his children.

They knelt for his blessing, and he embraced them, bidding them have patience, reminding them that nothing could happen without God willed or permitted it, promising they would all be merry in Heaven. He was returning to the boat; in a moment the vaulted archway would swallow him from their sight for ever. But before that moment came, Meg tore herself from Margaret's sustaining arm. Reckless of danger, caring nothing for the onlookers, filled with a sort of superhuman strength, she fought her way through the billmen, pushing aside their sharp weapons, and once more flung herself into her fathers' arms, kissing him again and again, crying aloud that she was proud he was to die in God's quarrel, begging his prayers that his family might be given a like fortitude if the same were demanded of them.

He said as though they were alone:

'My dearly beloved daughter, I never liked your manner towards me better than I do at this instant. For your dear love takes no regard of what the world thinks.'

(iii)

Never again would he be allowed visitors, but each day Meg sent her maid, Dorothy Colley, to beg for news of him. On July 5th, Dorothy brought to Chelsea his hair shirt and discipline; and secreted in the shirt Meg found a note, written with charcoal. There were loving messages for his wife, his children, and his grandchildren, and he concluded:

'I would be very sorry if my execution be delayed after tomorrow, for it is the octave-day of SS. Peter and Paul, and likewise the eve of the Translation of St Thomas, my heavenly patron. And therefore tomorrow long I to go to God. Pray you it may be so, with His good liking.'

On that same day his servant, John Wood, was discharged from attendance on the prisoner, and came to Chelsea where the family spent most of their time in the chapel of the New Building which the master of the house had built for his studies and devotions.

'Master Secretary came to see my master this morning,' John told them, 'to try if he could tempt him to recant. "Why," says master, "if you intend by this to ask me whether I have changed my mind, I may tell you I have changed it." But as Master Cromwell cried out all joyful and triumphant, says master, very solemn. "Whereas I meant to be shaven, now have I decided to let my beard share the fate of my head." '

'What a man for his jest!' wept Dame Alice, her homely face all blotched with tears. 'But do you mean, John – '

'Yes, mistress,' said the servant eagerly. 'They have told him that the King's Grace, out of his royal clemency, will not have him hanged and quartered but is content that he shall lose his head. Then says master merrily, "God forbid the King should use any more such mercy unto any of my friends." '

Late that night, an official of the Tower, Sir Thomas Pope, came to Chelsea to break the news that the prisoner must die next day. Pope himself was overwhelmed with grief, for he was devoted to learning and had always hero-worshipped the great humanist.

'It was I,' he lamented, 'who was ordered to inform him he must suffer before nine tomorrow morning. He thanked me heartily for what he termed my good tidings, and said that whereas he had always been much bounden to his Grace for the benefits and honours the King had heaped upon him from time to time, he was still more bounden to his Highness that it pleased him now to rid him of the miseries of this wretched world. Then I told him it was his Grace's pleasure that at his execution he should not use many words (for they are in dread of the impression he may make upon the people). Whereat he thanked me again, saying he had intended to speak somewhat, though in no wise as could offend his Grace, but that nevertheless he was as ready as ever to conform himself to the King's commands, so they did not violate his conscience.'

When Pope had gone, Margaret Clement drew Meg aside and said to her:

'We are all given liberty to bury our dear father in the Chapel of St Peter and Vincula in the Tower, but neither Mother nor any of your sisters can bear to come. Will you meet me, therefore, on the morrow, with your brother John, that we three may perform this last service?'

'Meet you there?' whispered Meg. 'But you are staying here tonight, and so we may go together, Margot.'

'I shall be at the Tower before you,' Margaret said steadily. 'There were women at the foot of the Cross.'

(iv)

The three of them, with Dorothy Colley, took a boat early next morning, but at the first stairs within the City walls they separated, Margaret and John joining the crowds which were swarming towards the high ground west of the Tower, and who were avid to catch the last sight and hear the last words of this famous citizen; and Meg and her maid going from church to church, arranging for Masses for her father's soul and distributing money contributed by every member of his family for the poor he had loved so much. Her purse was empty when at last she too turned her steps towards the Tower, whence folk were now streaming back again, many of them in mourning, the women in tears, all of them exchanging anecdotes of what they had seen and heard.

'Never was such a man for fun and humour. Said he to the Under Sheriff as he climbed the steps to the scaffold, "I pray you, Mr Hall, see me safely up, and for my coming down let me shift for myself." '

'He embraced the executioner. "My neck is short," says he. "Don't strike awry, for saving of your honesty." '

'He set aside the cup of wine Mistress Clement offered him. "My Master had gall, not wine, to drink." I heard him say the words.'

'I'll not soon forget his last words. His voice rang out clear as a bell. "I do protest I die the King's good servant, but God's first." '

They battered at Meg, those voices. Her numb despair was pierced with bitterness. London loved him, but London had not raised a finger to save him; London, like the Bishops and the Parliament and the Court, was cowed by the carrion beast that must feed on the best men in the realm. And what had he accomplished? That merry, gentle, and wise father of hers was just a carcase to be buried within prison walls instead of in the tomb he had built for himself in quiet Chelsea, a head to be food for crows on London Bridge. And at Greenwich Henry laughed and feasted and staged masques.

Meg and her maid had nearly reached the Ald Gate when Meg stopped abruptly, with an exclamation of distress.

'I have forgotten to provide a shroud,' she faltered. 'I dared not watch him die, and cannot even be trusted to remember his winding-sheet. And now I have no money left to buy one.'

'We will buy some linen from a mercer's,' said the practical Dorothy. 'For surely, mistress, they will give you credit.'

'I am far from home, and no one knows me here. But go, good Dolly, go and try.'

Meg stood waiting in the crowded street, jostled by the throng, her mind drained and numb again. Presently she saw her maid coming back to her in haste, and under her arm she carried a roll of fine linen. Flushed, breathless, round-eyed, Dorothy gabbled:

'I went in and asked the shopman for as much as I needed, and when it was cut I put my hand into the purse, meaning to feign surprise at finding it empty. I had it all pat what I would say; that I had come out in a hurry, my master being lately dead, and that if the mercer would trust me I would fetch the price of the linen within the hour. But – '

She stopped, licked her lips, and drew a shuddering breath. 'Upon my salvation, mistress, what I tell you is true. In the purse I found the exact price of the linen, neither a farthing more nor a farthing less.'

They stared at one another for a long moment. Then Meg turned abruptly without a world, and continued her melancholy journey towards the Tower. But it was not melancholy and longer. Vivid in her memory was a letter she had received from her father long ago, when he had been on some embassy abroad and she had written to ask him, very timidly, for money to buy something on which she had set her heart.

'I sent only what you ask, dear Meg, but would have added more, only that as I am eager to give, so am I desirous to be asked and coaxed by my daughter whose virtue and learning has made her so dear to my soul... '

He still, it seemed, wanted to be asked and coaxed. He was not a headless carcase; he was the father she had always known. He was so near to her that, within an hour of his death, he was aware of her need of the moment and had hastened to supply it, neither more nor less desiring to be asked in future for all her needs, and not for hers alone.

He, and not the tyrant who had murdered him, would have the last word.

Chapter Six

It was spring of the following year.

In the great Abbey Church of Peterborough, in a plain tomb without inscription, slept Catherine the Queen. At Greenwich her supplanter, Anne, laughed shrilly with the younger gentlemen at Court, the only ones whom her arrogance and vanity had not alienated, collected incongruous compliments, bit her lips as she looked in her mirror and saw the warnings that her youth was past, ordered new gowns, flung herself frenziedly into inventing new games; and tried to forget the scorching words Henry had cried at her when, late in January, she had miscarried of a dead male child:

'When you are on your feet again, I will speak to you. I see plainly that I shall never have an heir by you.'

In that same palace, in apartments lately vacated by Mr Secretary Cromwell himself for the purpose, modest little Jane Seymour was installed, chaperoned by her elder brother Edward, now a Gentleman of the Privy Chamber, and his wife, apartments connected by a secret passage with the royal ones. Here this pale English wildflower, with her buttoned-up mouth and kittenish manner, daily received visits from his Grace – but always in the presence of her relatives.

263

At Lambeth Palace Archbishop Cranmer paced often up and down the gardens beside the flowing river; but it was not for the sake of the air, nor did his short-sighted eyes admire the beauty of the spring. His timid soul was troubled; he was having to burn heretics who denied the Presence of Our Lord in the Blessed Sacrament, he who for many years past had denied it in his own heart. And the King, determined to show Christendom that he was more Catholic than the Pope, was talking of a new measure whereby the celibacy of the clergy should be declared a law imposed by God, and not, as hitherto, an appointed discipline. Mrs Cranmer who comforted his leisure hours, would have to be shipped back to Germany.

In his new country retreat at Stepney, Thomas Cromwell was busier than ever. He had obtained for himself some new posts; as Vicar-General this layman was placed above the Archbishop and Bishops even in Convocation; and as Visitor-General he had achieved the power necessary to fulfil his greatest ambition. The last Act passed by the Parliament which had sat since 1532, had been to create a Court of Augmentation, whereof Sir Richard Rich was Chancellor; its function was to deal with all lands and goods coming into the King's possession through the suppression or surrender of the monasteries. And as Visitor-General, it lay with Cromwell to suppress or spare at his pleasure.

So far he was content to deal only with the smaller monasteries and convents. For before he could attack the great ones, the ground must be prepared. He spent a great deal of time and thought on this preparing. Frightful tales were circulated, the kind of sensational stuff which could be depended on to appeal to the ignorant; the monks were guilty of unnatural vice, their houses were dens of error and superstition, they mulcted the poor for mortuary dues, they duped the people with sham miracles; idleness was the least of their crimes. If the King's Grace took their wealth from them, he would never more need to tax his subjects; and when the monasteries were suppressed, any farmer who cared to cart it away might have the stone free for repairing his wall or building a new byre.

To combat the influence of the Friars, who preached in market-places, Cromwell filled the outdoor pulpits of London with tame preachers who could be depended upon to say what they were told, and who entertained the people with the grossest stories concerning the Religious whom the English had always revered; and to make quite sure, Cromwell issued an order on his own authority that all should come to hear the preacher at Paul's Cross every Sunday, under pain of the King's high displeasure. Cromwell was using his own authority now even as Wolsey had done. He had imbibed a contempt for Henry and his precious conscience; little did he guess that already the old process was beginning in his master, and that Henry had reached the secretly resentful stage.

The King's own ante-rooms were not more crowded with petitioners than were Master Secretary's. The old nobility who had hated him as soon as he had risen to power, pestered him for some of the spoils that were pouring in, offering him bribes to settle on them by private arrangement mills, woods, or revenues of the monasteries suppressed. Form terrified abbesses and harassed abbots came endless presents, fat wethers, geldings, partridges, gloves, fruit, and fish, even the pathetic little gift of a cheese.

'Our slender income' wrote a prioress, 'is but sixty-six pounds by the year, wherewith we have to maintain not only ourselves but twelve poor persons; but if our house be allowed to stand, you shall have a hundred marks, and all our prayers during our lives.'

265

'Pleaseth your mastership,' wrote the Abbot of Waverley, 'I have sent your mastership the true extent, value, and account of our said monastery. Beseeching your good mastership, for the love of Christ's Passion, to help me in the preservation of this poor monastery, that we bedesmen may remain in the service of God with the meanest living that any poor men may live with in this world, so to continue in the service of Almighty Jesus.'

Cromwell did not trouble to answer any of these letters, not even the timid note from Archbishop Cranmer asking for particulars of the policy as it would be applied in the case of the monastery of Christ Church, Canterbury. But he took the bribes.

In the midst of all this business, in intervals of studying reports from the disreputable agents he had picked for the visitation of the monasteries, Cromwell found time to make the notes he called his 'Remembrances', notes scribbled on the backs of documents and letters, in a cipher to which he alone had the key. Some of them were very mysterious little notes, and they did not concern the monasteries; they concerned Anne, the Queen. Cromwell never struck at a victim in caprice or passion; he ticked off the lives of human beings in his memoranda as if they were items in an account. And the time was fast approaching when he would have enough 'evidence' to tick off the life of the woman of whom the King was weary.

He read the little notes, his piggy eyes twinkling and flickering under his arched brows.

'Item. Two hours alone with her brother. Incest?' 'Item. Asked one Mark Smeaton, a lute-player, why he was so sad. Told her because she did not look at him as she was used.' 'Item. Dropped her kerchief from the gallery at a tournament on purpose to be picked up by F Weston.' 'Item. Chided H Norris for not loving his wife, and told him not to wait for dead men's shoes. The King's?' Yes, he decided, he had plenty with which to catch Anne. He would go to the King (who was pretending not to know what his faithful Cromwell was doing in the matter), tell him there were conspiracies hatching, and ask for a general commission to inquire into them.

And at Westminster or at Windsor or at Woodstock, moving restlessly from place to place, was Henry the King.

He alternated between moods of self-pity, the only pity of which he was capable now, and bursts of maniac rage. On the receipt of the news of Catherine's death he had felt for a moment that all was well, for there was no longer any fear of war with the Emperor; and it was this relief, he told himself, that had caused him to put on a new suit of yellow, the colour of joy, and to give a great banquet. But then the Pope had gone and issued a Bull of Deprivation against him, and was urging Francis and the Emperor to carry it out. Everyone seemed to take delight in thwarting him, even God, his only Head. There was this constant rain which had ruined last year's harvest; there was the sweating-sickness which was rampant again. If war came, the Flemish trade would be lost, and England ruined. Even his Parliament, which ought to have been so submissive since he himself had picked the Members, had shown the most unnatural reluctance to pass the Act of Suppression which would give into his Grace's hands the monasteries, those hot-beds of treason. But he had taught Parliament a lesson they would not be likely to forget. He had sent for the Commons, the whole lot of them, to wait on him one forenoon at Greenwich; he had kept them waiting there in the gallery till evening; then he had stalked in and said to them:

'I hear that my Bill will not pass. But I will have it pass, or I will have some of your heads.'

He was beginning to have an obsession with heads. Sometimes in his dreams he was wielding an axe, and in waking hours he found himself studying the necks of those about him, Cromwell's, thick and short, Norfolk's, spare and sinewy, Anne's, long and thin, embraced by her jewelled collar. His eyes grew dark with anger when he thought of the head of Thomas More, mysteriously stolen from the pike on London Bridge. More who had defied him with that last cry on the scaffold:

'I die the King's good servant, but God's first.'

How could he be God's servant when he was not the King's? What blasphemous presumption to have promised himself Heaven, that blessed region thinned out in Henry's imagination, inhabited only by those who had bowed to his will.

But at a certain point in his self-pity and his anger, he returned always to Anne, for his obsession with her was now the obsession of pure hate. She was to blame for everything, this witch who had seduced him into marriage.

On April 30th, Henry returned to Greenwich for the junketings of May Day. It was observed that he was oddly silent, and that his flat eyes watched the Queen as she fished for compliments and laughed as though she could not control herself.

(ii)

He sat beside her in the royal gallery above the lists, his gross figure sprawling on the cushions.

Strangely there came to his mind another great tournament he had staged in honour of St Michael, long ago. He had been down there in his armour then, young, athletic, flat-stomached, avid for the sport in which he was so expert; here, where Anne sat now, Catherine had sat, irritating him by her lack of interest in the technicalities of jousting, but conformable to his will and always with the manners of a great lady. Over there Wolsey had watched the sport, Wolsey whom he had loaded with honours, and who, though he had wickedly failed his master in the end, had been such a good companion, had had such an air of majesty, unlike this brutish Cromwell.

Tears of self-pity welled up into his eyes, and began to roll down his great cheeks, as he remembered how many lances he had splintered that day, how skilfully he had unhorsed the man who had been plain Lord Thomas Howard then; but he brushed the tears aside, for a gentleman in a livery very familiar to him was presenting him with a note. He broke the seal and read it surreptitiously between his hands. It was brief, unsigned, and in Cromwell's writing.

'M S has confessed his own adultery and that of H N and others. I have lodged him in the Tower for further questioning.'

He rose abruptly. Down below, Lord Rochford, Anne's brother, and Harry Norris, now Keeper of the Privy Purse, were riding back to their pavilions from a joust. The King sent one of his gentlemen to tell Norris that his grace was returning to London immediately, and required his company upon the way. Norris, thus hastily summoned, had scarcely time to get himself divested of his cumbrous tilting armour, and arrived breathless and sweating, the cap worn under his helm still tied upon his head. The king said never a word until the cavalcade was out in the open country; then he turned and beckoned sharply to Norris who, wondering greatly, rode up to his side.

'We have heard a most detestable thing of you,' Henry said without preliminaries. 'That you have had carnal communication with the Queen.'

Norris was speechless from shock.

'Confess,' continued Henry, 'and you shall have a free pardon. We believe you are more sinned against than sinning.'

'I would rather die than be guilty of such a falsehood!' cried Norris, finding his voice, 'And I am ready to prove it false in combat with anyone who thus accuses me.'

The King turned away from him, and summoning his guards, bade them take Norris to the Tower.

(iii)

The usual preparations for a great banquet and an elaborate masque had been made, but the King did not return from Westminster. And wherever she looked, Anne saw eyes quickly averted from her; the whole palace seemed full of an excited, mysterious whispering which had nothing to do with the May Day revels. The very pages bowing her through doorways had an air of secrecy; even the young men with whom she flirted, who ministered to her craving for compliments, were forced and unnatural in their response to her coquetry.

'Where is Mark Smeaton?' she asked her father. 'I have a mind for some music.'

He stroked his smooth beard and answered brutally:

'If you would have him, you must seek him in the Tower, for there he lies tonight.'

Her sallow face blanched.

'The Tower! But on what charge?'

'You should know, for it seems you had a finger in that pie.'

He looked directly at her rudimentary sixth finger, half concealed by her hanging sleeve. He had no pity for her; all his life he had made traffic of everything, of his wife's flirtations, his younger daughter's liaison, his elder girl's ambition; he had go an earldom as a result, and now he was busy collecting some of the richer spoils of the monasteries. All he was concerned about at present was to dissociate himself from Anne in her coming destruction.

Next day the palace was abuzz with the news. In the Queen's apartments her uncle, Norfolk, with other commissioners, were subjecting her to a long interrogation; ears pricked in anterooms heard Norfolk tut-tutting, the Queen's hysterical laugh, her voice upraised in delirious protest. The commissioners emerged presently, carefully locking the door behind them, and gave orders that the Queen's barge was to be ready at five o'clock.

By that hour all London knew what was happening, and the river was packed with wherries and barges, the banks were black with people. In a silence more ominous than execrations would have been, in that same silence which they had maintained at her coronation, they watched her handed into the barge which had been Queen Catherine's and now was embellished with the sham coats and emblems of the Boleyns. In that dreadful silence her voice rang out clearly:

'I to be a queen, and to so cruelly handled!'

On the first of the flood she was rowed up-river, and by way of Traitor's Gate entered the Tower. She had a glimpse of hostile faces packing the Wharf, before her barge entered the covered channel, under the Tower of St Thomas, beneath the roadway which divided the Outer and Inner Wards and so to the ring in the wall where the boat was tied. The portcullises of the Bloody Tower grinned at her with their iron teeth; a raven croaked a greeting. She collapsed upon the flagstones, beating her hands against her brow, and asked the Constable whether she was to be confined in a dungeon.

'No, madam,' Sir William Kingston told her gravely. 'You are to occupy the same apartments as those in which you stayed before your Coronation.'

'They are too good for me,' she whimpered, not knowing what she said, rambling, half out of her mind. 'Jesu have mercy on me!'

And then, fraying the nerves of all who heard it, pealed out her hysterical laugh.

Those apartments were near the Bell Tower, looking out upon the river. Four matrons were appointed to attend her, female warders ordered by Cromwell to note down every word she said. Two lay on a pallet in her room at night, Kingston and his wife slept at her door, and the other two ladies in the ante-room. There was plenty to report to Cromwell; all her old courage had deserted her, and mortal fear unloosed her tongue.

At one moment she would buoy herself up with hope.

'I think the King does this to prove me. Was it not only last Sunday that Harry Norris told my Almoner he would swear I was a pure woman?'

'Why, madam,' one of her wardresses asked slyly, 'should any such matters be spoken of?'

'Because I told Norris that if anything befell the King, he, Black Harry as I call him, would look to have me. If I had any such thought, said he, my head would fly. And then I said I could make him if I would, and therewith we fell out.'

Then she would passionately protest her innocence.

'I hear I shall be accused with four men, and I can say no more but nay – without I should open my body.' With a wild gesture, she plucked at the lacing of her gown. 'Oh Norris, hast thou accused me? Thou and I will die together. And Mark here too. Oh my mother, thou wilt die with sorrow! Master Kingston,' she cried, clutching his arm, kneading it in frenzy, 'shall I die without justice?'

'The poorest subject of the King has justice,' replied Kingston; at which she fell once more into her wild laughter.

At dinner she would be very merry, and then immediately afterwards, forgetting what time it was, ask why supper was not prepared.

'I am glad my brother is here in the Tower with me. Who else is here?'

They told her Norris, Sir Francis Weston, Sir Richard Page, Sir William Brereton, and Mark Smeaton, and that Sir Thomas Wyatt had just been arrested.

'All my admirers,' she laughed. 'Oh how poor Tom doted on me when I first came over from France! What love poems he wrote me! As for Smeaton, he never was in my chamber but at Winchester, and there I sent for him to play the virginal. He is wearing irons, you say? That is because he is no gentleman.'

She might not have been so indifferent to the treatment of poor Smeaton had she known that Cromwell had extracted his confession from him by tightening a knotted cord round his head.

'I knew the most part of England prays for me,' she said, with a self-deception that was new to her. 'And if I die you shall see the greatest punishments fall on the realm within this seven-year. But I shall be in Heaven, for I have done many good deeds; ask Smeaton how many charitable sums I bestowed on him.'

And then, bursting into tears, the moaned:

'Would I had my Archbishop by me; he would solicit the King on my behalf.'

(iv)

Her Archbishop was being ferried across from Lambeth to Westminster in a state of stark panic, for he was summoned to present himself in the Star Chamber. He had been the Boleyns' chaplain; he was godfather to the Princess Elizabeth; he had raced through the annulment of Henry's first marriage and pronounced the second one valid; he had crowned Anne.

Of all this he was reminded (had he needed reminding) by those of the Council assembled in the Star Chamber; and having been thoroughly frightened, was given a private interview with Cromwell.

'I shall have work for you anon, my Lord Archbishop,' said Cromwell. 'That is if, as I hope and believe, you will show yourself a true loyal subject of his Grace.'

Tremblingly Cranmer protested his absolute devotion to the King.

'What is desired,' said Cromwell, 'is that the King's present marriage be declared null and void, and – '

'A pre-contract with her sister,' Cranmer interrupted, so eager was he to please.

Mr Secretary regarded him with a pained air.

'I fear you have been listening to gossip,' said he severely. 'Gossip which must go no further; do you understand? No, a pre-contract between the Queen and the Earl of Northumberland when he was Lord Henry Percy; I have endeavoured to get the admission from him, but he refuses to speak. Therefore we must get it from her; and you, who showed such talent in the case of the Nun of Kent, are surely the man to obtain it, especially as she believes you her true friend.'

Cranmer swallowed, and said yes, yes. He was ready to say anything to make sure of his own safety.

A week later, under orders, he went to visit Anne in the Tower. Both she and her brother had been condemned the previous day, their own uncle, Norfolk, presiding at their trial, and her one-time suitor, Northumberland, saying 'Guilty' with the other peers. She had astonished them all by the real dignity with which she had listened to the extremely detailed and obscene charges, and to her many enemies vying with one another in accusing her of

274

mocking at the King's Grace, at his dress, his literary hobbies, and his impotence.

But now when she saw Cranmer, her Archbishop, her man, her protégé, she broke down, and on her knees implored him to plead for her to the King.

He promised. He begged her to be of good heart; he was, he said, her very friend. And the King was merciful to all who confessed their crimes and asked pardon; no, no, it was not a matter of carnal communication with the lovers who had been condemned and four of whom had been executed this very morning, but a little matter of a pre-contract with him who was now the Earl of Northumberland. She was bewildered, but snatched at the chance of obliging the incalculable Henry. Yes, indeed she and Lord Henry Percy had plighted their troth before witnesses; and then she fell to rambling again, remembering the details of that incident long ago, raging against Wolsey as though he still lived, calling Percy a spineless fool.

When Cranmer left her she was gay.

'I shall not die,' she told her wardresses. 'But I think I shall be sent abroad. I would like to go to France again; I was happy there. Or perhaps the King will send me to a convent; but no, there are to be no convents left in England now, I hear.'

As for Cranmer, he was back at Lambeth, writing to the King. He was shocked to hear, he wrote, of the Queen's guilt, of which he was now quite convinced. 'I am clean amazed, for I never had better opinion of woman.' Next day he held his Ecclesiastical Court to decide the interesting question whether this woman whom he had so solemnly declared to be Henry's wife really were so. The King's Proctors argued learnedly that she was not, basing their arguments on Anne's pre-contract with Lord Henry

Percy; and casting up his eyes to Heaven, invoking the name of the Lord, and protesting that he had God alone in his thoughts, Cranmer pronounced sentence that the marriage between Henry and Anne was and always had been null and void, and that the Princess Elizabeth was a bastard. The fact that if Anne were not Henry's wife she could not be guilty of the adultery for which she had been condemned to death, was tactfully ignored by all concerned.

Again Cranmer was ferried across the river to Westminster, where he found Henry reading a tragedy he had composed upon his own misfortunes.

'We long feared this would happen,' he told Cranmer, when the Archbishop had related the sentence of his own court. 'Our conscience has been much disquieted. And becoming aware of her abominable treasons, we have befallen our body. We verily believe she conspired our death, like the sorceress she is.'

Then he grew cheerful, clapped Cranmer on the shoulder, told him that his tender conscience was now quieted, and went off gaily to watch his darling, modest, meek little Jane having her portrait painted by Hans Holbein.

(v)

By condemning Anne either to burning or beheading according to his august pleasure, he had left her deliberately in an agony of suspense. Now, Cranmer's comfortable sentence given, he sent word that out of his great mercy he was content that she should lose her head. Next day she requested the presence of Sir William Kingston to see her receive the Sacrament and to hear her protest her innocence afterwards.

276

'Master Kingston,' she faltered, 'I hear I shall not die afore noon; I though to be dead by this time, and past my pain.'

He was the King's servant, but not without pity; and he, like many others, was beginning to have a revulsion of feeling in Anne's favour, partly because of the courage with which she had faced her accusers, partly because of the King's disgusting frolicsomeness with his new love.

'Madam, you will have no pain,' said Kingston gently, 'the doing of it will be so subtle. For knowing your very great fear of the axe, his Grace has sent to Calais for the only one of his subjects who knows how to behead with the sword. And therefore your death must be deferred until tomorrow.'

She began to laugh again, that terrible hysterical laughter.

'He sent Wolsey rings when he was planning his downfall, and he sends me a sword. But that executioner is swift and sure; I saw him at his work once while I was in France. And I have but a little neck –' putting her two hands about it '– but alack that I must put off my jewelled collar and show what I never would have seen. The jesters will have no difficulty in finding a nickname for me in history, *la Reine sans-tête*.'

He was shocked by her levity, and begged her to think of her soul. She grew grave for an instant, and said:

'I do not fear the Divine judgement except for my treatment of the Princess Mary. I would go on my knees to ask pardon of her for all I have done and said against her; for belike my own sweet child will have the same treatment, being named a bastard. Go now, Master Kingston; I must think of my little speech upon the scaffold, and choose what head-dress I shall wear. Head-dress!' And she stuffed her fingers into her mouth to stifle that mad, painful laughter.

(vi)

The sun rose in glory over Placentia upon the morrow, and with it rose Henry the King.

The royal toilet had become a painful business nowadays, both for Henry and his gentlemen; rising from dream-ridden sleep, racked by the pain of his ulcerating leg, he was at his most bad-tempered early in the morning. But not this morning. He laughed and jested while they arrayed him in a new costume of yellow silk sewn with diamonds, white silken hosen as in the old days, with the new rounded toes. He must be heavily perfumed; his auburn hair and beard meticulously brushed; he crammed ring after ring upon his thickening fingers, playfully cuffing a gentleman who dropped one of the precious things, humming the love-songs he had composed for Anne.

The nightmare was over, he reflected thankfully; and all had turned out for the best. He was cured of his infatuation for a wicked, adulterous witch; Catherine was dead; and in a week he would be truly married at last, without Pope or Emperor to say him nay. He was back where he had started, perhaps not the 'Adonis of fresh colour' of his Coronation, but certainly his people's wealth and earthly joy; and best of all his tender conscience was at peace at last. Like Job he had been tried, and like Job he was rewarded. Long ago he had plunged his arms to the elbows in his miserly father's treasure-chest; now he could plunge them into those same coffers replenished, by the special providence of God (his only Head), with the spoils of traitors who, in the sacred name of religion, had dared defy him.

He heard his three Masses. He had ordered the Archbishop to celebrate the first of them (little guessing how his outwardly orthodox Cranmer hated the Mass in his heart), and he offered them in thanksgiving. At his side

278

upon a velvet cushion knelt his appealing little Jane; he glanced fondly at her bowed head, feeling so protective towards her, who today was to be trothed to him, who would never dare to laugh at him, who had chosen for her motto, *Bound to serve and obey,* who was the ideal wife as described by St Paul, and who would bear him strong sons and prove his virility.

He was breakfasting on fish (for it was Friday), when he heard that for which he had been listening; the voice of a single great cannon booming out from the Tower.

He had a moment, just one fleeting moment, of uneasiness, almost of remorse. But here was Cranmer kneeling beside him, discreetly congratulating him on his deliverance from a wicked adulteress; and at the moment when the bleeding head and body of Anne Boleyn were being bundled into an arrow-chest (the provision for a coffin having been forgotten), Henry's huge hand clasped the timid white fingers of Jane Seymour, plighting his troth.

EPILOGUE

Fall of Night

On January 27th, 1547, Henry the King lay dying. The England he had ruled for nearly forty years was no longer a province of a united Christendom, and the very face of it had changed. Villages had shrunk, the populations of towns increased; fine new mansions had arisen, built of sculptured stone from some demolished house of God, by a rack-renting gentry who squeezed from their tenants every penny they could get so that they could make a good show at Court. The walls of these mansions were hung with rich altar-cloths, cupboards displayed gold chalices turned into drinking-vessels, copes of Eastern stuff skilfully embroidered with the needle now did duty as bedspreads or as my lady's Sunday gown.

Roofless walls filled with rank weeds marked the spot where small holders had lived, once the tenants of the easy-going monks who never raised rent who had taken wainloads of their own corn into the markets if the price of it rose there, and sold it to the poor below market price, who could always be relied on to lend seed or malt to some householder whose little patch had failed.

On the roads, churned up by the endless procession of carts carrying to the royal melting-pot in London lead stripped from abbey roofs, patens, censers, sanctuary lamps, cruets, processional crosses, and images (those treasures which Sunday by Sunday had brightened the dull lives of the peasants), hordes of beggars slunk along, self-respecting yeomen ruined by the enclosure of common and waste lands, widows, the old and infirm, almsmen and women whom the charity of the pious dead had supported. For the first time in history, poverty had become a crime; to beg one must wear a badge emblazoned with King Henry's arms to show his royal munificence.

The poor man shivered in the January cold; the monastery woods, where he had always been able to get free firing, had been cut down for the sale of their timber. The wayfarer paused wistfully by some ruined gatehouse where in the past he had been welcomed and received. Swelling the troops of mendicants were men and women who had been the stewards of the accumulated charity of generations; monks and nuns turned adrift into the world they had renounced, some making a long and painful journey to the coast to seek shelter in houses of their Order overseas, some searching for relatives long dead, some looking for work where there was none.

In town and country the wind whistled round heaps of rubble become common quarries, where once had stood the most noble architectural monuments of England. In the cloisters garths still showed black patches where bands of workmen sent from London had built fires of choir stalls, reredos, and rood for the melting of the head torn from the roofs. They were silent now, those ruins, but not so long ago they had echoed to the crash of sledge-hammer and crow-bar; they had been noisy with the voices of foreign merchants following like vultures in the footsteps of the royal Visitors, haggling at auctions, held on the spot, to buy cheap and sell dear, illuminated Mass-books, psalters, manuals, antiphonals, the results of a labour of love which had occupied some monk for a lifetime, and now to be sold to grocers for wrapping up their goods.

A farmer, ploughing his land, often came across human bones, the bones of saints scattered when their tomb had been rifled for the croziers and pontifical rings buried with them.

On heaths and at crossroads there dangled from gibbets other bones, picked clean by the crows, a reminder of that day when Lincolnshire and the North had risen as one man under the banner of the Five Wounds, demanding the restoration of the monasteries where, as they wrote in their songs, they had had in time of need both ale and bread, and succour great in all distress. Not a town in all the country from the Humber to the Scottish Marches, form the German Ocean to the Irish Sea, but had its gates decorated with the grinning skulls of simple folk who had risen in the Pilgrimage of Grace. From the broken gates of the great Benedictine abbeys of Reading and Colchester, the heads of their abbots looked down; and on Glastonbury Tor, rising above the most sacred religious house in England, a house spared by every early invader because of the tradition that it had been founded by St Joseph of Arimathea, bung the frail bones of the last Abbot, hung, drawn, and quartered at the age of eighty-four.

In the ante-room of the King's Bedchamber at Whitehall, Archbishop Cranmer rustled up and down in his silk cassock, waiting for an unexpected summons, turning over in his mind some passage from the superb Litany and Communion Service, both in English, he had been composing in secret these many years past. They need not be secret when Henry died; in his determination to abolish the Mass he loathed, Cranmer would have as allies all the new rich who had become so on the looting of the monasteries, the seizure of colleges, hospitals, chantries, schools, parish guilds, and tithes. For only by getting rid of the ancient belief that Church property was sacred could they feel secure.

That carving of a phrase, that polishing of a sentence, that exact choice of a word, how such work had delighted him! And now at long last, when he was nearly sixty, he would be acclaimed for what he was, a master of prose.

When he was young he had read some exquisite composition to Black Joan, but all that lusty barmaid of the Dolphin had been concerned about was the catching of a husband who was a Fellow of his College, not knowing, stupid girl, that the University did not admit married Fellows. And the second Mrs Cranmer had never learned English, and merely had smiled her fat smile and said 'Ja! Ja!', when he had read her some great line.

He shivered a little, and went to the fire. How narrowly had he escaped the fate of his patron Cromwell when he had married his Grace to another woman who had never learned English, the plain, big German woman, Anne of Cleves. But he *had* escaped. He had declared the marriage null and void, just as he had declared that of Anne Boleyn, and of Catherine before her. And it was he who had entrapped yet another wife, Catherine Howard, into confessing her adultery. All through the years he had remained in Henry's favour, watching the fall of so many men and women who had made the mistake of laughing at the King behind his back, of playing their own hand, of thinking they held the whip.

In the gallery beyond the ante-room, Edward Seymour, Earl of Hertford, uncle of the sickly little boy who was soon to become King Edward VI, walked arm-in-arm with his ally Paget, plotting to get the Protectorship into his own ruthless and capable hands directly the old King died. Already he had destroyed his principal rivals, the Howards, or at least was on the verge of doing so. He had whispered to Henry of a conspiracy, of the Howards quartering the Royal Arms upon their own; and the Earl of Surrey, Norfolk's son, had paid the supreme penalty on Tower Hill. Norfolk's own death warrant awaited the King's signature; and Cranmer, the useful, pliant Cranmer, must get that signature from the dying fingers.

In an alcove of the same gallery, Hertford's younger brother Thomas talked heart to heart with Catherine Parr, the Queen. She wept, this small, motherly woman, widowed before Henry had picked her for his sixth wife; she wept with compassion, for she was tender-hearted, but she smiled through her tears as Thomas Seymour consoled her. Theirs was an old love, and now they could be married at last. They looked into each other's eyes and felt that it was almost too good to be true.

And in his bed lay Henry, a vast corrupting mass of bloated flesh.

For some time now he had become so unwieldy that they had had to enlarge doorways, so helpless that they had invented a sort of machinery to lug him from place to place. The small waist of which he had been so proud had swollen to fifty-four inches; the legs of which he had boasted were elephantine. His physicians had implored him to take to his bed; he would not; he dared not. It was blasphemy to imagine that he, Vicar of Christ, Defender of the Faith, Supreme Head of Church and State, he who had broken every opposition to his royal will, who had cut down every enemy, was face to face with an enemy he could not burn, behead, hang, draw, and quarter, the last enemy, Death.

Even though he could smell the stench of his own putrefaction, and saw men turn white and sick with it when they approached him, he would not accept the monstrous fact. He was only fifty-five; he was good for another ten years at least, even if he were not, as in his megalomania he half believed, immortal. And no one had dared to tell him until this evening, when Sir Anthony Denny, a Gentleman of the Bedchamber, obviously sent by greater men to do the job they shirked, had flung himself upon his knees and faltered:

'May it please your Majesty, your Majesty is in such case that to man's judgement your Majesty is not – not like to live.'

The flat eyes had gleamed with a faint reflection of that wrath which had made the bravest quail.

'What judge had sent you to pass sentence on us?'

'Your Majesty's physicians. Is there,' Denny timidly inquired, 'any godly man with whom your Majesty would confer?'

'Cranmer; but he not yet. We will sleep a little, and then we will advise upon the matter.'

Sleep was all he needed. He would have his burning forehead bathed from a basin of agate he had taken from Westminster Abbey, his parched mouth refreshed by spiced wine from a chalice torn from the Shrine of St Thomas of Canterbury (now known by royal order, as 'that high traitor, Thomas à Becket'), he would sleep, and wake revived. There was something particular he had to do – what was it? Ah, the signing of Norfolk's death warrant, that was it. Norfolk who had persuaded him to marry one niece who was a witch and another who was a wanton, Norfolk who had been the most corrupt of that army of officials who had cheated their King of half the monastic spoils. Yes, Norfolk's white head would fall tomorrow; but in the meantime, sleep.

The merciful dullness was slow in coming, held off by the pain of the sores which covered his body and the agony of his ulcerating leg. He longed for comfort, and who should comfort him but Kate, the wife he had chosen in the autumn of his days, who gave him the wholehearted love and devotion he had never known since the time of the first Catherine, who did not expect him to be virile, in whose tender affection he could repose. Yes, God had been good to him at last; he was no longer Solomon but David, seeking neither riches nor honour, but understanding and wisdom. Chancellor Audley had referred to him as David, he remembered, when proposing an Act whereby it should be lawful for a subject to reveal any lightness in 'the Queen for the time being,' and high treason for an unchaste woman to marry the King.

The drugged wine was working. It must be, for when he tried to raise his hand to signal to his attendants to call his wife, he found he could not. Yet his sense of hearing had become abnormally acute; through the open door of his chamber he could hear a woman weeping. It must be Kate, poor, devoted faithful Kate, broken hearted because she feared she was going to lose him.

His livid lips soundlessly formed the name:

'Kate.'

He thought that a woman came and stood beside his bed, looking down at him with china-blue eyes. She was speaking, and he could hear every word distinctly, though he did not wish to hear them.

'My most dear lord, king, and husband, the hour of my death now approaching I cannot but choose, out of the love I bear you, to advise you of your soul's health, which your ought to prefer above all considerations of the world or flesh whatsoever. For which yet you have cast me into many calamities, and yourself into many troubles. But I forgive you all, and pray God to do so likewise. For the rest, I commend unto you Mary our daughter, beseeching you to be a good father to her. Lastly, I make this vow, that mine eyes desire you above all things. Catherine the Queen.'

Catherine of Aragon's last letter to him, her last defiance – 'Catherine the Queen'. He had got back at her after her death by ordering Hilsey, Bishop-designate of Rochester, to declare in her funeral sermon that she had acknowledged she had never been Queen of England. And he had forgiven her; though other matters had made him forget his intention to give her the most magnificent funeral ever seen, he had bestowed on her as goodly a monument as any in the world, the great Abbey Church of Peterborough, spared for the purpose when he had accepted from Parliament all the other Religious Houses as a sacred trust.

He wished she would go, the ghost of this squat little woman in her Spanish mantilla; she had never had any tact. It was true she was no longer speaking, but the spectre of her there beside his bed conjured up things he hoped he had long forgotten.

Who had given those monstrously mischievous instructions to lap her body in lead the very day she died? They had refused to allow any of her own attendants near her corpse, and had ordered the chandler of the house to embalm her. And then making matters worse by saying that it must be done in haste – when it was mid-winter, and when she had not died of anything likely to accelerate corruption. Of course the chandler had talked, a lot of nonsense about her heart being black, and a preposterous rumour had got round that she had been poisoned. To stop such malicious tales from spreading overseas, he had refused her doctor and confessor a passport, and to make quite sure had clapped them into the Tower.

'You lie in peace at Peterborough, Kate,' he tried to cry at her, 'and I have been a good father to Mary – since I broke her will.'

Thank God he had not had Catherine buried here in London. It would have been hideous to have seen the candles on the hearse above her grave mysteriously light themselves on that morning when the great cannon in the Tower had informed him that Anne Boleyn had met the fate she deserved.

He tried to turn his head away form the phantom standing between the curtains of his bed, but all movement had become impossible. Weak tears welled up in his eyes as he still cried soundlessly for his wife, for his last and true love, for Kate.

'I am here, if it please your Grace.'

Catherine of Aragon had gone, and in her place stood Catherine Howard, romping, sparkling, bubbling with life, the girl he had named his Rose without a Thorn, the bride whose motto he himself had chosen, *No other will but his*. Even in public he had not been able to keep his amorous hands off her…

That terrible morning when Cranmer had put into his hand a paper while he was at Mass. Only the day before he had ordered a national thanksgiving for the chaste and happy life he was leading with his new young spouse, the sweet eighteen-year-old whom Norfolk, her uncle, had commended for her pure and honest condition. And all the time, from the age of fourteen, she had been a wanton; and the old Duchess of Norfolk had been her bawd.

He had burst into tears on reading Cranmer's evidence against her. He had always been too tender-hearted to be present when any unfaithful spouse was confronted with her infidelities, but the scene had been described to him when his Rose without a Thorn had been arrested, dragged by force, struggling and screaming to her barge, shrieking for mercy when she had passed beneath Traitors' Gate. They ought not to have told him such things; they knew how sensitive he was. He had deferred her execution for two whole days in order that she might have leisure to reflect on the state of her conscience; and she had repaid him by her shameless declaration on the scaffold that though she died a queen she would rather be the wife of the low physician, Culpepper, once her chamber-boy.

'Mercy! Mercy! Mercy!'

It was not her voice now; it was a man who screeched the words into his dying ear; it was a voice from Hell. Yes, there you are burning, Thomas Cromwell whom I always called a knave, Cromwell the brewer's son, Anne of Cleves, outshone in beauty all other women as the sun does the moon. They bungled your execution, Cromwell; they had to hack again and again at your horrible plebeian neck. You rot in the same grave with Anne the witch and her incestuous brother; but I shall lie in splendid state at Windsor beside my dear little Jane.

Jane. Such a very tenuous shape it was that seemed to stand between the bed curtains now. He smiled at it; and then he frowned. His modest, meek English wildflower, who had chosen as her motto, *Bound to serve and obey,* had had the insolence to tell him that appalling rebellion called the Pilgrimage of Grace was a judgement on him for his spoilation of the monasteries. But he had forgiven her when she had borne him a son; and perhaps it was a blessing in disguise when she had died nine days later. The Lord had given, had given and the Lord had taken away; and she had been a little insipid.

Then again the tears trickled down his bloated cheeks as he thought of Jane's son, his only son by six wives, so sickly, so solemn, so afflicted by a certain ominous rash...

The phantoms had gone; he was awake; but he found he was only just in touch with the material world. Someone was rustling beside him, whispering, offering him a paper and a quill. Again he tried to lift his hand; he would sign Norfolk's death warrant if it was the last thing he did. Norfolk had wilfully misunderstood him at the time of the Pilgrimage of Grace. Of course he had never meant to offer the Pilgrims the royal pardon if they would disband and then, immediately they disbanded, lay the kingdom under martial law. Norfolk had made God's Viceregent odious to his subjects; Norfolk must die.

But he had lost all his power of movement. He could only stare at the hand lying flaccid on his mountainous belly, his eyes, dazzled by the flashing of the diamond on his thumb, the Regal of France, given four centuries past by Louis VII to the Shrine of St Thomas of Canterbury.

He heard a deep, slow thunder; it was his heart labouring, but he thought it was the bells of London tolling for his end. So few left of all those myraid bells which had pealed for his Coronation. Down every navigable river in England they had been floated in barges, broken and packed in barrels, to be sold for export or fashioned into guns. Here in London the bells of St Martin le Grand, which of old had set the time of curfew, all the other parishes taking it up; the bells of the Priory of Holy Trinity; of the Black, White, the Grey, and the Crutched Friars; of the Charterhouse; of the great Benedictine convent in Bishopsgate; of the Priory of the Knights Hospitallers of Jerusalem – all were dumb. Even the Jesus Bells of St Paul's Cathedral had been lost by him to some courtier in a game of dice.

He forgot Norfolk's death warrant. There was his own will to be made…no, no, he had made it already. 'In the name of God, and of the glorious and blessed Virgin, Our Lady, St Mary, and of all the Holy Company of Heaven…that there by provided all manner of things requisite and necessary for daily Masses for our soul, while the world shall endure… ' He could rely on Cranmer, so orthodox, so devoted to the Holy sacrifice, to see that these Masses were said; and suddenly he knew his need of them.

The breath began to rattle in his throat, and his lips, cracked, edged with foam, tried to mumble:

'Our Lady of Walsingham, pray for me!'

His fading senses had a last vision. The great priory which for five hundred years had attracted pilgrims from all over Christendom; himself walking barefoot along the Holy Mile from the Slipper Chapel to the Shrine. But it was gone. It had been the first of the greater priories to be despoiled; its famous image of Our Lady had been burnt at

Chelsea as a kind of retort to the challenge of Sir Thomas More; its Slipper Chapel was now a barn and smithy; its masonry had been used for mending the King's highway.

Crying like a lost child, Henry the King went down into the dark.

One hand holding up his silken skirts, and in the other Norfolk's death warrant, Archbishop Cranmer tiptoed into the ante-room, and shook his head at Edward Seymour whose eyes fastened greedily upon the document.

'No, my lord,' he said in a reverent undertone, 'his Majesty was unable to sign. But he passed very peacefully in the faith of Christ, and now has entered into Life Eternal.'

Jane Lane

A Call of Trumpets

Civil war rages in England, rendering it a minefield of corruption and conflict. Town and country are besieged. Through the complex interlocking of England's turmoil with that of a king, Jane Lane brings to life some amazing characters in the court of Charles I. This is the story both of Charles' adored wife whose indiscretions prove disastrous, and of the King's nephew, Rupert, a rash, arrogant soldier whose actions lead to tragedy and his uncle's final downfall.

Conies in the Hay

1586 was the year of an unbearably hot summer when treachery came to the fore. In this scintillating drama of betrayals, Jane Lane sketches the master of espionage, Francis Walsingham, in the bright, lurid colours of the deceit for which he was renowned. Anthony Babington and his fellow conspirators are also brought to life in this vivid, tense novel, which tells of how they were duped by Walsingham into betraying the ill-fated Mary, Queen of Scots, only to be hounded to their own awful destruction.

JANE LANE

HIS FIGHT IS OURS

His Fight Is Ours follows the traumatic trials of MacIain, a Highland Chieftain of the clan Donald, as he leads his people in the second Jacobite rising on behalf of James Stuart, the Old Pretender. The battle to restore the king to his rightful throne is portrayed here in this absorbing historical escapade, which highlights all the beauty and romance of Highland life. Jane Lane presents a dazzling, picaresque story of the problems facing MacIain as leader of a proud, ancient race, and his struggles against injustice and the violent infamy of oppression.

A SUMMER STORM

Conflict and destiny abound as King Richard II, a chivalrous, romantic and idealist monarch, courts his beloved Anne of Bohemia. In the background, the swirling rage of the Peasants' Revolt of 1381 threatens to topple London as the tides of farmers, labourers and charismatic rebel hearts flood the city. This tense, powerful historical romance leads the reader from bubbling discord to doomed love all at the turn of a page.

JANE LANE

THUNDER ON ST PAUL'S DAY

London is gripped by mass hysteria as Titus Oates uncovers the Popish Plot, and a gentle English family gets caught up in the terrors of trial and accusation when Oates points the finger of blame. The villainous Oates adds fuel to the fire of an angry mob with his sham plot, leaving innocence to face a bullying judge and an intimidated jury. Only one small boy may save the family in this moving tale of courage pitted against treachery.

A WIND THROUGH THE HEATHER

A Wind Through the Heather is a poignant, tragic story based on the Highland Clearances where thousands of farmers were driven from their homes by tyrannical and greedy landowners. Introducing the Macleods, Jane Lane recreates the shameful past suffered by an innocent family who lived to cross the Atlantic and find a new home. This wistful, historical novel focuses on the atrocities so many bravely faced and reveals how adversities were overcome.

OTHER TITLES BY JANE LANE AVAILABLE DIRECT
FROM HOUSE OF STRATUS

Quantity		£	$(US)	$(CAN)	€
☐	BRIDGE OF SIGHS	6.99	12.95	19.95	13.50
☐	A CALL OF TRUMPETS	6.99	12.95	19.95	13.50
☐	CAT AMONG THE PIGEONS	6.99	12.95	19.95	13.50
☐	COMMAND PERFORMANCE	6.99	12.95	19.95	13.50
☐	CONIES IN THE HAY	6.99	12.95	19.95	13.50
☐	COUNTESS AT WAR	6.99	12.95	19.95	13.50
☐	THE CROWN FOR A LIE	6.99	12.95	19.95	13.50
☐	DARK CONSPIRACY	6.99	12.95	19.95	13.50
☐	EMBER IN THE ASHES	6.99	12.95	19.95	13.50
☐	FAREWELL TO THE WHITE COCKADE	6.99	12.95	19.95	13.50
☐	FORTRESS IN THE FORTH	6.99	12.95	19.95	13.50
☐	HEIRS OF SQUIRE HARRY	6.99	12.95	19.95	13.50
☐	HIS FIGHT IS OURS	6.99	12.95	19.95	13.50

ALL HOUSE OF STRATUS BOOKS ARE AVAILABLE FROM GOOD BOOKSHOPS
OR DIRECT FROM THE PUBLISHER:

Internet: **www.houseofstratus.com** including author interviews, reviews, features.

Email: **sales@houseofstratus.com** please quote author, title and credit card details.

OTHER TITLES BY JANE LANE AVAILABLE DIRECT
FROM HOUSE OF STRATUS

Quantity		£	$(US)	$(CAN)	€
	THE PHOENIX AND THE LAUREL	6.99	12.95	19.95	13.50
	PRELUDE TO KINGSHIP	6.99	12.95	19.95	13.50
	QUEEN OF THE CASTLE	6.99	12.95	19.95	13.50
	THE SEALED KNOT	6.99	12.95	19.95	13.50
	A SECRET CHRONICLE	6.99	12.95	19.95	13.50
	THE SEVERED CROWN	6.99	12.95	19.95	13.50
	SIR DEVIL MAY CARE	6.99	12.95	19.95	13.50
	A STATE OF MIND	6.99	12.95	19.95	13.50
	A SUMMER STORM	6.99	12.95	19.95	13.50
	THUNDER ON ST PAUL'S DAY	6.99	12.95	19.95	13.50
	A WIND THROUGH THE HEATHER	6.99	12.95	19.95	13.50
	THE YOUNG AND LONELY KING	6.99	12.95	19.95	13.50

ALL HOUSE OF STRATUS BOOKS ARE AVAILABLE FROM GOOD BOOKSHOPS
OR DIRECT FROM THE PUBLISHER:

Order Line: UK: 0800 169 1780,
USA: 1 800 509 9942
INTERNATIONAL: +44 (0) 20 7494 6400 (UK)
or
+01 212 218 7649
(please quote author, title, and credit card details.)

Send to: House of Stratus Sales Department   House of Stratus Inc.
24c Old Burlington Street   Suite 210
London   1270 Avenue of the Americas
W1X 1RL   New York • NY 10020
UK   USA

PAYMENT

Please tick currency you wish to use:

☐ £ (Sterling)   ☐ $ (US)   ☐ $ (CAN)   ☐ € (Euros)

Allow for shipping costs charged per order plus an amount per book as set out in the tables below:

CURRENCY/DESTINATION

	£(Sterling)	$(US)	$(CAN)	€(Euros)
Cost per order				
UK	1.50	2.25	3.50	2.50
Europe	3.00	4.50	6.75	5.00
North America	3.00	3.50	5.25	5.00
Rest of World	3.00	4.50	6.75	5.00
Additional cost per book				
UK	0.50	0.75	1.15	0.85
Europe	1.00	1.50	2.25	1.70
North America	1.00	1.00	1.50	1.70
Rest of World	1.50	2.25	3.50	3.00

PLEASE SEND CHEQUE OR INTERNATIONAL MONEY ORDER.
payable to: STRATUS HOLDINGS plc or HOUSE OF STRATUS INC. or card payment as indicated

STERLING EXAMPLE

Cost of book(s):..................... Example: 3 x books at £6.99 each: £20.97
Cost of order: .... Example: £1.50 (Delivery to UK address)
Additional cost per book:.............. Example: 3 x £0.50: £1.50
Order total including shipping:.......... Example: £23.97

VISA, MASTERCARD, SWITCH, AMEX:

☐ ☐ ☐ ☐ ☐ ☐ ☐ ☐ ☐ ☐ ☐ ☐ ☐ ☐ ☐ ☐ ☐ ☐

Issue number (Switch only):

☐ ☐ ☐

Start Date: **Expiry Date:**

☐☐/☐☐   ☐☐/☐☐

Signature: _____

NAME: _____

ADDRESS: _____

COUNTRY: _____

ZIP/POSTCODE: _____

Please allow 28 days for delivery. Despatch normally within 48 hours.

Prices subject to change without notice.
Please tick box if you do not wish to receive any additional information. ☐

House of Stratus publishes many other titles in this genre; please check our website (**www.houseofstratus.com**) for more details.